to Simon and Debbie

real smallholding gurus

OTHER BOOKS BY PHIN HALL

The Omnifex Chronicles Series
Montgomery's Trouble in the Underworld
Montgomery's Battle with Atlantis *(coming soon)*

Guide to Self-Publishing Online *(coming soon)*

Cover-to-Cover Series
Judges 1-8: The Spiral of Faith
Judges 9-21: Learning to Live God's Way
The Creed: Belief in Action

VITAL - Spiritual Disciplines Series

What the Bible Says Series

For more information, and to receive a free
eBook & audiobook, visit

www.phinhall.net

No Time To Stand And Stare

Phin Hall

Lundarien Press

Published by Lundarien Press, UK
www.lundarienpress.com
Copyright © Phin Hall 2015

ISBN 978-1-910816-14-1 (paperback)
978-1-910816-13-4 (ePub)
978-1-910816-12-7 (mobi)
978-1-910816-15-8 (audiobook)

STEEPLEFORD

MAP KEY

1 THE FARMHOUSE
2 BUTCHER SHOP
3 THE HEADMISTRESS
4 THE VILLAGE STORE
5 ST BARTHOLOMEW'S
6 THE VICARAGE
7 THE GREEN MAN
8 THE OLD SCHOOL
9 THE OLD POST OFFICE
   & FORGE
10 STEEPLEFORD GREEN

THE SMALLHOLDING

A POULTRY FIELD
B GOAT SHED
C HORSE FIELD
D THE STABLES
E LUCY & PIGLETS
F MAJOR TOM
G MORE PIGS
H THE TOP FIELD

N

River Bray

to Embercombe Hill

CONTENTS

What is this life if, full of care,
We have no time to stand and stare?
No time to stand beneath the boughs,
And stare as long as sheep and cows:
No time to see, when woods we pass,
Where squirrels hide their nuts in grass:
No time to see, in broad daylight,
Streams full of stars, like skies at night:
No time to turn at Beauty's glance,
And watch her feet, how they can dance:
No time to wait till her mouth can
Enrich that smile her eyes began?
A poor life this if, full of care,
We have no time to stand and stare.

'Leisure' by W H Davies

NOT A REAL MAN

Sebastian's bedroom window looked out on an unbroken canvas of brickwork, and it was the most wonderful sight in the world. At least, it was to him. And every morning, before breaking into the day's routine, Sebastian would spend just a few minutes gazing at the expanse of patchwork orange. There were no curtains or blinds to obscure this glorious view, since there were no overlooking windows through which people might peer in at him and, at night, he would often lie in bed looking out at the brickwork, illuminated by a nearby security light, and feel safe. There was no other word for it; that was how the stability of this unchanging vista made him feel: *safe*. Safe in the city, that triumph of human dominion, where concrete, steel and brick had tamed, if not conquered, the wild terrors of nature.

It wasn't that Sebastian was opposed to nature; he understood that the food he ate had some kind of connection to the world beyond London, but it was as distant a connection as between the treacherous waters of the ocean and a cool pint of beer, and he was happy to keep it at that distance. But life in the city was all he had ever known. And it was all he *wanted* to know. The city kept him safe, and the view from his window, this wall, this solid sheet of bricks and mortar was a constant reminder of this.

Today, however, there was no time to stand and stare at the view, not if he was to avoid being late for his train. Not that he'd mind being late. In fact, he'd like nothing more than to avoid the journey, and its destination, altogether, but he knew he wouldn't get let off that easily. His friends would make sure of that.

'Bloody friends!' he muttered, as he folded a crisp, white shirt into his suitcase with practised care. And he muttered the words with no small amount of venom as he thought back to the previous night, when this nonsense, this *nightmare*, had kicked off.

It had been Thursday evening, his twenty-fourth birthday, and they'd bought him presents.

'Presents!' The voice had cut through the hum of the bar and Sebastian jerked round to see the blonde-dreaded Alison Jabber, aka Brillig, surging towards him with a large, well-wrapped package clutched to her chest.

Sebastian set down his London Pride, still feeling somewhat put out at having paid for this first birthday pint himself, and leaned away from the approaching gift. 'I've only just got here!'

'So?' said Brillig, her Leeds accent making it sound more like '*sore*'. She perched on the bench next to him as the others shuffled up to make room. 'I've been dying to see how you'd react all day. It'd be proper unfair to make me wait any longer.'

'Yeah, come on!' said DeVere - Justin to his parents, DeVere to his mates - leaning forwards and almost knocking his lager over. 'I've got good money riding on this.'

'Money?' Sebastian frowned round at the eager, almost hungry looks in his friends' faces. His concern deepened. 'What's going on?' he asked, failing to sound breezy and nonchalant. 'Why are you all staring at me like that?'

In answer, Brillig nudged his drink out of the way and dumped the package on the table in front of him. It looked like a pair of wellies.

'It looks like a pair of wellies,' said Sebastian with a strained laugh. No one else laughed. Nor did they say anything, though their eager faces seemed to wilt slightly. With a slowness born of unenthusiastic resignation, he teased off the wrapping paper to reveal, as expected, a pair of rubber wellies. They were an uninspiring shade of green. 'Um,' he began. 'I... er. Yes, well, thank you.' He paused, but no one else volunteered to fill the silence. 'I was right. It, it *is* a pair of wellies.' He smiled. Another pause, longer this time, and still nobody came to his rescue. He sighed. 'So... why have you given me a pair of wellies?'

'You'll have to, like, open your card to find that out,' said Diesel, whose full and much despised name was Denise Selborne. She was in her late-twenties and bore the panda-like makeup of a lifelong Goth.

On cue, Brillig thrust out an envelope towards him. As Sebastian opened it and drew out the card, something small slipped out and fluttered to the floor. He picked it up. It was a train ticket, with the customary orange bands at the top and bottom, for travel from Clapham Junction, a station with which Sebastian was familiar, and Barnstaple, somewhere with which he was not.

'Barnstaple?' he said. 'Isn't that north of the river somewhere? Up near Edgware?'

'You're thinking of Barnet,' said Little Pete, whose name really was Pete. 'Barnstaple's in Devon. Why don't you just read the card?'

Sebastian stroked his chin, clean-shaven just forty-five minutes before. 'Devon? That's flipping *miles* away, isn't it?'

DeVere shrugged. 'Couple of hundred or so. Just read the card, it'll explain everything.'

'It says it's only valid for tomorrow...' said Sebastian, peering down at the ticket again. 'Did someone put it in the envelope by mistake?'

'*Just read the card!*' shouted Little Pete from across the table, jabbing an aggressive finger at the item in question before slumping, arms folded, back into his seat, looking mildly embarrassed at his outburst.

Sebastian picked up the envelope and, pulling out the card, began to read it in silence.

'Read it out loud, then,' said Diesel. 'We all wants to hear.'

Despite the fact it was clear to Sebastian that they were all well aware of the contents, he cleared his throat and read. '*Dear Sebastian* - being me - *we all hope you have a great birthday* - thanks for that...' He paused, his eyes scanning the next sentence.

'Keep going then!' said Brillig, nudging his shoulder, causing a second train ticket to slip out of the envelope onto the floor.

'*However,*' he continued, making no move to pick it up, '*the days that follow may not be so enjoyable. Your challenge, should you choose to accept it...* Someone's scribbled, *"You don't have a choice!"* above it in red pen?' Sebastian glanced at DeVere, who was grinning at the ceiling, the red core of the biro behind his ear clearly showing. '*Your challenge is to spend one week living and working on a smallholding in Devon to prove you're a real man.*' Sebastian flashed a look of indignation at his assembled colleagues. 'To prove I'm a real man? What are you saying?'

'I'd've thought that was obvious,' said Little Pete. 'We're saying you ain't a real man.'

Sebastian gave the group another round of his offended glare, waving the card at them. 'This is a joke, right? You're just messing with me?' For a moment the burst of laughter from his friends gave him a glimpse of hope. But it was just a glimpse. And just for a moment. But he could see the truth in their eyes. They weren't joking! 'What do you mean, I'm not a real man?'

'Well, you're not are you?' said Brillig, ruffling Sebastian's hair. Instinctively, he pull a comb from his jacket pocket and starting putting it back in order, leaning slightly to check his reflection in the window over Diesel's shoulder.

Little Pete grinned at him. 'You're a bit, you know, metrosexual.' DeVere snorted into his pint, spattering the table with beer.

'What?' said Sebastian, pausing with the comb halfway through his fringe. 'I am *not* metrosexual!'

'Come on,' said Brillig. 'You're like the *ultimate* metrosexual. If you Google "metrosexual" you'd find a ton of photos of *you*. And in most of them, you'd be combing your hair.'

Sebastian paused, comb poised above his head, a few stray strands of hair still caught in it. He dropped his arm, slipping the comb back into a pocket. 'You're talking rubbish,' he said. 'In what way am I...' he could hardly bring himself to say the word, '"metrosexual"?'

'Apart from combing your hair every five seconds?' said Little Pete.

'Obviously.'

'Well, there's your clothes,' said DeVere, reaching past Brillig to give the fabric of Sebastian's shirt a tug between forefinger and thumb. 'I don't know anyone who buys the sort of stuff you wear, except those androgynous freaks you see on the front of magazines.'

'There's nothing wrong with buying a few decent threads.'

'True,' said Brillig, glancing down at her own work clothes. Sebastian's eyes followed hers, noting the mark on her top where she had spilled mayonnaise at lunchtime and the long ladder down the right calf of her tights. He looked up to see her staring back, her eyes narrowed. 'But I bet you ironed that shirt before you came out, didn't you?'

'Of course. Everyone-'

'Despite the fact you ironed them before you put them in your wardrobe?'

'Yeah, but… hang on,' said Sebastian. 'How do you know that? Have you been spying on me?'

'And then there's all that stuff on your desk,' said Diesel, pointing a black-polished finger nail in his direction. 'I've never seen that many bottles of, like, creams, lotions, moisturisers and perfumes and that outside a chemist. I don't even know what half of them are for.'

Sebastian pulled a face at this outrageous display of ignorance. 'They're just products, Diesel. They're necessary, especially if-'

'I bet you pluck your eyebrows,' interrupted Little Pete.

'And shave your chest,' added Brillig, trying to peer down his shirt at the area in question. Sebastian leant back in his chair, a hand clamped across his collar.

'Do you go to a professional to get your nails

done?' That was DeVere.

Little Pete leaned in for a closer look. 'Are you actually wearing eye makeup?'

'So many bottles on your desk,' said Diesel, her eyes focused somewhere above Sebastian's head. 'I think one of them was, like, shampoo or something. Why would you ever need shampoo in the office? It's not like there's a shower in-'

Sebastian held up his hands to stem the eruption of comments. 'Yes, alright! I get the picture. So I like to look after myself a bit, and take a little pride in my appearance. So what? It doesn't mean I'm not a real man.'

Little Pete smacked a hand on the table, clearly enjoying himself. 'Come on, Sebastian! You're a Victorian duchess trapped in a man's body.'

'I'm not going.'

'You what?' said Little Pete, thrown by this sudden change of topic.

'To this... smallholding, or whatever it is. I'm not going.'

'Told you!' said DeVere, sounding smug and thrusting out a hand to Brillig. 'Cough up, then. You owe me twenty quid.'

Brillig slapped his hand away and leaned closer to Sebastian. 'Why don't you want to go?'

'Why *would* I?' said Sebastian, looking at her as though she'd asked him why he might not fancy swimming in the Thames. 'It sounds awful. I literally couldn't think of anything worse. Countryside. Animals. Mud. Weird village people... and I bet there's no internet or mobile reception.'

'No doubt,' said DeVere. 'I bet it's like the Dark Ages out in those parts. I'm fairly sure the people are all hairy like apes. Some of them probably have tails.'

'Shut up, DeVere!' Brillig flashed a glare at him before turning back to Sebastian. 'We were all aware, when we chose your present, that you wouldn't want to go. But we all agreed that you *need* to go. Wait!' She held up a hand to forestall Sebastian's interruption. 'Yes, it's going to be dirty and smelly. Yes, it's going to be way out in the countryside in some small, probably fairly backward, village. Yes, it's going to be hard, unpleasant and generally grim. But this is what you need to do to prove, once and for all, beyond doubt, that you are a real man. And while we'd love you to prove it to us, ultimately, you need to prove it to yourself.'

'But...' Sebastian began, trying to think up an excuse. 'But I've got work. The boss'd never give me a week off at such short notice. You wouldn't, would you, Sheila?' He turned to his left where a middle-aged woman was slumped, drinking something blue through a straw. Her silence was not unusual - Sheila was woman of less than few words - and it remained unbroken as a grin spread across her face that failed to raise Sebastian's hopes.

'Of course she would!' said Little Pete. 'Sheila's chipped into the pot, same as the rest of us. It's all sorted.'

'Surely not?' said Sebastian, directing the question to the boss, as she wiggled her eyebrows in confirmation. 'But I've not packed!' He picked up the second train ticket and waved them at the staring faces. 'There'll be no time tomorrow.'

'I'll come and help,' said DeVere. Sebastian glanced across to find him picking his nose. 'Won't take long to stuff some old clothes into a rucksack.'

Sebastian shifted his chair out of range of these nasal activities. 'No thanks,' he said. 'I can do it myself. And anyway, I don't have any "old clothes". Or a rucksack.'

Brillig patted him on the knee, like a well-behaved child. 'That's that sorted then.'

Sebastian tried one last attempt to wriggle out of the unwanted gift. 'But who'd feed my cat?'

'You don't have a cat,' said Diesel. 'You don't have *any* pets. You're scared of them, remember? You told us, like, a thousand times.'

DeVere jabbed a finger at Sebastian. 'Yet another reason to prove yourself, mate. There's all kind of animals on the smallholding. Apparently.' Sebastian looked around the group and sighed. Every face was focused on him, eyebrows raised in silent anticipation.

'Okay, fine!' he said, in the voice that suggested it wasn't *that* fine. 'I'll go. But if I die-'

'Boom!' Brillig beamed at him, holding out a hand to DeVere. 'That's twenty pounds, I believe.'

DeVere fished a crumpled bank note from his pocket and tossed it at her. 'Tough luck, mate,' he said, slapping Sebastian on the back with his nose-picking hand. 'Looks like you're off to Devon. Pete!' he shouted, making Sheila jump and start coughing into her blue drink. 'It's your round. Get a move on!'

'Get a move on!' Sebastian peered through the rain across the deserted platform to see Brillig waving to him. Catching his eye, she shouted again, 'Come on. It's leaving any second.'

Sure enough, as he struggled towards her with his umbrella in one hand, shielding his sculpted hair from the wet, and a bulging suitcase in the other, the guard appeared from the rear doors of the train. He glanced up and down the platform before blowing on his whistle.

'Hold up!' called Sebastian.

The guard turned to peer at him, eyebrows clenched in a frown. 'Quickly then!'

'See you, Brillig,' shouted Sebastian over his shoulder. 'Thanks for coming to see me off. At least one person cares.'

'Oh, it's not that,' she said, already turning away. 'One of us had to check you actually got on the train. I just happened to draw the short straw. Laters.' And then she was gone, hurrying towards the stairs and the cover of the underpass.

Feeling a wrench of loneliness, tinged with a stab of apprehension, Sebastian stepped onto the train and the door hissed shut behind him. And as the train pulled away from the station, he sat looking out of the window at the streaks of rain and the solid, safe bulk of the city slipping away behind him.

2

PHEASANT PIE

The journey was a misery. Although it brightened up around Basingstoke, and the evening sun etched the surroundings in a rich orange glow, Sebastian's already low mood sank with every strange-sounding station from Overton to Pinhoe. The sun also sank, casting its thinning light across the fields as they stretched away on every side. Fields, he couldn't help noticing, that were filled with animals. *Large* animals. He turned away from the view, his imagination conjuring up terrors of what the week ahead might contain. A week that last night, after a few beers, hadn't seemed such a big deal, but today seemed like some horrific, Herculean ordeal.

He changed at Exeter St Davids, drinking in the brief exposure to the noise of the busy platform. But it was short-lived and he soon found himself huddled up on the Barnstaple train, as it wound its way from one deserted station to another, each one with a more alien name than the last.

It was almost midnight when Sebastian emerged onto the road outside Barnstaple station, his suitcase clutched in front of him like a leather shield. No one else was in sight and no cars moved along the silent road. The few street lamps cast too-small patches of light, making the darkness beyond them even darker.

'It's like a third-world country,' he muttered, 'or

the Middle Ages. Maybe that train was a time machine.'

He glanced round as headlights burst from a nearby turning, accompanied by the roar of an engine, and shrank back from the curb as a large Landrover jerked to a stop in front of him. He noticed the mud crusted up the side of the vehicle and then his reflection in the driver's window. He didn't look happy and, even worse, his hair was a bit dishevelled. Glancing down, he pulled his comb from a pocket, but when he looked back, the window had been lowered, and instead of his reflection, he found himself staring at a large, black moustache. Sebastian gasped in surprise and took another step back.

The mouth below the moustache chuckled at him.

'"Hello" to you, too!' it said and, as the driver leant through the window, the face beyond the hair came into view, dark eyes glinting in the glow of the nearest streetlamp. 'The name's Neil Symes.' Sebastian, frozen and staring in incomprehension, made no response. 'You must be Sebastian, right? Sebastian Cooper?'

Somehow these words made an impact on Sebastian's confused brain. 'What?' he said, gathering his thoughts and realising that this man, with his filthy tank-like car, must be here for him. 'Yes, that's me. I'm Sebastian.'

The man chuckled again and opened his door. Sebastian backed away a little further as Neil unfolded himself onto the pavement. He was least a few inches shorter than Sebastian's own six foot one, but he was about twice as wide, and as he reached out a large hand to take Sebastian's suitcase, his bicep bulged, stretching the sleeve of his wax jacket, and he freed the case from Sebastian's grip with impressive ease.

'Right then, Sebastian,' he said, his Devon accent as heavy and broad as his body. 'In you hop and we'll get you back to the farm.'

'*Back?*' thought Sebastian as he crept around the front of the vehicle and wrestled with the passenger door handle. 'As if I'd come to a place like this if I'd ever been here before!' Disgusted by the state of the passenger seat, which appeared to be covered in a crust of dirt and offcuts of the countryside, he brushed the worst of it off to join the compacted layers of rubbish in the footwell and climbed aboard. Neil jumped in next to him and, not bothering with his seatbelt, jammed the Landrover into gear and it lurched into the road.

'So,' said Neil, breaking the uncomfortable silence that almost drowned out the drone and rattles of the vehicle. 'Been to Devon before?'

Sebastian shook his head. 'No.'

'Ah, you're in for a treat then, and no mistake.' This seemed to Sebastian to be highly unlikely, and though he opened his mouth, he could find nothing inoffensive to say so closed it again without a word. Neil cleared his throat, which Sebastian suspected was to disguise another chuckle. 'Eaten, have you? There's half a pie back at the farm, if you fancy a bite.'

'I had a sandwich on the train,' said Sebastian. 'I'm fine. Thank you.'

'A *sandwich?*' Neil spoke the word as though it was an entirely new concept to him. 'You had a sandwich? You had to be travelling for six hours, lad, and all you've had is a sandwich.'

Sebastian's shrug was hidden in the darkness. 'Yes,' he said at last. 'It was egg and cress.' And the silence spread out again, filling his world with the sounds of the four-by-four as it sped along the street.

Neither of them uttered a word as they turned onto the main road towards somewhere called South Moulton.

The journey seemed to last an age, though it couldn't have been more than ten minutes. Just as Sebastian thought it would never end, and that the loud rattling from below his seat was some defect that would soon drop him through the floor onto the tarmac speeding beneath them, Neil spoke.

'Right then, lad. We're just up here.' And without bothering to signal, he slewed the vehicle left off the main road and onto a narrow, uphill avenue. On the ancient-looking sign opposite, Sebastian made out the words: 'Steepleford ¼ mile'.

'Steepleford?' he said, frowning at the unfamiliar name. 'Is that where we're going?'

Neil chuckled again. 'Course it is! Didn't your friend, Alison, tell you where you'd be staying?'

'Alison? Oh, you mean, Brillig. No. She didn't tell me anything. All I got was a couple of tickets, a pair of boots and told to get on the train.'

More coughing erupted from the driver's seat and this time Sebastian was even more certain it was to cover Neil's laughter.

'Well, you never know. Here we are,' he added, turning right onto a driveway. 'Home, sweet home.' One of the headlights had stopped working, but the other lit up a flash of brickwork, which almost brought a smile to Sebastian's face, but then it was gone as Neil swerved the Landrover round, and the light settled on an expanse of plants and netting before the engine died and darkness reclaimed the view. Sebastian frowned. That brief glimpse of the outside did not look at all appealing, and the plants looked ragged and ugly, nothing like the carefully tended parks of London, and even *those* were not really his "thing".

Neil leapt out and dragged the suitcase from the back before heading towards the house. Following him, Sebastian tripped over something on the dark, uneven path - a root maybe or some other hazard - and would have fallen over had he not hit the broad and very solid bulk of Neil.

'Aye, you'll be wanting to watch your step along here,' said Neil. Sebastian could almost feel the man's moustache bristling with amusement.

'Sorry,' he muttered.

Ahead of them came the sound of a handle being turned and a door creaked open, bathing the path ahead with a dull, yellow light. Standing in the entrance was the silhouette of a woman, who called out, her accent the twin of Neil's, 'You found the place alright, then?'

Sebastian, realising this comment was directed at him, replied, 'I guess. Though I didn't really *find* it, as such. I spent all evening being a passenger while everyone else drove.'

'Well, come on inside and I'll fix you up with some of this pheasant pie before you set up your tent.'

'I'm fine, thanks.'

'Aye,' said Neil, ushering Sebastian ahead of him through the door. 'He's not hungry, love. Apparently he had a *sandwich* on the train.' Again he spoke the word as though it was some strange, mythological entity. 'Egg and cress, wasn't it?'

Ignoring him, Sebastian wiped his shoes on the doormat, though it probably only made them dirtier, slipped them off and placed them on an empty shoe rack, surrounded by a pile of filthy boots. Then he straightened up and turned to his hosts.

'Sorry?' he said. 'Did you just say "tent"?'

It was a thing of nightmares. Spindly limbs clawed and snapped at him, and at every moment the tent's wing-like folds threatened to envelop and consume him. The wind wasn't helping either as, on the rare moments when Sebastian made any progress, it would snatch and pull at the tent, causing it to billow out, pulling up pegs that were hardly in the ground, whipping up guy-ropes like angry serpents and generally making the whole thing impossible.

'This is impossible!' he shouted, but there was no one to hear. After Neil had handed him the bag of tent parts, he'd flicked a switch, lighting up the area of grass in front of the house and disappeared into the warmth. Sebastian looked up at a nearby window and thought he saw someone watching him in the room beyond, but his view was obstructed as the wind picked up the far side of the tent, causing it to rear up over his head. He stepped back, trying to avoid it, but tripped over the poles that were strewn across the ground and landed in a heap of metal and canvas, a pole jabbing into the soft skin beneath his left eye, the instructions slipping from his fingers and blustering away on the breeze.

It started to rain.

Sebastian felt the anger welling up inside him and was almost overcome with an urge to smash the tent - to tear at it and stamp on it, to reduce it to a tattered mess - but he was worried *he* would come off worse. How could his friends have done this to him? How could they ever have imagined this would be anything less than a brutal torture? How could they even call themselves his *friends*? He tried not to imagine them all tucked up in their nice, cosy beds back in the city. And failed. Which only made him angrier.

He snatched up one of the metal poles, raising it above his head and the damp mess of his hair, and was about to bring it crashing down on the flapping sheets, when he heard a cough. Looking up, Sebastian noticed the farmhouse door was open and Neil stood watching him from the entrance.

'I take it you weren't a boy scout, then?' he said. Sebastian made no reply, but lowered the pole slowly, letting it slide from his fingers onto the wet ground. 'Come on, then. Let's get you inside. We'll put you up in the guest room instead.'

Sebastian gestured to the tangled mess of the tent. 'But what about–'

'Ah, don't worry about that old thing. Should have ditched it years ago. Just leave it there, lad.' And with that, he disappeared back into the house. Almost tearful with gratitude, Sebastian trudged back inside, leaving the hated tent to the mercy of the wind and rain.

'Are you sure you won't have a slice of this pie?' asked Neil's wife as he entered the living room. She had introduced herself as Virginia, and Sebastian's first impression of her was all about her hair. It wasn't so much that it was unkempt, more that it looked as though it had been clawed out of a hedge and then shovelled in a tangled heap onto her head. She had tied it up out of her face with a blue and white chequered tea-cloth, but a tentacular clump had managed to slip from its grasp and hung down over her right eye. She kept blowing at it with little effect. It took most of Sebastian's remaining willpower to keep from suggesting some products that might help tame its tangled coils. She was wearing a faded dressing gown over a pair of navy dungarees, and holding out a plate with a generous triangle of pheasant pie, its lattice top gleaming temptingly. Sebastian checked his watch, disturbed to find it smeared with mud. He pulled out a hanky to wipe the glass and was shocked to find it was almost one in the morning.

'I shouldn't really,' he said. 'It's pretty late and I won't have time to digest it properly. Thanks, though.'

Virginia frowned, still holding out the plate. 'No time to digest it? What else has your body got to do while you're snoozing away?'

'And besides,' said Neil, settling himself into an armchair overloaded with crochet-covered cushions, 'you'll need all the energy you can get for tomorrow!' There was a clatter as Virginia placed a fork on the plate, still held out to him.

Sebastian sighed and accepted the pie, before sitting, or rather collapsing, into one of the kitchen chairs.

'So then, Sebastian,' said Virginia, perching nearby and trying to tuck the stray tentacle back into the tea-towel. 'Neil tells me you've never been to Devon before.'

He paused, fork halfway to his mouth. 'To be honest, I've only been out of London a few times, and all of them were as a kid.'

'Really?' asked Neil, peering round the back of the armchair. The kitchen and living room were part of a single space, the wall between having been knocked through, and although Sebastian couldn't work out exactly what it was, it felt like something in the room was missing. Something *important*.

'Why would I?' said Sebastian, half a laugh in his

voice. 'There's everything anyone could possibly need in the city. Why venture out into the... the...' He waved his fork at the surroundings, noticing the piece of pie had fallen off, as he sought for a term that wasn't too derogatory.

'The *real* world?' suggested Virginia. She raised her eyebrows, causing the strands of hair to flop back down.

Sebastian coaxed the pie back onto his fork. 'Okay. That's not *exactly* the phrase I was searching for.'

'You don't like the countryside?'

Sebastian felt a shadow of irritability returning and took a deep breath, steeling himself to tell her *exactly* what he thought about the wretched countryside. But before he could utter a word, Neil spoke up from his armchair.

'Leave the poor lad to eat his pie, Virg. It's late and we have to be up at five-thirty.'

'*Five-thirty?*' said Sebastian. The pie fell off the fork again. 'In the *morning*?'

Neil was hidden by the back of the chair, but Sebastian could hear him chuckling again. 'Don't worry yourself,' he said. 'It's only us that's got an early morning. You can get up when you're ready.'

Sebastian speared the pie and ate the rest in silence. When he had finished, Virginia took his empty plate and set it down next to the large Belfast sink.

'Right,' she said as Sebastian got to his feet. 'Your room's straight up the stairs, second door on the left. Neil's already put your suitcase up there,' she added, as he peered around for it.

'Thanks,' he said. 'And thanks for letting me stay in your house. I don't think I'd've survived the night in the tent.'

Neil chuckled again. 'I don't reckon you'd have got it set up before morning.'

'There's space for your clothes in the wardrobe,' said Virginia, 'and you've got your own sink. Not that you'll use it, of course, if you're anything like Neil. You boys never seem to bother with unpacking clothes, and the lengths you go to to avoid washing...' She left the sentence unfinished, as though the lengths were too extreme even to mention.

For a moment, Sebastian was about to correct this assumption, but he couldn't be bothered. He was too tired and too miserable. He felt as though he was trapped in some kind of medieval purgatory, and, even worse, he had a bit of pheasant stuck in his teeth and suspected he had forgotten to bring his floss.

'Thank you.' he mumbled, and trudged up the stairs. As he settled into his bed, his worries and anxiety about what awful experiences lay in wait for him tomorrow threatened to keep him awake for hours, but as he rested his uncombed head on the too-soft pillow, he slipped into unconsciousness in moments.

A COUNTRY WEIRDO

It was quarter past eight when Sebastian opened his eyes, and immediately closed them again. Sunlight was lancing through a gap in the curtains and it felt as though it was boring into his face. This confused him as he wasn't used to sunlight invading his bedroom, but as he sat up and peered blearily at his surroundings, he remembered this wasn't *his* room. It wasn't his flat. He wasn't entirely sure if it even counted as his country, since he felt so far from home. He sighed.

'I really hate this place!' he said, then grimaced as he realised he'd said it out loud and hoped his hosts hadn't heard. He strained to listen, but couldn't hear any sounds from the house. Hopefully they were both out somewhere, and he recalled they had to be up super-early for some reason. 'Ridiculous.' he said, out loud again.

Opposite the bed was a dressing table, and Sebastian caught sight of himself in the ornately ugly mirror. He looked awful. His eyes were puffy and shadowed, his hair looked as though it'd been paused mid-explosion, and there was the clear mark of a bruise on his cheek, a token of his fight with the feral tent.

Dragging himself out of bed, he went to open the curtain, but thought better of it. The view, whatever it happened to be, would only upset him. Instead he shuffled across to the sink, where, on a small shelf that was barely up to the job, he had arranged the various bottles, tubs and pots that were part of his essential, everyday ablutions. He selected some shower gel, shampoo, conditioner and body scrub, together with some hair wax, deodorant, his shaving bag, toothbrush and paste, and his comb.

He looked at himself in the mirror again, the various products clutched across his chest, a towel on his shoulder.

'I guess it'll just have to do,' he said, and, after fiddling awkwardly with the door handle, let himself out onto the landing.

There were still no signs that Neil or Virginia were in the house, but he called out anyone to let anyone listening know he would be using the shower for a bit. There was no reply.

The bathroom was something of a surprise; specifically the bath itself. Although he had come across houses with baths before, neither the home he grew up in nor his own flat had one.

'Disgusting things!' he muttered as he lined up his collection of products on the basin. Then, as he looked at the room in the mirror, he realised there was no shower. Not even one of the rubbish ones that get built into the bath taps. Nothing. He span round, his eyes darting around the room as though, through his desperate searching, he might bring one into being. 'Now what am I supposed to do?'

The answer turned out to be squat in the bath and "shower" bits of himself at a time beneath the taps. It wasn't the most effective way to wash, especially since Sebastian hated to miss a single inch of his body, but eventually, after only slipping over and hitting his head twice and scalding himself just once, he finished the job and emerged from the tub.

Wrapping the towel around his waist, he opened up his shaving kit and found he had failed to pack his flannel. This was exactly why he hated having to leave in a rush! Who knew what else he'd forgotten to bring? Next to the bath was a tall cupboard, which he presumed might be where such things were stored. And sure enough, hidden among a pile of towels, most of which were worn paper thin, was a flannel. It had a faded picture of a horse on it. There was also a shower attachment for the bath taps.

'Typical!' he said, snatching up the ugly flannel and shoving it in the basin.

Twenty minutes later, having completed his washing, styling, shaving and perfuming, and dressed in a poloshirt tucked into grey cargo trousers, the pockets loaded with necessities, Sebastian emerged from his room and headed downstairs. There was no sign of Neil or Virginia, except for a handwritten note left on the kitchen table. The writing was a messy scrawl of the kind he produced when trying to use his left hand when drunk, but his name was clearly legible at the top of the page. He picked it up and attempted to decipher the rest.

'Help yourself to… Frankfurt? *Breakfast!*' he read aloud. 'Bacon and… sal.. sausages in the fudge… *fridge*. Please called… *collect* the eggs from the… hens and take… them to the village stove. *Store*. The Village Store. Right out of the drive. Right… at the crossword… *road*… crossroad. Thanks.' Beneath this was a scribble that he assumed was either Virginia or Neil's signature, though he couldn't work out which.

Glancing around the kitchen, Sebastian decided not to bother with the fridge; not because he didn't fancy bacon or sausages, but because there were a couple of large dead birds of some description, hanging from a length of thick, orange string tied to the handle. Instead, he made himself a mug of coffee - black - and some toast - dry - before pulling on his shiny, new wellies, making sure his trouser bottoms were safely tucked inside. He then headed out of the farmhouse.

Sebastian's experience of chickens, which was limited to pictures in books or on egg boxes and brief appearances on television, was sufficient to help him find the henhouse. It was inside a large, scrub-covered run surrounded by a rusting wire fence to the left of the driveway. As he approached the gate to the enclosure, the dozen or so chickens turned to watch him, their heads moving with arrhythmic jerks, their bodies unmoving. He flicked the latch and inched the gate open, trying to keep an eye on all the birds at the same time, just in case. Satisfied that they weren't about to attack him, he pulled the gate closed behind him and picked his way step-by-step towards the henhouse, taking care to avoid sullying his clean boots in anything unsavoury.

He took so long to reach the small shed-like building that the chickens, clearly deciding he was neither food nor threat, returned to scratching at the dirt and pecking at the invisible scraps they unearthed.

'Right,' said Sebastian, causing the chickens to pause and fix him with their one-eyed stares again. 'Whereabouts do you lot lay your eggs, then?' As far as he could see there was only one entrance to the henhouse; a small door at the top of a miniature ladder. He crouched down, bending his head to peer inside, but it was too dark to see anything. Holding his breath, he eased his head gently through the entrance, taking care not to let his face, or worse his hair, touch the edges.

Something exploded from the darkness; a crazed mound of feathers, squawking as though it had been kicked, which launched itself at Sebastian's face in a flapping frenzy. Sebastian swore loudly, tumbling backwards onto the ground, his arms desperately trying to protect himself from the crazed chicken.

'Get off!' he screamed in the voice of a howling child. 'Not my face!' But the chicken had gone, scurrying across the enclosure still squawking away. Sebastian didn't move, but stayed curled up in a protective ball until his breathing slowed and his panic subsided. He reached up and gripped hold of part of the henhouse that jutted out from the main body, pulling himself up off the ground. As he did so, the panel he was holding moved and he noticed it was attached to the side of the building by a series of hinges. Carefully, in case it revealed further feathered furies, he raised the lid and found himself staring in at a series of sectioned areas, each filled with golden straw, amongst which were a number of speckled, brown eggs.

'Who'd have guessed?' he said, wishing *he* had before he'd landed on his back in goodness knows what filth. He drew a pair of bright, yellow washing-up gloves from his back pocket. 'I may not know much about the countryside,' he informed the chickens, as they watched him snapping the gloves onto his hands, 'but I *do* know where eggs come from!'

One by one, with as much care as possible, he lifted the eggs from the nesting boxes until he had all thirteen nestling in his arms. He looked around, but couldn't see anything to carry them in - all the containers were taken up with water and what he presumed was some kind of chicken food, though it looked more like piles of gravel - so, taking care not to drop any of the eggs, he tiptoed back across the enclosure.

Half way to the door, he spotted the chicken that had attacked him watching him with what he interpreted as a hostile expression (though, to be fair, none of them looked over-friendly), so he gave it a wide berth. With some difficulty he fumbled the gate open with a combination of fingertips and boots, and escaped from their lair. As he was prodding the latch back into place the 'Psycho Hen', as he now thought of it, squawked again and scurried back towards the henhouse to lay in wait for the next unsuspecting trespasser.

'Turn right out of the drive,' he repeated to himself, and left the property, heading uphill towards, he presumed, the centre of the village. He had only glimpsed this road yesterday, in the Landrover's headlight, but it was much as he recalled; a narrow strip of tarmac bordered on the left by a high hedge in which he recognised clusters of nettles lurking amongst the other plants, which were no doubt just as unpleasant. You didn't get roads like this in the city, not even in the backstreets. Thinking of London pulled a veil of homesickness over Sebastian, lowering his already damaged mood. He sighed and shook his head, trying to clear it, while also keeping the eggs steady.

As he neared the brow of the hill, the hedge on the left gave way to a gate and then a building. It had the look of an old house, but its front was almost entirely filled by a large window, the space behind it shrouded in shadow. Above the glass the word 'butcher' had been written in large, ornate capitals of flaking paint. Sebastian caught sight of his reflection and approached the window to take a closer look. His polo shirt had, hopefully, mud down the left sleeve and was all skewed across his shoulders.

'What a mess!' he told his reflected self. 'And you don't smell so good either. I think you might have-' Distracted by a movement beyond the glass, he paused and, refocusing, leaned in closer to see what it was.

At first all he could make out was a few indistinct shapes: a till on a counter, something large hanging from the ceiling, a glass display cabinet. Then, with a shock, he saw the man. He was huge - broad shouldered, thick necked, his head bald and gleaming, his beard like something out of the Bible. If it wasn't for his white shirt and striped apron, and the straw boater perched on his head, he could have been a Hell's Angel. In one hand he held something large and shiny, and with a start Sebastian realised it was a cleaver. The man was wiping his other hand slowly across his apron, leaving a dark smear in its wake. And he was staring straight at Sebastian in a way that looked even more hostile than the Psycho Hen. Sebastian jumped back in shock, causing one of the eggs to bounce off his forearm and tumble towards the paving slabs. Instinctively he tried to slow its fall with his foot. The egg burst apart, coating his boot with its contents and spattering the window with globules of yolk.

A sound escaped from Sebastian's mouth as though he was being strangled and, not waiting for the massive and heavily-armed butcher to burst onto the scene, he hurried up to the crossroads, leaning backwards as he did so to make sure no further breakages occurred. Turning right, he passed a hairdresser called *The Head Mistress*, where a small cluster of ladies chattered together, the domes of wall-mounted dryers hovering above their heads like something from a Fifties movie. Their conversation stilled and their faces followed him as Sebastian scurried past to the neighbouring Village Store. Nudging the door open with his boot, he dashed inside and jammed the door shut with his back, the bell above it dancing and ringing out his arrival.

Sebastian ran his eyes around the interior of the shop. On the three sides facing him, shelves filled the walls from floor to ceiling, laden with everything from bags of sugar and tea to bottles of bleach and sink plungers. Against one, a wooden ladder had been left, waiting for a customer to request something high up.

An oak-topped counter formed a U-shape in front of these shelves, stacked high with goods, except for a gap in the centre, where Sebastian saw the top could be lifted up to allow easy access to the till and the doorway beyond. In the space made by the U, there were a few large baskets with things like mops, brushes and other items that were not ideally shaped for the counter-top or shelves. The floor beneath them was a checkerboard of worn linoleum. It looked so old-fashioned that Sebastian wondered if they still rationed some of the goods they sold, butter maybe or chocolate. It was very *Open All Hours*.

'Those for me, are they?' came a voice, but Sebastian couldn't see who it belonged to. It was certainly female and he imagined her as a middle-aged, busty shopkeeper, full of gossip and suspicion, dressed in some old-fashioned dress, her large and no doubt hairy arms left bare. He stepped away from the security of the door and ventured into the U.

'Hello?' he said, his voice sounding uncertain. 'Who's there?'

Without warning a head popped up from behind a stack of loaves on the counter, making Sebastian jump and almost drop further eggs. 'Me, of course!'

His first thought was how different she was from his imagined shopkeeper. Far from the gossipy, old bulldog woman, this was, well, a *girl*! He hadn't even considered that someone so close to his own age, in fact a few years younger, would be living so far from city life. And she was pretty. *Definitely* pretty. Sebastian had come across girls with red hair and freckles before and, for most of them, it hadn't worked in their favour. But for this girl, who he noticed, as he stared at her open-mouthed, had the green eyes to match, it *did* work. The hair was of a darker shade of red, which lay somewhere between curly and straight, and the freckles were concentrated around the area below her eyes and across the bridge of her nose, highlighting the soft lines of her face. Her clothes, however, were dreadful, consisting mostly of the sort of boring dress he'd imagined on the middle-aged version of the shopkeeper, which entirely failed to show off the body which lay beneath.

Sebastian shook his head in an attempt to dispel the thought of her body, and coughed to cover his embarrassment.

'Something up?' asked the girl, with a lopsided smile that Sebastian couldn't interpret.

He croaked something unintelligible, then cleared his throat and tried again. 'Sorry. You're just... not what I expected.'

'Why? What did you expect.'

He tried not to think about the imagined shopkeeper. 'Nothing,' he said, his voice higher than normal.

'I'll take that as a compliment!' The girl looked at him a moment, her head tilted slightly to one side, before lifting up the hinged counter top and striding towards him. She stopped uncomfortably close. 'You going to answer my question then?'

Sebastian swallowed, wondering what she meant. 'Your question?'

'Are those for me?' She indicated downwards with her eyes. When there was no response, she added, 'The eggs?'

'Eggs?' said Sebastian, sounding confused. He looked down at the objects nestling in his arms as if he'd never seen them before. 'Oh, the eggs! Yes, of course. They're for you. For the shop. I'm supposed to bring them here. And here they are! Twelve eggs.'

'What happened to unlucky number thirteen?' she asked, pointing to the globules still clinging to his boot. He followed her finger and noticed a blob slide off onto the lino.

'Er...'

The girl raised her eyebrows. 'You didn't think to put them in an egg box or anything? They *are* made for them, you know. The clue's in the name.'

Sebastian shrugged. 'I couldn't find one.'

The girl ducked back behind the counter and emerged with a couple of said boxes. 'Let's get them into these before you drop any more.' One at a time, she plucked the eggs from Sebastian's arms and tucked them into the boxes. 'So, you must be the guy from London, yes? The one staying with the Symeses?'

'Who?' he asked, the skin on his arms prickling

with awareness as the girl slid her fingers under an egg.

'Neil and Virg.' She gestured with the egg in the direction of the crossroads. 'At Larkin Farm.'

Sebastian nodded. 'My name's Sebastian.'

The girl placed the first full box on the counter, then turned back, locking eyes with him, her stare intense and confident. 'I'm Emma,' she said. Sebastian broke her gaze. Why couldn't she be called Deirdre or Pauline or something like that? Not Emma! Emma was up there with Amy and Lucy as one of his favourite girls' names. 'So what brings you all the way here from the city?' asked Emma, opening the other egg box and filling it from Sebastian's arms. He tried to ignore the contact with his bare skin.

'Huh. I was more *forced* here than "brought". This really isn't my sort of thing.'

'What isn't? Collecting eggs?'

'All of it! Collecting eggs, doing other farm stuff, being miles from the city, surrounded by trees and fields and all the weirdoes who live in the country.'

'*I* live in the country,' said Emma, placing the last egg in the box and closing the lid. 'Does that make *me* a weirdo, too?'

Sebastian felt his cheeks flush and he rubbed a hand across his forehead self-consciously. 'What? No, of course not. I didn't mean-'

'Are you going to take those off?'

'Sorry?' said Sebastian, confused.

She pointed to his hand, still pressed against his brow. 'Those gloves. Why are you wearing them, anyway?'

Sebastian's eyes focussed on the yellow of the glove. Remembering what it had been touching, he jerked it away from his face. 'Eurgh!' He tried to wipe his brow on his shoulder, but failed. 'I put them on so I wouldn't have to touch those dirty eggs. They come out of chickens' backsides, you know!'

She raised her eyebrows and frowned at the same time, which only managed to make her look even more attractive. 'Do they really?'

'Yeah,' said Sebastian, pulling off the gloves and folding them into his back pocket. 'I try not to think about it when I'm actually eating them, and I reckon the ones from the supermarket are properly sterilised, but *these...*' he gestured to the egg boxes, 'these are straight from the source. Grim! You'll want to wash your hands,' he added.

'I could,' she said, and, before he could react, she seized his now uncovered hands in her own and pulled him forward so her mouth was next to his ear. She was tall. He couldn't breathe. Though the dress concealed her form in its dowdy folds, he was all to aware of the shape of her body as it pressed against him. He was worried he was quivering, ever so slightly, as she whispered in his ear. 'But I'm a country weirdo, remember?' Although her voice bore the same accent as Neil's, it seemed different somehow, lilting, almost hypnotic. She paused a moment, her breath stroking his hair, before drawing back a few inches to look him in the eye, her hands still gripping his. She frowned a little as though trying to work something out. Sebastian noticed the green of her eyes was edged with a ring of dark brown. She was so close, and he felt himself melting in the warmth of her breath on his cheek.

'Are you wearing perfume?' she asked in a loud voice, breaking the spell as she stepped back and let go of his hands.

'Sorry?' said Sebastian, desperately gathering his thoughts. 'Perfume?'

'Yes, perfume. You are, aren't you? You're wearing perfume. Is that what men do in London?'

Sebastian held up his hands, defending himself from this accusation. 'I'm not wearing *perfume*.' Emma raised cynical eyebrows, but said nothing. 'I'm *not*! It's just normal products. *Men's* products.'

'Men's perfume?'

He bristled. '*Scents!* Deodorant, eau de toilette, aftershave… that sort of thing. Women don't wear aftershave.'

'Don't you believe it!' said Emma, her smile revealing straight, white teeth. 'Some of the women round here definitely do.'

'That reminds me. Do you have any dental floss?'

Behind him the bell burst into its chirpy, fitful ringing and he span round, half-expecting to find the gigantic butcher with his blood-spattered knife.

'Alright, you two,' said Neil. 'Thought I might find you in here.'

Emma shrugged. 'Of course,' she said. 'This is my home.'

'I was talking to young Sebastian. Everything alright with them eggs?'

Without meaning to, Sebastian glanced down at his boot and the evidence of his egg delivery mishap. 'Kind of.'

'Good.' Neil clapped his large hands together. 'Right then. You can't hide in here all day, chatting up Miss Standfield. We've got plenty to be getting on with.' He yanked the door open, a broad smile on his face. 'It's time to feed the pigs.'

4

MANICURE AND MANURE

'I wasn't,' said Sebastian, glancing over his shoulder to check the shop door was closed.

Neil didn't pause as he crossed the road. 'You weren't what?'

'I wasn't chatting her up.'

'Course you weren't!' said Neil, in the voice that suggests you believe the opposite. 'Right. Jump in the back and we'll head on down.'

They had stopped next to the strangest, and filthiest, looking vehicle Sebastian had ever seen. It looked like the blighted offspring of a Landrover and a motorbike. Just visible beneath the swathes of caked-on muck, there were small patches of green paint. Attached to the back of this manure heap on wheels was a trailer, filled with dirty sacks, containing who knew what, a mess of straw and a dog.

'What is this contraption?' he asked, flapping a hand at the vehicle, then, remembering Emma had touched them after handling the unwashed eggs, he ferreted around in his pocket and pulled out a bottle of alcohol gel.

'It's my quad bike,' said Neil, sounding, to Sebastian's ears, far too proud of the horrible thing.

'And you want *me* to get in *there*?' he pointed at the trailer while rubbing the gel over his hands. 'Does this thing even work?'

Neil pulled a bundle of keys from his wax jacket and jangled them. 'Oh, you bet it does. And yes, in you get.' Sebastian made no move towards the trailer, but just stood in the road, staring at the jumbled contents. And the dog. Neil followed his gaze. 'Ah, don't worry about old Tank. He won't bite you. Probably.'

'I wasn't worried about it biting me,' said Sebastian, 'more that it might give me fleas or something.'

'*It?*' Neil gave him a look of disbelief. 'He's a *he*. And no, *he* won't give you fleas. Come on.' And with that, he swung a booted leg over the seat of the quad bike and started it up. On the pavement beyond, an old man watched impassively, sucking on a pipe and breathing out great clouds of smoke. Catching Sebastian's eye, the man nodded at the trailer. Sebastian sighed and clambered aboard, perching in amongst the dirty clutter and the messy dog, and touching as little of it as possible. Without warning the quad bike shot forwards, nearly pitching him back out into the road, but instead landing him squarely on his backside in the straw. He swore. 'Did you say something?' called Neil over his shoulder.

'Nothing,' Sebastian shouted back as he pulled out the alcohol gel again. 'Just getting comfy.'

Neil signalled with his left arm and swerved across the road, causing a small lady riding an antique looking bicycle, its basket full of flowers, to swerve out of the way. Sebastian turned to watch as she mounted the pavement behind them, amazed she didn't end up in the hedge.

'Sorry, love!' shouted Neil, over the drone of the quad bike, but made no attempt to stop as he headed down the hill towards the farmhouse. 'So you're not a dog person then, lad?'

'What? No. Not really.' He looked at Tank, who was facing into the breeze as they sped down the hill, tongue lolling out to one side. 'Not at all, in fact.'

'Do you like cats, then?'

Sebastian thought back to his great aunt Joan's house, which he used to get dragged along to occasionally as a child. She'd had a cat, a fat, old tabby called Tiddles. *Tiddles*, for goodness' sake! Thankfully the wretched thing was long dead, but even now Sebastian could almost taste the smell of stale cat urine that pervaded every inch of that house. It was a horrible beast, which would sidle up to Sebastian and start rubbing itself up against him, leaving clumps of hair on his clothes. Eventually, he would give in and pat it ever so slightly, and Tiddles would immediately lay on the floor, legs stretched out to expose its large belly. Sebastian would stroke it, tentatively, knowing that any second the cat would turn from purring adoration to claw-thrashing hatred without warning.

Sebastian touched his forearm, absentmindedly, thinking about the many scratches that had criss-crossed his skin over the years. Damned cat!

'Definitely not!' he replied. They carried on down the hill, past the farmhouse on the left and the next two houses, after which they had hedges on both sides with tall trees forming a canopy above them, throwing the surroundings into a dappled shade. Sebastian didn't like it. It was all far too green for his tastes.

Neil shouted again, turning to look at Sebastian over his shoulder, which was most disconcerting. 'So, what *do* you like? You got any pets back in London.'

'I have a spider plant,' shouted Sebastian, gripping onto the sides of the trailer and making a mental note to put the washing-up gloves back on to avoid running out of alcohol gel. As they approached the bottom of the hill and the main road, the wind that rushed past him, tugging at his clothes and pulling at his hair, was filled with Neil's laughter.

Fifty metres or so from the T-junction, the quad bike slowed almost to a stop, before turning right through a gap in the hedge and doubling-back along a dirt track. The ground was uneven and, though Tank seemed to be unshakeable, as though he was nailed to the trailer floor, Sebastian was tossed around with the sacks and straw no matter how hard he gripped onto the sides. To his relief, the path ahead was blocked by a vehicle, which, even though his vision was blurred by the constant juddering motion of the quad bike, he recognised as the Landrover which had brought him to the farmhouse last night. Just before they reached it, the path widened out on both sides and Neil pulled up behind it as he jammed on the brakes. He cut the engine and turned to Sebastian.

'Well, that was fun!' he began, then paused as he took in the sight of Sebastian, whose face was set in a terrified grimace, his hands still gripping the sides of the trailer. A smile slowly spread across Neil's face. 'You look like you've just seen a ghost,' he said.

'If I did,' said Sebastian, 'it was probably my own. I think you dislodged it when we were bouncing along the track back there. It is an actual, proper track, isn't it? Or did we just take some short cut across a building site?'

Neil's face looked suddenly serious. 'So you believe in them, then?'

'In what? Building sites?'

'In *ghosts!*' Neil spoke the word in a loud whisper,

accentuating it with a flick of his fingers. Sebastian stared at him, uncertain whether he was just winding him up. After all, this was a genuine, real-life countryside person and they believed all kinds of things, didn't they? He was pretty sure they were all pagans or Druids or something.

'Um...' he said, trying to find the right words that would cause the least offence. 'I'm not entirely closed-minded about that sort of thing... but I can't say I've ever really given it much thought.' Neil's eyes narrowed, his moustache drooping solemnly, but he made no response. 'So, er...' said Sebastian, filling the awkward void. 'Do *you* believe in... um, you know, ghosts and that?'

'Load of old nonsense, if you ask me!' said Neil, chuckling again as he climbed off the quad bike. 'Right then, these pigs won't feed themselves. Grab that green plastic bag for us, and we'll head on up.'

Shaking his head, Sebastian half-climbed, half-fell out of the trailer. 'One moment,' he said, pulling his comb from his back pocket. It had snapped on the journey down, but he did as good a job as he could with the larger of the two halves. Tucking it into a different pocket, he took out the alcohol gel and squeezed some onto his hands. 'Oh no!'

It was such a desperate sounding cry, that Neil, who was busy sorting through a pile of what looked like ice cream tubs, dropped them and span round.

'Everything okay?' he asked, his voice etched with concern. 'What's happened, lad?'

Sebastian lifted up a hand, its palm facing Neil, its finger spread. 'I broke a nail! It must have happened when I was gripping the trailer as we jolted over all that rubble. I can't believe it!'

'A *nail?*' It was now Neil's turn to look uncertain whether Sebastian was being serious. 'You broke a nail? They do grow back, you know.'

'But I only had them done last week. Up in Soho. It cost me forty quid.'

If anything Neil's face looked even more stunned. 'What do you mean, you had them *done?*'

Sebastian, having tucked his alcohol gel away, pulled out his trusty washing-up gloves and started tugging them on. 'Just the usual stuff, you know. Buffing, polishing, tidying up the cuticles and all that. A manicure.'

Neil clearly *didn't* know, but, with a brief raise of his eyebrows, turned his attention back to the containers. As Sebastian walked over, carrying the green plastic bag, which turned out to be empty, Neil rattled the lid off a metal bin and started scooping out piles of large, grey pellets into the bag with one of the ice cream tubs.

Sebastian took a moment to glance around the place. There wasn't much to see to the right of the track, just a load of trees on a hill that climbed up to the road they'd come down. On the other side, the ground levelled off into a couple of fields that stretched away to what looked like a small river, about a billionth of the size of the Thames - the only river Sebastian knew to compare it with. He couldn't quite make out what was in the first field, as a long, low building blocked most of his view, but in the second, he saw a couple of brown horses chewing at the grass and wearing covers over their heads. Another large building and a row of trees obscured the rest of the smallholding, but Sebastian got the impression it went on a long way, and although he was used to the massive structures and spaces of London, the size of this place made him feel small and vulnerable. To him, it was a vast, alien terrain, full of unpredictable creatures and dangerous obstacles. And the quad bike, of course.

After eight or nine ice cream tubfuls, Neil clanked the lid back on and tossed the container back with the others, then grabbed the sack in one large hand and strode off up the track beyond the Landrover.

'So, these pigs,' said Sebastian, hurrying along behind him, 'are they dangerous at all? Only I've seen films where gangsters use pigs as a way to dispose of bodies. And a friend of mine, Little Pete, told me a story the other night about a farmer who fell into his pigsty and there was nothing left of him but a pair of wellies.'

'Glad to hear you've done your research,' said Neil over his shoulder. 'I'd not heard about the farmer's boots, but they sure do eat pretty much anything. I wouldn't go lying down in their run, if I was you.'

'So they *are* dangerous, then?'

Neil just chuckled, a sound that was beginning to get on Sebastian's nerves, and followed the path as it curved uphill. Sebastian was about to repeat his question, when he caught a glimpse of something moving up ahead between the trees. And it wasn't just the sight that gave him pause, but, as he passed the broad trunk of a nearby tree, his sense of smell and sound came under assault as well.

The pigs had obviously heard them approaching and piled out en masse, but when Neil shook the bag of pellets, which were presumably pig food, they went into some kind of squabbling, squealing frenzy. As Sebastian drew closer, he realised that they were much smaller than he had expected, about the length of one of his arms, though with a much bigger girth. But it wasn't their size that surprised him so much as the colour.

'Aren't pigs pink?' he said, as they came to a halt a few feet away from where the creatures jostled and snorted.

Neil turned. 'Some are, yes. Yorkshires, Chester Whites, that sort of thing, even Tamworths, I guess, though they're more orangey.' Sebastian nodded, though he had no idea what he was talking about. 'But these here,' Neil reached out and patted one of the pigs on the head, 'are Berkshires. Beautiful, black piggies.' For a moment Sebastian was on the verge of offering him the alcohol gel, but thought better of it.

'And are they all this small?' he said. 'I was expecting something a bit… bigger.'

'Something more like Lucy?' asked Neil. He pointed further up the hill and for the first time, Sebastian noticed the presence of a monster. It looked about the same size and weight as the quad bike, and he was sure it would be strong enough to pull the trailer with hardly any effort, though Sebastian certainly wouldn't be hopping in for the ride. Its muddy, black hide was covered in a thick mat of bristles, from its bat-like ears to its chewed-up-rope-like tail. Its face was shaped like a ski jump, its snout pushed up and sniffing at the air, and what Sebastian reckoned to be rows of teats dragged along in the muck beneath its vast belly.

He opened his mouth and closed it, struggling for words, and eventually settled on, 'Lucy? You named *that* thing Lucy?'

Neil beamed at the beast. 'That's her. Beautiful girl, ain't she, our Lucy? And these,' he brandished a hand at the still squabbling hoards of piglets, 'are her cuddly little babies. Shall we give them their breakfast?'

'Er, I'd rather not,' said Sebastian, taking a step back.

Neil chuckled again. 'It weren't a question. Come on, and mind out for this wire.' He bent and pointed to a run of wire about six inches from the ground. 'It's electric.'

Sebastian looked at the thin strand by Neil's finger. It looked thin and not very fence-like. 'Is that all that's stopping them getting out?'

'Aye. They don't like to get too close. It won't kill you, but it'll give you a nasty shock!' As if to emphasise the point, one of the piglets edged forward to sniff at Neil's finger and its snout brushed against the wire. There was a sound like someone snapping a piece of bamboo and a definite spark, followed by a sound somewhere between a high-pitched bark and a gunshot.

Neil laughed and stomped over the wire, nudging the piglets out of the way with his boots. They made Sebastian think of the pig-munched farmer's boots, so he decided to step over well away from the seething mass of bodies. However, as he edged along the boundary, the pigs followed him, leaving no safe gap to cross.

'They're not letting me in, Neil!' he said. In answer, Neil reached into the plastic sack and brought out a handful of pellets, which he tossed away up the hill. As they hit the stony earth, the piglets threw themselves on them in a snorting, bustling turmoil, which only made Sebastian think even more about that unfortunate farmer.

'Hurry up, then,' said Neil. 'That won't keep them

away for long.'

Cautiously, as though stepping onto a minefield, he lifted his left foot and placed it on the far side of the wire. The ground here was mostly thick mud where the pigs had churned it up and done goodness' knew what to it, but it felt firm enough, so Sebastian stepped in with the other foot as well.

Neil held out the sack. 'Good lad. Give us a hand scattering this lot around would you. I'm going to check the water.'

'Where do you want me to scatter it?' asked Sebastian, eyeing Lucy nervously as she shuffled down the hill.

Neil waved his hand towards the area furthest from the piglets as he marched away. 'Oh, over that side will do. Just scatter it around as if you're sowing grass seed.'

Sebastian, who had never sowed seeds of any variety in his life, headed off to the indicated area, pleased to get away from the man-eating swine. In his relief, however, he failed to notice the tree root sticking up from a patch of mud and tripped. He just managed to keep himself from falling over, which would have been nothing short of a disaster of personally apocalyptic proportions, but in doing so, he trod on the bottom of the sack, tearing the corner. He yanked it up, trying to stem the eruption of pellets with a gloved hand, but it was too late. The piglets were already aware.

As one, the writhing herd charged towards Sebastian, snorting and squealing, their snouts twitching and their mouths dripping with saliva and half-chewed pellets.

He swore. Loudly. A spontaneous outburst, born

of panic. Then the creatures were all around him, snuffling at the ground around his boots, biting at the sack which slipped through his unresisting fingers onto the ground. One of them nudged at his ankle, while another, bullied by one of its siblings, forced its way between his legs. Sebastian tried to back away, but there was a pig right behind him.

'Don't try and move!' shouted Neil, hurrying back down the hill towards him, but Sebastian had already picked up one foot and suddenly there was nowhere to set it back down again, except on one of the bristle-covered backs snaking around him. And then he felt it, a nudge in the back of his knee, and he knew that it was all over. He was going down and no one could save him. Thankfully, most of the pellets had fallen in front of him, so he mostly landed on the ground. He hardly felt the impact; his one thought was to get away from the feeding frenzy and the razor sharp teeth, and get to the safety of the path. He scuttled backwards, pulling off a remarkable speed for someone propelled by only their heels and elbows.

'Wait!' shouted Neil, 'You don't want to go that way!' But Sebastian wasn't interested. He was headed away from the piglets, so it was the *only* way he was interested in. 'That's their toilet!'

For a split second, Sebastian paused, his eyes flicking to the ground on either side. It was certainly more sludgy here. And some of those lumps of earth looked much more like...

'Crap!' he shouted and, catching sight of the path only a couple of metres away to his right, launched himself over it sideways. He almost made it. It would have been a perfect landing had he not twisted slightly and ended up with his cheek pressed against the electric wire.

He knew then why the piglet had made such a fuss.

5

GLUTEN INTOLERANCE

'It wasn't *that* bad!' said Neil, chewing on a piece of bread and watching Sebastian from across the table. They were back in the farmhouse kitchen where Virginia had prepared them a lunch of ham, cheese, fruit and bread, together with a large jug of what Sebastian was surprised to find out was beer. *Homebrewed* beer apparently. He had experienced homebrew before during his student days at UCL and, while he couldn't remember *everything* about the evening in question, he did remember whispering promises of abstinence to the toilet he ended up hugging, and the two-day hangover that caused him to receive a D for handing his assignment in late.

He took a sip of his orange squash. '*Not that bad?*' he said, emphasising every word. 'It was bad enough that I needed a complete change of clothes and a shower. And I now have another mark on my cheek to match the one from the tent.'

'We don't have a shower,' said Neil, frowning over his massive sandwich.

Virginia reached over to turn Sebastian's head a little. 'Let's have a look at it, then.' Sebastian leaned forwards, brandishing his injured cheek. 'Oh, it is quite red, isn't it? Still, another inch higher it would've been your eye. You were lucky!'

'Like I said,' Neil pointed with his sandwich and a

slice of tomato flopped out onto his plate, 'it's not *that* bad.'

'Because the electric wire didn't burn my eye out? Lucky old me.' Sebastian shook his head and continued the careful operation of slicing the bread. This wasn't something he was used to as all the bread he bought came pre-sliced. In his mind, he had imagined producing an even, coaster-straight piece of bread, but the reality was turning out more like a lump of wood that had been hacked at with a blunt axe.

'Here,' said Virginia. 'Let me.' Sebastian handed her the knife and, in a matter of seconds, she had not only tidied up the mess he'd made of the loaf, but produced a perfect, thick slice. She flicked it onto his plate with the knife.

'Thanks.'

'He broke a nail, too,' said Neil, scooping out an alarming amount of mustard from a small jar and adding it to his half-eaten sandwich. 'Show Virg your nail, lad.'

Sighing, Sebastian held out his hand towards her, tilted so she could see the nail in question. 'I clipped it and filed it down after my shower,' he said, 'but it still feels a bit strange.'

'Apparently it cost him, what was it, forty pounds to have them done?'

Virginia frowned. 'What do you mean, *done?*'

Sebastian opened his mouth to speak, but Neil beat him to it. 'Oh, you know, Virg. Buffing, polishing... er, sorting out his canticles.'

'*Cuticles*,' Sebastian corrected.

'Aye, them too.'

Virginia looked down at her own nails, which Sebastian saw were dull and cracked, with tips of varying lengths, and a few spots of red here and there where they had once been painted. 'Forty pounds, eh?' she whispered. 'Well, I never.'

Neil chuckled into his mug of beer. 'Don't you start getting any ideas, love!'

'I could give you a manicure, if you want,' said Sebastian, concentrating on making sure the butter was evenly distributed across his bread.

'Really?' she asked.

Sebastian nodded. 'Of course. I'm pretty sure I know what I'm doing.' He gestured to her hands with the buttery knife. 'I reckon I could sort them out with the equipment I've got upstairs.'

Virginia opened her mouth, but no sound came out. She appeared, to Sebastian, to be having some kind of internal struggle as she tried to work out what to say. Eventually the words found their way out. 'I don't think so,' she said. 'It's very kind of you, Sebastian, but... well, I'm a farmer's wife. There's no point in having some fancy manicure when you could end up elbow deep in a goat an hour later, or have to claw your way through a log pile after an escaped chicken. It'd be a waste of both our time. But thanks.' She looked again at her nails, a wistful expression crossing her face. 'Anyway,' she said at last, 'what're you boys up to this afternoon now you've fed the pigs?'

Sebastian raised his eyebrows at Neil, who downed the rest of his beer in one go and clanked the glass onto the table. 'Actually,' he said, wiping a couple of drips from his chin with the back of his sleeve, 'we didn't get them *all* fed, thanks to that messing around with Lucy and her little uns. We've still got the weaners and Major Tom to feed.'

'Major Tom?' said Sebastian, his heart sinking at

the idea of having to face yet more terrifying beasts.

Virginia smiled. 'Major Tom's our boar.' She must have caught Sebastian's anxious look, as she continued, 'Don't worry yourself about him. Old Tom wouldn't hurt a fly. He's just a big, cuddly softy.'

As far as Sebastian could see, as he loitered outside Major Tom's enclosure some thirty minutes later, the only correct part of Virginia's description was the word 'big'. The bit about the flies might also have been true, since, as he approached, a great buzzing cloud burst from what Sebastian recognised from recent experience as the pig's toilet area.

The pen was smaller than that of the piglets and their mother, and rather than being situated on the hill among the trees, this one was on part of the flat area between the hill and the river, which Neil informed him was called the Bray. In the field behind him, the horses still ambled around in their face masks, while on the far side of Major Tom's enclosure, there was another large field before the tall boundary hedge cut off the view beyond. Neither that field nor the enclosure ahead were grassy like the horses', but were instead a sea of churned up earth and stones. The sun was high above the valley, sparkling on the brisk ripples of the Bray and the stagnant surface of a muddy wallow in the run ahead. It did not smell wonderful.

Too worried by the pig to care about these untamed surroundings, Sebastian watched as Neil swung a leg over the electric wires. There were two this time, one low like before, the second about two foot off the ground. Sebastian paused in front of them, clutching another plastic sack of pellets in his washing-up gloved hands, and considered Major Tom. Perhaps 'big' *wasn't* that accurate a word. 'Gigantic' might have been more appropriate, or even 'monstrous'. Like Lucy - Sebastian still couldn't get over Neil's choice of that name for a pig! - Major Tom was black, no doubt being the same breed, but he was much broader and looked far more menacing. As the bore swaggered towards Neil, the creature's vast bulk swaying beneath, it seemed somehow primal, a terror from an ancient world. Sebastian recalled a history lesson at school, where his class had been told that, back in the days when people rode horses and used swords, pigs had been used in battle. When the enemy cavalry came galloping in, the pigs would be released, scaring the horses and tearing at their bellies with long, razor-sharp tusks. And though Major Tom didn't have any tusks, that did nothing to allay Sebastian's fears.

'Come on,' called Neil as he poured water into a metal container. 'The poor bugger's waited long enough for his food already.'

Steeling himself, Sebastian tiptoed over the electric wire and crept across the run. 'Where shall I put it?' he asked, his voice barely a whisper.

Neil looked round and waved a hand. 'Oh, anywhere's fine.'

Although the boar didn't move with the same speed or agility as the piglets, Major Tom did manage to get up to a decent trot as he heard the sound of the pellets hitting the muddy ground. As he approached, Sebastian dumped the last of the pellets in a heap and backed hurriedly away behind the pig ark, taking care not to touch the dirty corrugated iron roof with his clean clothes.

'So is this thing the father of the ones that attacked me earlier?' he asked.

'*Attacked?*' Neil chuckled as he sauntered over to lean against the opposite side of the ark. 'Course he is. And he sired the weaners we're going to feed next.' He beckoned Sebastian to join him. 'Come and see here.'

Sebastian edged around the back of the ark, so he wouldn't have to squeeze past the bulk of Major Tom, to find Neil pointing at the end of the boar that wasn't busy chomping away at the ground. Beneath the creature's not-very-curly tail and seeming to force his back legs apart were two large bulges, about the size and shape of a couple of mangos.

Black, hairy mangos.

'Are those...' He nodded at the bulges. 'Are those his...'

'They're his *balls*, lad' Neil announced, thumping Sebastian on the shoulder in pride. 'And what a pair of beauties, eh? No wonder he makes such fine, little piggies with those crackers to work with. Did you know there's almost half a pint of pig-maker in each one?' Sebastian, who did not know that, and didn't really want to either, pulled a suitably disgusted face. 'Go on,' said Neil. 'Give them a little pat.'

Sebastian's head swivelled to face him. 'That's not going to happen. Not even with these on.' He brandished his gloves. 'Anyway, shouldn't we be feeding the rest of the pigs?'

'Alright, alright. You're keen all of a sudden.'

'I'm really not,' said Sebastian, heading back towards the electric fence, taking a course that ensured the most distance from the boar, while avoiding entering the toilet zone. 'I just want to get it done and out of the way so I can get back and have another shower.'

'Shower?' said Neil. 'We don't even have a

shower.' He began to head back too, but then stopped and called to Sebastian. 'Here, can you guess how long the Major takes to impregnate one of ours sows? Just the delivery, you know, the end game?'

Sebastian turned back with an expansive shrug. 'I dunno. Twenty seconds?' he suggested, hating himself for joining in.

'Twenty seconds?' said Neil, incredulous. 'There's almost a full pint in there, remember. Try again.'

Sebastian raised his eyebrows, drawn in against his better judgement. 'So longer then? A minute, maybe? Two minutes?'

'Try *twenty* minutes!'

'Twenty minutes?' said Sebastian, shaking his head as he turned to leave. 'Twenty whole minutes?' Distracted slightly, he missed his footing and slipped in a patch of mud or probably something worse. Thankfully there was a handy electric wire there to support him. He was surprised to find out that the washing-up gloves provided almost no insulation whatsoever.

'You'll have to take those gloves off,' said Virginia as she loaded bags of flour onto the kitchen table. It was just after five that afternoon on a day Sebastian was starting to think would never end. How many different jobs could there be on a smallholding? The answer was clearly *a lot*, and this evening's chore was bread-making. He was not entirely ignorant of the process, and in his mind it mostly involved clouds of flour, so he had come suitably prepared. On his head was a shower cap of the disposable, clear plastic type, and, though he had failed to bring one himself, it turned out the farmhouse was home to a single apron, which he also had on. Apparently it was the apron Neil used when he did his summer barbecues and was designed in such a way as to make the wearer appear to be naked except for black underwear, complete with fishnet stockings and suspenders. And enormous breasts. No doubt it was meant to be amusing, since Neil had laughed hugely when Sebastian put it on, closely followed by his washing-up gloves.

He held them up for inspection. 'They're a clean pair.'

'They may very well be a clean pair,' said Virginia, not pausing in her preparations, 'but you can't make bread wearing washing-up gloves.'

Sebastian was about to argue, but decided it wasn't worth the hassle. 'I still don't get what the point is,' he said as he wrestled with the gloves. 'You can buy bread in the supermarkets for next to nothing. They use it as a loss-leader or something, to get people into the store to buy all their other groceries. There's no way you can make your own bread any cheaper.'

'Do you always buy whatever product happens to be cheapest?' asked Virginia, crossing over to a tall cupboard and lifting out a large bowl

Sebastian shrugged. 'The cheapest *bread*, yes.'

'But what about other things?' She placed the bowl on the table and gave him a knowing look. 'What about shampoo or aftershave or… body butter, whatever that is?'

'Body butter?' said Sebastian. 'It's for super-moisturising your body.' Virginia's face was blank. 'You know. For after you've had a shower… or a bath.' The face remained blank. 'It's quite common. A lot of people use it.'

'Not anyone *I* know,' said Neil from the lounge.

'Certainly not any *men!*'

'I just happened to notice it when I was cleaning in your room this afternoon,' said Virginia, ignoring him. 'That, and a lot of other items I'm not very familiar with. You like being clean, don't you?'

'Who doesn't?' Sebastian only just managed to stop himself glancing across to where Neil had settled into his armchair, pawing over a crossword with his back to them.

'Well, you'll enjoy bread making, then,' said Virginia. 'There's nothing like it for getting your hands clean!' She started laughing at the look of disgust on Sebastian's face. 'So, would you?' she asked.

'Would I what? Enjoy making bread? I doubt it.'

'No.' Virginia turned to open the fridge and Sebastian was pleased to note the dead birds had been removed. 'Would you buy the cheapest toiletries?'

'No way,' he said, drawing out the remaining half of his comb and redoing his hair. 'I've made that mistake before. Never again!'

She turned back and laid something wrapped in brown paper onto the table. 'Well, it's the same with me and bread. I've tried that cheap stuff before. Terrible it is, the texture of damp polystyrene and with just about as much taste. Like you say: Never again!' She smiled at Sebastian and noticed he was peering at the brown paper package. 'That's yeast. Fresh yeast from the baker in Barnstaple. There's nothing quite like it.' She clapped her hands together. 'Right. Let's get started.'

Sebastian surveyed the various items that had been laid out across the table, surprised at the quantity of ingredients involved. Apparently the plan was to make two different types of loaf, a batch of rolls and some pizza dough for their evening meal. Virginia began by introducing him to the flour.

'What's the point of having so many types?' he asked, looking at the five bags lined up on the table. 'Flour's just flour, isn't it? White, powdery stuff.'

'Ah, you're thinking of *plain* flour,' she said, picking up a bag and opening it for him to inspect.

'Or cocaine,' suggested Neil, rustling his paper. 'Crazy for that stuff, you city types.'

Virginia ignored him. 'You use this stuff for making sauces and that sort of thing.'

'Do I look like I make my own sauces?' Sebastian pulled the face of someone who didn't.

She closed the bag and placed it to one side. 'Well, plain flour isn't much use for making bread. It's not strong enough. Not enough gluten.'

'I've head of that,' said Sebastian, who was feeling out of his depth already. 'A friend of mine, Diesel, is gluten intolerant.'

Virginia nodded as though she'd expected something of the sort. 'Well, you get gluten in wheat. It's what makes dough elastic and ensures it rises properly, makes it strong. This here,' she indicated another bag, 'is strong white bread flour. We'll use this to make the rolls. If you measure out two pounds, I'll get the water.'

And so the baking began. As the work progressed, Sebastian found it less and less enjoyable, and he hadn't been that keen to start off with. The weighing scales looked like something from the reign of Queen Victoria, a brass monstrosity with crude, black weights in a series of archaic measurements that required a degree in Maths to work out. The feel of the dry flour on his hands set his teeth on edge; it was worse than talcum powder, which he considered a despicable travesty that he wouldn't let within a mile of his skin.

Virginia filled a blue and white striped jug with lukewarm water, while Sebastian measured out the fresh yeast, which he did not like the look of at all. Or the smell. Or the weird way it felt like it was eating through his skin as he crumbled it over the flour. When it was all mixed together, Virginia divided the dough into two large chunks and demonstrated, with practised ease, how to knead one of them. She made it look so easy, in fact, that Sebastian went at his piece with something almost verging on eagerness, but it wasn't long before he found himself in a mess. A sticky, stretchy, impossible-to-get-off mess.

'This is flipping awful!' he said, trying desperately to scrape the tacky dough from one hand with his just-as-dough-covered other hand, but the more he tried, the worse it got. 'Mine must be too watery or something.'

'It's *exactly* the same as mine,' said Virginia, whose dough was now shaped into a perfect dome. She held out her hands, which didn't have even a speck of flour on them. 'Like I said, there's nothing like bread-making for getting your hands clean. You've just got to keep working it.'

Sebastian sighed and carried on squeezing and folding the mess of dough that was now entirely caked around his hands. It was almost worse than feeding the wretched pigs, though only almost. Eventually, after what felt like hours of messy misery, the dough began to slowly release its hold on his fingers and stick to itself instead.

'Well, that's weird!' said Sebastian, as a large strand of the stuff stretched out from his palm and came away with a dull slap. 'It's like witchcraft.' He regretted the words as soon as they were out of his mouth. Together with assuming all country folk were pagans, he also had a vague notion that most villages had witches in them. Witches who would meet by a full moon to cast creepy spells, ride around on broomsticks and dance naked in the forest. He tried not to imagine Virginia in such a situation. He cleared his throat. 'It's not though, of course!' he said, smiling to cover up his embarrassment. 'It's just…' He held up the springy ball of dough in his now clean hands. 'How did it do that?'

'Gluten,' said Virginia, as if that cleared up the confusion. 'Pop it into this bowl, then. We'll cover it up and leave it to rise. And we can get on with the next batch.'

Three times more Sebastian had to go through the hideous ordeal of dough kneading, first with a mixture made from white bread flour, rye flour and milk, and the second containing something called spelt.

'I've never even heard of it,' he said, as he measured out nine ounces onto the scales. Ounces! Who uses *ounces* anymore? Another time travel effect of coming to the countryside. 'What's this stuff actually made of, you know, grain-wise?'

Virginia's brow creased in puzzlement. 'It's spelt. That's what the grain's actually called. It's an ancient type of wheat, I think. Been around for thousands of years.'

'How's it spelled?' shouted Neil from the other room.

Virginia rolled her eyes. 'Once you've got your nine ounces, add it into the bowl of bread flour and crumble in the yeast.'

When they finally had all the dough made,

including the one for the pizzas, Sebastian realised for the first time just how hungry he was after the day's labours. Unfortunately, this ordeal was not yet over as Virginia announced that the first batch of dough was ready.

'Ready for what?' he asked, dreading the answer. He felt as though he'd been stood in this kitchen forever, and his back, which had rarely ached before, was killing from leaning over the table for so long.

'We need to knock it back,' said Virginia, sounding far too much like she was enjoying herself for Sebastian's liking. No matter how much better this turned out to be than the cheap bread he bought from his local supermarket, it couldn't possibly be worth this much effort.

He shrugged. 'Knock it back? I thought that had something to do with drinking shots.'

'Well, in this case, it means getting all the air out of the dough.' Sebastian shrugged again, an action that was becoming so common, it was probably contributing to his bad back. 'Basically we've got to knead it again,' she explained.

Sebastian's shrug slumped and he looked almost on the verge of tears. 'We've got to knead it? *Again?* What on earth for?'

'Like I said, we've got to get the air out. It makes sure the yeast is spread throughout the whole lump of dough so that, when it rises again, the air bubbles are even and small.' She looked at Sebastian and smiled in a kindly sort of way at his dejected expression. 'You'll see,' she said.

Seventy minutes later, leaving Virginia to load the loaves, rolls and pizzas into the cooker's two large ovens, Sebastian slumped onto the sofa, having first removed his apron and the shower cap so he wouldn't get too much flour on it. Not that it would matter, since it turned out to be covered in dog hairs. As if reading his thoughts, Tank, who was curled up like a scruffy pillow at the other end of the sofa, raised his head to peer at Sebastian, and started wagging his tail. Sebastian shifted out of its reach and looked around the lounge, taking in the sideboard covered in papers, the fireplace over which stood an ugly ornament display and a photograph of Neil and Virginia smiling out on their wedding day, and the stack of old newspapers beneath a pile of moss-covered logs. It was then that he noticed what was missing from the room.

'Hey, where's your telly?' he asked, sitting up and looking around as though it might be concealed behind one of the awful Toby mugs on the windowsill or under one of the mismatched cushions.

The newspaper drooped slightly, revealing Neil's face as far as his moustache. 'We don't have a telly,' he said. 'Never seen the need.'

'Never seen the need?' Sebastian almost couldn't take it in. 'But *everyone* has a telly! Surely. I mean… How do you find out what's going on in the world? How do you get your entertainment? On the internet?'

Neil's face, what could be seen of it, frowned. 'Internet? Oh, you mean like on a computer? No, we don't have one here.'

'No internet?' Sebastian's voice, already raised, cranked up a few tones higher. 'But… How? What do you *do* in the evenings?'

'Well, I've got my paper,' said Neil, brandishing it as evidence. 'And there's books. Virg always picks up a few rubbishy romance novels from the library when she goes to town for the market.'

'They're not rubbishy,' said Virginia, wandering through from the kitchen still wearing her oven gloves. 'They're beautiful.' Neil grunted. 'We play games sometimes, too.' added Virginia.

'Games?' Sebastian's gaming was entirely played out on the computer. Surely no other type of game was worth bothering with.

'Of course.' Neil snatched up a deck of cards from the shelf below the coffee table. 'Ever played Cribbage, lad?'

He hadn't. And he didn't.

That night, as he lay awake in his bed, listening to the strange sounds of the countryside, or rather the eerie lack of the normal sounds of London, he found it impossible to sleep. And yet he felt so weary. Maybe he was *too* tired to sleep; he'd heard of that sort of thing.

Instinctively, he grabbed his mobile phone from the bedside table to look it up, but, as on the thousand other times he'd checked, there was no reception here whatsoever. It was as though the village was lined with lead. Or as though all the satellites had ceased to exist.

'Bloody time-travelling train,' he muttered and turned over onto his side to face the window, but it made no difference. There was no light outside to coax him to sleep, no bricks and mortar to comfort him. There was only the stifling darkness of somewhere without light. Somewhere wild. Somewhere dangerous. Somewhere humanity had not fully conquered.

He found his mind drifting back to the pigs and his near addition to their breakfast menu. In the darkness, his brain projected images of their sunken eyes, their muscular bodies, their mouths salivating, teeth bared. He thumped the pillow.

'I'm never going to get to sleep!'

He was wrong. He dropped off barely three hours later.

SUNDAY BEST

Sunday was usually a day of rest for Sebastian, not for any religious reason, but simply because he enjoyed the opportunity to relax at home without having to rush out to work or to see friends and family. He suspected he would not get off so lightly today.

Having dragged himself out of bed, he was surprised to find he wasn't aching from the rigours of the previous day. He felt quite limber, in fact, nearly ready to face the day.

But only nearly.

Having avoided the view yesterday morning, he decided to give it a go, on the off-chance it wasn't all bad. He tugged the curtains apart and sunlight barged into the room. Directly beneath him was the patch of grass where he'd failed to erect the tent on Friday evening. Separating this from the narrow strip of tarmac that wound up the hill to the village, was a rock wall, hung with a carpet of green and blue plants. Beyond the road and the far hedge, the upper fields of the smallholding dropped away towards the river and the green-hued trees that climbed the hill beyond, their leafy branches swaying gently on the backdrop of a crystal clear, blue sky. The sun was somewhere behind him, but its presence could be felt in the clear-etched shadow cast by the house, the bright green of the fields and the dancing light on the troubled surface of the

Bray. It wasn't a patch on the view from his bedroom back in London.

After a few seconds he turned away and, with his armoury of products and equipment, he headed to the bathroom. Finding it occupied, he returned to his room and sat on the bed, still clutching his grooming kit in his arms. After ten minutes or so, he heard the bathroom door open.

'All yours!' shouted Neil, banging Sebastian's door on his way past.

The atmosphere in the bathroom was about as offensive as he'd imagined it would be, but after working out how to open the sash window and spraying a few bursts of cologne around, it no longer felt as though his eyes were on fire.

This was Sebastian's third shower since arriving, not including yesterday morning's debacle. He jammed the rubber ends of the shower attachment onto the taps and turned them on, holding a hand under the head to check the temperature. Satisfied that he wasn't going to get scalded or chilled, he climbed into the tub and began to wash himself, laying down in the bath, so he didn't spray the walls, something he'd learned yesterday lunchtime; the carpet still hadn't dried out.

Once completed, he got dressed in dark grey chinos and a crisp, blue shirt, and headed downstairs.

'Morning,' said Neil and glanced up at the clock in the lounge, an ugly ceramic affair with too colourful flowers painted across it. 'You're up early.'

'Early?' Sebastian looked at his watch, a sleek handcrafted timepiece in silver and blue that probably cost more than everything in the room put together. 'It's almost eight. I thought you country people got up with the sun.'

Neil smiled. 'Well, you're up early for a city lad, anyway.'

'Grab a chair,' said Virginia, busying herself around the kitchen. 'Help yourself to cereal. The toast's on its way.' Sebastian sat down and, as he did so, noticed that Neil wasn't dressed in his usual scruffy clothes. Instead he was wearing a brown suit, in a style that might even have been in fashion once upon a time, complete with a shirt and a tie that no doubt hailed from the same epoch. He glanced at Virginia to see that she too, instead of wearing the dungarees she'd had on the previous day, had on her smart clothes, specifically a dress that reminded him of the shapeless thing Emma had been wearing the day before.

Thinking of Emma, he asked, 'Should I take the eggs up to the shop?'

'Oh, that's sweet of you,' said Virginia, setting a plate and a knife in front of him, 'but it's not open on Sundays. You can just bring them in here before church instead. There's a couple of empty egg boxes by the shoe rack. Get stuck in,' she added. 'And there's plenty of tea in the pot.'

Sebastian did so, and as he served himself tea and cornflakes, he considered Virginia's words. Something in there had seemed odd, but in his disappointment about not returning to the village shop today, it took him a while to work out what it was.

'Before *church*?' he said suddenly.

The toast popped up from the massive toaster and Virginia caught it. 'That's right,' she said. 'Don't worry, though, there's plenty of time. The service here doesn't start until half ten.'

'But… *church*? You're going to church?'

'Course we are,' said Neil. 'It's Sunday! Don't you

go to church in London?'

Sebastian wasn't sure what to say. Unlike pagans and witches, this wasn't something he'd expected. 'Well,' he said at last, as Virginia placed a loaded toast rack on the table, 'I've been to church, of course… but I can't say it's a *regular* thing.'

Neil looked surprised. 'Oh. Everyone goes round here.'

'Everyone?' said Sebastian, just stopping himself from adding, *'Even Emma?'*

'Of course,' said Neil, winking at him. 'Even young Emma.'

Sebastian, pretending he hadn't heard, turned to Virginia, who had finally stopped scurrying around the kitchen and joined them at the table. He cleared his throat and pointed to the toast. 'Is this the bread we made last night?'

'That it is,' said Virginia, sliding the rack towards him. 'Shouldn't really toast bread that's less than a day old - too soft in the middle - but I thought you'd like a little taste.' Despite the fact Sebastian had far from enjoyed the endless kneading the evening before, he had been slightly disappointed that there hadn't been time to taste the fruits of his labour. But Virginia had insisted that eating bread when it was still warm would make him sick. It sounded like nonsense to him, but he couldn't be certain.

He selected a piece of toasted rye bread, dropping it onto his plate and blowing on his fingers. 'Hot!' he said, in response to a look from Neil. He turned to Virginia. 'I suppose it is safe to eat though? It won't make me sick?'

She pushed the butter dish towards him. 'Just give it a try.'

Sebastian did so, knifing on a thin layer of butter before taking a bite. His face reflected a number of emotions as he chewed his first mouthful: surprise at how different the texture was to the cheap stuff he was used to, thoughtfulness as he tried to work out what was unusual about the taste, insight when he realised it was an underlying sourness that accentuated its nutty flavour, and pleasure at simply enjoying a nice piece of toast.

'Well?' said Virginia, clearly eager to hear his verdict. 'What do you think? How does it compare to that sliced polystyrene of yours?'

'Compare?' said Sebastian, speaking with his mouth full, but covering it with the back of his hand. He swallowed and, for what seemed like the first time since he got on the train at Clapham Junction, he smiled. 'It's a completely different creature altogether. It's… I've…' he struggled for the right words, finally settling on, 'It was surprisingly acceptable.'

Neil snorted into his breakfast.

Sebastian's momentary good mood was dampened somewhat by his egg-collecting duties. Apparently this was to be his daily task during his stay at the smallholding and, as far as he could see, its sole redeeming feature was that it came with a visit to the village shop. Though not today, of course. Today it had no redeeming features whatsoever.

This morning he was slightly better armed both with equipment, specifically his gloves and two empty egg boxes, and with experience, after the previous day's ignorance and chicken attack. He peered around as he entered the enclosure, but could see no sign of the Psycho Hen. It must be lying in wait again inside that little laddered doorway, so, keeping well away from that entrance, Sebastian crept up to the nesting area lid and raised it cautiously, checking the straw-filled compartments were clear. Once satisfied, he lifted it fully and, placing the open egg boxes on the edge, he started filling them. Thirteen eggs again; one more than the boxes could take, but it would still be easier than carrying an armful up the hill. With the first box full, he closed the lid and placed it on the floor, then started on the second. He'd only added one and was picking up another, when something leapt into the nesting box from the dark recesses of the henhouse and, with a loud squawk, pecked him on the finger. Hard. Again, the gloves did little to protect him and the beak cut through the rubber and jabbed into his flesh.

He swore loudly and his fingers jerked, crushing the egg in his hand. But the Psycho Hen hadn't finished. Emboldened by its successful attack, the bird flapped forwards again, but Sebastian wasn't going to be pecked a second time. He lurched backwards, snatching his hands away, and managed not only to keep his balance, but to avoid treading on the full box of eggs. Unfortunately the other box wasn't so lucky and he watched powerlessly as the wooden lid came crashing down, almost in slow motion, straight onto it, crushing both cardboard and egg.

'Damn you, Psycho Hen!' shouted Sebastian as the wildly squawking bird rocketed out of the henhouse door and scurried across the run. A few minutes later he returned to the house, carrying one box full of eggs, five loose eggs and a crumpled heap of egg-spattered cardboard to go with his equally egg-spattered glove.

He was no longer smiling.

Neil was standing just inside the backdoor,

polishing a black shoe. He chuckled as he caught sight of Sebastian.

'What happened to you?' he said.

'What happened to you?' asked Emma, jabbing him in the ribs with an elbow as Sebastian sat down next to her on the hard pew.

St Bartholomew's Church was situated on the imaginatively named Church Street, straight over the crossroads from Holders Hill, the road that led down to the smallholding. On the right hand side was the village green and on the left, hidden by the rambling branches of an ancient yew tree, was the smallest church Sebastian had ever encountered. The walls and even the roof were made of grey stone and, at one end, there was a squat steeple. It had no spire, but it clearly had a bell and someone had been ringing it as though announcing the arrival of an invading army. Beyond the huge wooden door was a handful of dark pews which were almost filled by the sixty or so people sitting in them.

To Sebastian's silent and, he hoped, concealed delight, there was only space in one pew, which was occupied by Emma and one, older woman. And now here he was, sitting next to her.

He nudged her back. 'What do you mean, what happened to me? When?'

'Yesterday,' Emma whispered, her voice only just audible above the erratic organ playing. 'I was expecting you to come back to the shop.'

Sebastian was determined to be a bit more assertive than on their first meeting, though it was difficult to accomplish this in only hushed tones. 'Why's that then?' he asked, trying on a winning smile.

'Did you miss me?'

'Hardly. It's just I spent about twenty minutes looking for this,' she pulled a pack of dental floss from somewhere and passed it to him, all the time facing straight ahead, 'and I was hoping it wasn't a wasted effort.'

'Oh…er, thanks,' he said, taking the proffered item, his winning smile forgotten.

'That's two pounds fifty, please. You can drop off the money tomorrow.' Without warning, Emma placed a hand on his knee, tapping it with her index finger. Then she leaned close to him and whispered, 'Do you realise you've got egg or something on your trousers?'

He swallowed, but tried to hide it by scratching his cheek. 'Yes.' He didn't know what else to say. Then, just as he thought of something, the vicar appeared from somewhere. This puzzled Sebastian for a moment as the church didn't have space for many hiding places. The vicar was much younger than he had expected, probably in his late-thirties, and his square, heroic chin sported a manly growth of dark stubble. If he wasn't wearing a robe and everything, Sebastian might have found his film-ready features intimidating, but he *was* wearing a robe. A long, black one, even more shapeless than Emma's flowery one, though he suspected the body beneath the robe was as film-ready as his face.

'Please rise,' called the vicar, his voice echoing off the bare stone walls, and Emma's hand slipped from Sebastian's knee.

With the exception of a friend's wedding the previous September, Sebastian hadn't been to church since he was at school, and even then he'd not actually paid any attention, but used to scribble rude words in the pew bibles and play hangman with whomever happened to be sitting next to him. As a result, this morning's service caught him somewhat off-guard. The congregation kept standing up and sitting down without warning, and suddenly speaking out in creepy unison, repeating strange phrases that were unfamiliar to him. It was like they were deliberately trying to catch him out.

And then there were the hymns. Sebastian had nothing against organ music and had enjoyed singing along when they played Jerusalem on the radio a few months earlier, but the songs they dragged out for this service were clearly from the duller, less-catchy end of the hymnal. Bizarre words that would have had Shakespeare scratching his balding head were married to melodies that consisted either of fewer than five notes or of rambling, tuneless dirges that dropped off either end of his vocal range. And everyone else's by the sound of it.

At some point the vicar mounted the pulpit to speak, but Emma's knee was touching his own making it impossible for Sebastian to concentrate on the sermon. Not only that, but Sebastian had noticed a large man, sitting across the aisle and a couple of pews forward, who kept turning round and staring at him. It took him a moment, and the glint of the man's bald head, to realise it was the butcher, whose window he had defiled the previous morning. Having noticed the man looking at him, in what he took to be a somewhat unfriendly fashion, Sebastian tried his hardest not to make eye contact or even glance in his direction, but it was like trying not to look at something unpleasant and his eyes kept sliding sideways to find the butcher still glowering at him. He made a mental note to clean that egg off the window, preferably when the shop was closed.

Sebastian suddenly realised the vicar had stopped talking and was now heading towards the ridiculously ornate altar that stood, laden with symbolic items, in front of the large stained glass window, and, after some more to-ing and fro-ing between the vicar and the audience - or was it an assembly? - Sebastian found himself with the others at the altar rail, not out of any real desire to partake in the Communion, but simply because that seemed to be the done thing and he'd already messed up enough of the standing and sitting. So he copied Neil, who was kneeling next to him, holding out cupped hands into which the vicar placed a piece of what looked like flattened packing material, but which turned out to be rice paper. Sebastian chewed on the tasteless item, wondering if this was what shop-bought bread was like to Virginia. Then, to his horror, he watched as the people along the row all sipped wine from a silver cup. The *same* silver cup. All of them. Drinking out of the same cup.

He felt paralysed as he watched the cup progress from an old man with dirty-looking teeth and a sore on his lip, to Virginia and then to Neil. What could he do? He couldn't refuse. But nor could he drink something that was no doubt filled with the spittled dregs of a load of strangers - country folk, no less, who could be carrying who knew what germs and filth. As the vicar drew up in front of him, Sebastian lifted his hand to steady the goblet of disease and, taking care not to actually make any contact with the rim of the vessel, tried to mime taking a sip. It almost worked, until the vicar tilted it suddenly and a little of the lukewarm contents made it past his lips. Instinctively, he spat it back in, wishing he had some mouthwash to go with the dental floss, and hurried back to his seat, hoping the next person in line for the cup hadn't noticed.

At last the service came to an end and, as the vicar marched down the tiny aisle and through the oversized door, the muted drone of conversation started up and people began filing out behind him. Not meaning to, Sebastian's gaze flickered across the aisle and met that of the large butcher. He was certain it was the same man, with the same beard and everything, but it was hard to tell without the knife. And the blood smeared across his chest. To his relief, the butcher frowned and looked away.

Sebastian turned to Emma. 'There's a guy over there,' he whispered, indicating with a flick of his head, 'who doesn't seem to like me for some reason.'

'Well, he's clearly a good judge of character,' she said, picking up a small bag from under the seat. 'What did you think of the service, then? I noticed you were struggling a bit to keep up.'

Uncertain how to respond, he opted for, 'It was different.'

'Churches in London do things differently, do they?'

He shrugged. 'Um... I guess. Yeah.'

'Weird,' said Emma. 'I thought services were the same all across the country - same words, same readings, same choice of hymns even.' Having no idea if this was true or not, Sebastian chose to say nothing. 'So are you going to the pub for lunch?' asked Emma.

'The pub? I don't know... I shouldn't imagine so. Neil's probably got some hideously messy job lined up to ruin more of my clothes - something involving mud or manure no doubt. You know, yesterday, I ended up electrocuting myself twice, once on my cheek, just under-'

'Is this a long story?' interrupted Emma. 'Only it's starting to sound like it could be and I was wondering if you were going to start moving any time soon.'

Sebastian looked round to find Neil and Virginia were already on their way out of the church. 'Oh, right. Of course. Sorry.' He turned back to find her smiling. It was the sort of smile Sebastian associated with people who feel they've got one up on you. She clearly enjoyed making him feel uncomfortable and he'd fallen for it. Again. Cross with himself, he marched off up the short aisle without saying 'good bye'.

The Green Man public house was only a brisk walk across the village green and, despite Sebastian's gloomy prediction of how his day would be spent, it turned out the Symeses *were* taking him there for lunch.

'My treat,' said Neil, tugging off his tie and undoing his top button as he walked. 'A kind of "Welcome to Steepleford" meal.'

The idea of a 'welcome' at this point in his stay, reminded him of just how long he still had before he could return to the city. It already felt like he'd been stuck in this village for weeks, and a wave of homesickness swept over him at the eternity stretching away between now and the following Saturday. He pushed out an unconvincing smile.

'Thank you,' he muttered, aware of how ungrateful he sounded.

The interior of the Green Man was almost exactly what Sebastian had expected, though the sawdust in his mind was replaced with an ancient rug full of age old cigarette burns and worn paths that wove between the tables, through which terracotta tiles could be glimpsed. The fifteen or so tables, like the chairs around them, were of assorted styles and designs, no two of which were the same, and their once-varnished surfaces had been eroded to smooth, bare wood. Various ancient items, once used either for farming or torture, black and white pictures of long dead countryfolk on the unchanged backdrop of Steepleford, and many layers of nicotine-yellow paint conspired to hide the wood panelling that lined the walls, and the few windows had obviously not been cleaned during the reign of the current monarch, letting in a strangled light as though the sun were shining through a pint of warm beer. The black oak beams that spanned the ceiling were hung with pewter tankards, naked, unlit bulbs and what even Sebastian recognised as perishing hop plants, while at the far end of the room a fire smouldered in its cast iron surround, despite the fact it was May and the sun was blazing outside.

It was like something from the sixteen-hundreds, the kind of place one might expect to find fletchers, wheelwrights and coopers all supping mead together after a hard day doing whatever medieval thing such people did. The effect was spoiled somewhat by the bar, which was hung with glossy adverts for alcopops and housed an impressive collection of space-age lager dispensers instead of the expected brass beer handles. That and the fact that it was empty.

Sebastian looked at his watch. It was ten past twelve.

'Where is everyone?' he asked Neil.

'Where they always are,' said a voice from the empty bar. Sebastian turned to see the landlord's head rising up from below the polished oak surface, followed by a red bowtie, a checked shirt and a brown cardigan. It was like a parade of Sebastian's most hated clothing, and somehow he knew that, hidden by the bar's wood panelling, was a pair of corduroy trousers. Probably mustard yellow ones. The face above this fashion travesty continued, 'Anywhere that ain't here supporting the only pub for miles around. I've told them, if they don't use it the old place'll be knocked down and turned into flats or some modern age discotheque, but do they care?' Sebastian opened his mouth to attempt a response, but the flow continued unabated. 'No. That's the answer. No. No one cares that the pub's struggling, that we can barely afford to heat it,' the landlord gestured to the fireplace, 'or that we haven't been able to refurb the place since the old man ran it. Oh, they come in when it suits them, of course. Wandering in at half ten at night, looking for a swift couple of pints, complaining about the price. They'll be sorry when it's gone and no mistake. Table for three is it, Virg?'

'Yes, please, Donny love,' said Virginia, unfazed by the abrupt change in flow. 'We're here for lunch to welcome Sebastian to the village.' She indicated Sebastian, as though there could be any question who she was referring to.

Sebastian forced out another smile. 'Hi.'

'Ah,' said Donald, nodding to himself, 'you must be the lad from up London way. What on earth brings you down to this God-forsaken backwater?'

'I was wondering that myself,' Sebastian replied, the words spilling out before he could run them past his internal filters.

Donald laughed, a curious sound made up of rasping intakes of breath. 'Welcome to Steepleford, anyway,' he said, 'and welcome to the Green Man. You only just made it. A few more weeks and it'd no doubt have some strangers from town living in it like the old school. Not that anyone'd mind, of course. No one cares about the place anymore. No one ever comes here for lunch these days.'

Sebastian span round as the pub door slammed open behind him. Silhouetted in the doorway was the figure of Emma, another woman standing close behind her.

'Thought you weren't coming here,' she said, at an embarrassing volume. 'I hope you're not stalking me, Sebastian!'

NO USE CRYING

It wasn't the worst lunch Sebastian had ever experienced. That prize went to the occasion Sebastian's parents had left him at his gran's house when he was nine. He'd not wanted to be there. She'd not wanted him to be there. He'd wanted to be out playing with his friends. She'd wanted to be out heading to an afternoon of bingo. The resulting lunch consisted of leftovers from the fridge - half an egg, a mouldering piece of cheese, a slice of pepperoni pizza and some taramasalata - and three cheese crackers that had gone soft and lost their 'crack', all eaten while sitting on her lumpy sofa in dusty silence.

Lunch at the Green Man wasn't *that* bad. But it was bad.

The first problem was the menu. It wasn't the fact it was printed on cheap paper with beer marks that had smeared the ink. It wasn't the poor spelling evident throughout in words like 'Sousage' and 'Haddack'. It wasn't even the awful font that attempted, and failed, to look 'fun'. The problem was the choice of meals, which were as follows:

1. Sousage and chips
2. Haddack and chips
3. Ham, Egg and chip
4. Moroccan Rabbit and Sweet Potato Tagine

5. Sousage an Egg and chips
6. Beaf Burger and chps

'Moroccan rabbit and sweet potato tagine?' said Sebastian, turning the flimsy piece of paper over to see if there was anything on the other side. There was a letter printed on it upside down, complaining about the price of council tax. He gave Neil a puzzled look.

'Donald went on a course,' said Virginia, as though the landlord had caught an embarrassing disease. 'He only attended once and that's the dish they cooked.'

Neil leant across the table to Sebastian and spoke in a whisper. 'Trust me, it's awful. It tastes like someone else ate it first. Someone ill. Who washed it down with a pint of their own pi-'

'Ready?' Donald was standing by the table, though Sebastian hadn't seen him arrive. Neil glanced up at him.

'Donald,' he said.

'Neil,' replied the landlord. Afterwards, that was the only thing Sebastian could recall the two men saying to each other.

'I'm having the haddock and chips, please, Donny,' said Virginia, 'and Neil's having the ham, egg and chips. Sebastian?'

He looked down at the menu again, still uncertain what to choose.

'Spoilt for choice, is it?' asked Donald.

Sebastian wasn't sure how to answer. 'It's not *exactly* that...'

Donald stepped round the table to tap at the menu with his pencil. 'I'd recommend the rabbit tagine,' he said, pronouncing the word "taggeeny". 'A favourite with the locals. Well, I say it's a favourite, but of course no one actually bothers coming here to eat, but if they did, I reckon they'd go for the tagine because it sounds fancy. Though to be fair it'd probably put most of them off, on account of them being plebs who wouldn't know "fancy" if it knocked them down in the street and stole their shoes, but it is something of a speciality of mine.'

Sebastian was confused. 'Stealing people's shoes?'

'The taggeeny.' Donald tapped the menu again, causing it to fold back on itself. Sebastian looked up at him and saw, almost hidden by his grumpy exterior, a clear look of pleading in his eyes. On a table in the corner, half-hidden from view by Donald's mustard yellow corduroys, he noticed Emma was shaking her head at him in warning. That settled it!

'Sure,' he said. 'I'll go for the tagine.'

Donald frowned. 'Eh?'

'Er, the taggeeny?'

'Splendid.' Donald headed back to the bar, his feet scuffing along the already worn carpet tracks. Sebastian was horrified to notice he was wearing tartan slippers.

The second item, or rather items, that spoiled the lunch were the pair of ancient locals who entered the pub at this point, staggering to the bar as though they were already drunk. They clambered onto a pair of tall stools and leant against the bar, motionless.

Donald emerged from the doorway and, without so much as a 'Good afternoon' or 'The usual, is it?', he poured two pints of lager and placed them on a couple of ancient beermats.

'Six pounds twenty,' he said at last.

At the mention of the price, which sound very reasonable to Sebastian, the old men became suddenly animated, reminding him of the Covent Garden human statues, who would burst into life when given a coin.

'Six pounds twenty?' said one of them, clutching his bald head. His drawling Devon accent was so thick, it was almost unintelligible. 'Six pounds twenty? Prices gone up again, Sid. Did you hear? Prices gone up again, I tell thee!'

'Outrageous!' croaked his companion. 'Time was when you could go out drinking with only a shilling.' He peered around at the room in general, his eyes magnified by his thick lensed glasses. 'A shilling, I said! Not these days, though. Oh no. Robbing us blind, they are, Harry. Robbing us blind!'

And although they paid for their drinks, scattering fistfuls of change across the bar, their mumbled complaints carried on unabated.

'Who're these guys?' asked Sebastian, gesturing to the two old men with his eyebrows.

'Him on the left is Harry,' said Neil, 'and the other's Sid. They're always in here.'

'But I thought Donald said no one ever came in here.'

Neil shrugged. 'That's Donald for you. He's just a whining old git.'

'Be nice!' said Virginia, nudging him in the ribs as Donald shuffled over and dumped three sets of cutlery on the table and a bowl containing a few sachets of sauce. 'Thanks, Donny.'

The third issue, though Sebastian couldn't work out if it made his lunchtime better or worse, was Emma. She was sitting far enough away that conversation would have been awkward, but close enough that he could hear her talking. She was also right in his line of vision, which was distracting. Very distracting. Thank goodness she was wearing another shapeless dress. Not *that* shapeless though…

'Sorry, what?' he said, realising Virginia had been talking to him. He tore his gaze away from Emma.

'I asked how you were finding things here, now you've settled in.'

'*Settled in?*' He didn't mean it to sound quite so outraged. 'I… you've got to remember, except for a few times as a kid, I've never been out of the city.'

'Why ever not?' she asked, 'What're you afraid of?'

'Nothing,' said Sebastian. 'Well, except for spiders.'

Virginia ignored this. 'You shouldn't be afraid of the countryside.'

'Or spiders,' added Neil. 'Nothing scary about spiders.'

Sebastian laid his hands flat on the table top and leaned forwards. 'I am *not* afraid.'

'Except of spiders,' said Neil, miming a spider with his fingers and scuttling it across the table towards one of Sebastian's hands. He jerked it away.

Virginia ignored him again and patted Sebastian's other hand. 'You don't need to be afraid of the countryside,' she said. 'It's just nature and that. All very peaceful and normal out here.'

'I am *not* afraid of the countryside!' said Sebastian, frustrated by the certainty this was not true. 'And it's not just peaceful - it's… it's dead. There's no life here. You know, back in London, it doesn't matter what time you go out, there's always something going on. There are always people around, traffic, things to do, places to go, fun to be had. But here?' He gestured to the world beyond the grimy windows. 'There's nothing. It's deader than in the middle of the day than London is in the middle of the night. I bet nothing ever happens here, just the same handful of people living the same boring day over and over again. It's not normal… it's… it's *medieval*.' He stopped and looked at his hosts, worried for a moment that he had upset them. Neil, however, just looked amused, the ends of his moustache stretched into a broad smile. And Virginia was doing the kind of face that you'd expect on a counsellor just before they say, "And how does that make you feel?" He sagged, all the fight suddenly gone out of him. 'There's not even any internet here.'

'There's internet up at the shop,' said Emma from across the room, where she was grinning at him. 'You're welcome to come and use it once you've finished your chores this afternoon.'

'Er… thanks.' Sebastian turned back to his hosts with a frown, 'Chores? Not the pigs again?'

Neil shook his head. 'No, no. Nothing too strenuous today. We'll be milking the goats, is all.'

'And making some cheese,' added Virginia. 'Lovely, delicious, soft goat cheese.' She closed her eyes and smiled dreamily. 'Ooh, I can taste it already!' In his mind, Sebastian could taste it as well. Goat cheese. Surely the worst kind of cheese on the planet. He wasn't sure if there was such a thing as pig cheese or dog cheese, though there probably was, but even they couldn't be as terrible as *goat* cheese. He had made the mistake of trying some when he was out with his parents a few years before. He'd opted for the goat cheese and fig tart as a starter, which turned out to be a mistake. It tasted like goats smell, or at least as Sebastian imagined them to smell, since he'd never actually seen a goat in the flesh. After his first mouthful, he had pushed the rest of the starter away, untouched. This abstinence proved futile, however, as the rest of the meal was marred by the goaty taste that lingered long after the tart had been finished by his mother. He could almost taste it now. If he was expected not only to make it but to eat some as well... he couldn't think of anything worse.

'Your rabbit taggeeny,' said Donald, sliding the plate onto the table in front of Sebastian. He opened his mouth to thank the landlord, but the sight of the food strangled the words in his throat and all thoughts of the taste of goat cheese vanished from his mind. Donald dumped the other two meals in front of Neil and Virginia and shuffled away, disappearing through the door behind the bar.

'What's that muck?' came a loud voice from the bar and Sebastian looked up to see Sid - or was it Harry? - pointing across at him. 'Not that God-awful rabbit thing, is it? He tried to foist some of that filth on us once, didn't he?'

His companion nodded. 'Dreadful stuff,' he said, gurning a face to match. 'Couldn't think of anything worse. Tasted like someone else had eaten it first... someone who hadn't liked it much either.'

'That's what I told him,' said Neil, but the two men had turned back to the bar, their loud complaints about the landlord's cooking and general inadequacies battling for supremacy.

Sebastian picked up his fork and, after wiping it first on the paper napkin, skewered a piece of what he presumed was rabbit, sniffed at it and teased it off the fork with his teeth. Even Sid and Harry's endless complaining paused for moment as the room seemed to hold its breath.

The silence was broken by Neil chuckling at the look of horror that spread across Sebastian's face.

'Why don't I order you something else?' he said.

The goat shed was built into the lesser of the two buildings on the smallholding, which opened onto the first and smallest of the three fields that ran along the bank of the river. This field was mostly given over to various birds, including chickens, geese, what Sebastian assumed were turkeys, though he wasn't certain, and a number of strange, red faced birds with fat, grey-feathered bodies.

'What are those things?' he asked, pointing at the birds.

Neil paused in the entrance to the goat shed. 'The chickens?'

'No. I know what chickens look like. Those funny grey things.'

'You mean the guinea fowl?' suggested Neil.

'Possibly. Those other greyish ones are turkeys, yes?'

Neil raised his eyebrows. 'Well, look at you, knowing all about poultry! Turkeys, guinea fowl, chickens, geese and quail, though you can't really see them from here. They're the small birds in that separate run, there. And these,' he drew Sebastian's attention towards the interior of the shed, 'are our milking goats.' He stepped onto the straw covered floor and Sebastian edged in after him, keeping a wary eye out for any sudden movements from within.

On the ride down from the house, after Neil had shrugged off his Sunday best and emerged in his normal working clothes, Sebastian had worried about what might await him in this shed, and his imagination had been delighted to furnish him with images of demonic terrors with glowing eyes, long, curved horns to pierce his flesh, and charging furies hell bent on butting him into a broken, quivering mess. He was almost disappointed by the tranquil reality of the goat shed.

Instead of the creatures of nightmare he had envisioned, there were two piles of golden-brown fur, one nestling in the hay, another lounging on a wooden shelf, a leg draping over the edge. Neither had horns. They were about the size of large dogs and eyed Sebastian with a languid curiosity as they worked their jaws in a lazy chewing motion.

'This here is Marge,' said Neil, indicating the one in the straw, and Sebastian was pleased to hear this creature, at least, had a normal, animally sort of name. 'And this one's Amy.'

Sebastian snorted. 'Ridiculous!'

There was a door in the far wall and the goats, once roused from their afternoon stupor, ambled through this after Neil, followed at a safe distance by Sebastian. The room beyond was a stark contrast to the goats' living quarters. Instead of straw, the floor was grey-painted concrete with a central channel running from the rear wall to the front, where it disappeared through a hole in the blockwork. The walls were also painted, in white, and the whole area had a lingering smell of bleach about it. On one wall hung a coiled length of hosepipe, attached to a brass tap. On another were two tiled benches, about knee-height from the floor, on which the two goats had hopped and were loitering with an air of resigned expectation.

Sebastian's eyes were drawn to the two bags of tight, pink skin and long, horn-shaped teats that protruded from between their hind legs.

'Are you really expecting me to... *milk* these things?' he asked, his face echoing his distaste.

Neil chuckled. 'Course. There's nothing to it. In fact, I reckon you'll enjoy it once you get into your stride.'

The only stride Sebastian wanted to get into was one that took him away from the goat shed, preferably back to the train station, but instead he inched closer to where Neil was drawing a short stool out from beneath one of the benches.

'Which one's this?' he asked.

'This little beauty is Marge,' said Neil, running an affectionate hand across the goat's flank. 'She's a champion milker. Gives up to three quarts of milk most days.'

There was an expectant pause, and Sebastian felt some comment was expected of him. 'Really?' he said, trying to sound impressed while wondering if a quart was a lot.

Neil placed a stainless steel bucket beneath Marge. 'Pull up a stool, lad, so you can see what's going on down here.' And once Sebastian was perched next to him, he reached under the goat and took hold of one of the teats. The goat didn't even seem to notice, but was contentedly nibbling from at a bucket of food. 'Look at that! Not even a flinch. Good girl, Marge. Right, now, can you see what I'm doing here?' he asked, but didn't wait for a response. 'I'm pinching the top of the teat between finger and thumb, look.' He did this a few times to make sure Sebastian had seen. 'That closes it off, making sure the milk won't escape back up into the udder. Then all I do is squeeze out the milk using my free fingers. He demonstrated, causing a spear of white milk to jet into the bucket with a gong-like clang. 'See? Then you release your grip to allow more milk to drop into the teat and go again.' He repeated the action a few times, and the sound of the milk hitting the bucket rang around the room.

He turned to look at Sebastian, a grin peeking out from beneath his moustache. 'Give it a try,' he said. Sebastian opened his mouth to reply, but made no sound nor any move towards Marge's udder. 'Come on. Get involved, lad.'

'Fine!' said Sebastian, in the way that suggests it isn't, swallowed and reached out a hand towards the goat's underside.

'You haven't got them things on again, have you?' said Neil, shaking his head at the sight of the bright yellow washing-up glove.

Sebastian gave him a look. 'Of course I have. These are a new pair.'

'Marge won't like *them* on her.'

She didn't.

Where before the goat had been indifferent at Neil's touch, as though unaware she was even being milked, the moment Sebastian's gloved hand made contact with her skin, a hoof nipped up and flicked it away. His next two attempts were similarly rebuffed. Marge's investigation of the food bucket, however, continued uninterrupted.

'You're going to have to go in without them,' said Neil. 'Skin on skin, lad.'

Sebastian sighed and began to tug off his gloves, his head hanging forward dejectedly, until he got too close to Marge and got clipped across the forehead with her hoof. It took all his wherewithal not to jump backwards off his stool.

'You'll need to look,' said Neil as Sebastian reached gingerly beneath the goat, his face directed at the adjacent wall. 'That's right. Don't brush at it - hold it like you mean business.'

To Sebastian's relief, Marge made no attempt to kick his hand away as he made contact with the teat, but the sensation was far from pleasant. It was like touching a warm, hairy balloon, one made from skin and filled with milk. Gritting his teeth, he squeeze the teat as gently as he could. Nothing happened.

'Remember to pinch the top,' said Neil, 'or you'll be milking her in the wrong direction. We want it to come *out,* remember.'

Sebastian, who was entirely ambivalent about whether or not any milk came out, tried again, pinching the teat where it joined the udder. With a deep breath, he contracted his other fingers and was surprised to hear that same ringing clang as the milk spurted out into the bucket.

'I did it!' he said, turning wide eyes on Neil. 'I actually just did it.'

Neil patted him on the back. 'Give it another go,' he said, 'just to check it wasn't a fluke.'

A second jet of milk nailed into the bucket. And a third.

'Look!' said Sebastian, his disgust forgotten for the moment in the light of his success. More milk filled the bucket. 'How many quarts is that?'

Neil laughed at Sebastian's reaction. 'Alright, alright. Leave some for me to milk out. Why don't you go over there and get started on Amy? Poor girl must be bursting.'

With an eagerness that belied his hatred of all things to do with the countryside, Sebastian scuttled across to the other bench, his stool in one hand and an empty milking bucket in the other.

Sliding the bucket under Amy, he got himself

comfy and, after a couple of false-starts, he got into his stride, the milk clanging into the bucket in a steady rhythm, one jet to every four or five of Neil's.

'How are you going so fast?' Sebastian asked, 'Your bucket must be almost full!'

Neil shrugged without affecting his pace. 'Practice, I guess.' He leaned back to watch Sebastian for a moment. 'Try using your left hand too. That's why God gave them two teats. Two teats, two hands, gets the job done twice as quick.'

Sebastian watched Neil's double-handed action for a while, then lifted his left hand to give it a go. Not watching what he was doing, he caught hold of Amy's right hind leg. Her reaction was instantaneous. Up flicked the other leg, her hoof knocking his hand away before dropping down onto the rim of the bucket. The clatter of its fall echoed around the room and, though Sebastian had barely achieved quarter of a pint, the milk went everywhere! But mostly, it ended up in his lap.

Neil coughed, covering his amusement. 'Aye,' he said, 'that can happen sometimes. Goats is funny creatures.'

'Look at me.' Horrified, Sebastian held up the bucket in his hand and used it to indicate the wet patch spreading from his belt down towards his knees. 'I'm covered in the damn stuff.'

'Well, you know what they say about spilt milk?' said Neil, whose silent laughter had forced him to stop milking Marge.

'Don't get it all over your trousers?' suggested Sebastian, shoving the bucket back on the bench and trying to flick his hands dry. The action startled Amy, who turned to look at him and bleated loudly in his face. He jerked backwards in alarm, barely keeping from slipping off the stool. 'It sounds like a sheep trying to neigh!'

'You alright?' asked Neil, still chuckling as he resumed milking. 'Going to be able to carry on and get that bucket filled?'

Sebastian shrugged as he got himself settled back in position. 'I guess,' he said, 'though I'm going to have to change when we get back. And I'll need a shower.'

'Well, you'll be hard pushed to get one back at the house. Nothing wrong with a nice hot bath, though.' Neil paused, glancing across at Sebastian as he began milking Amy again, one-handed. 'Here, let me give you a hand with that.' And with a quick twist of his arm, he squirted milk at Sebastian.

Sebastian almost jumped to his feet, but managed not to in an attempt to keep from startling the goat. 'What the hell?'

Neil burst out laughing, causing Marge to look at him in evident surprise. 'Any of that go in the bucket?' he said, before sending another jet towards Sebastian. 'There you go, lad. Must be almost full!'

Jerking up his left arm to shield himself, Sebastian attempted to return fire, but managed instead to squirt milk at himself. Mostly in his eye.

'Eurgh! Some of that went in my mouth,' said Sebastian, trying not to gag at the warm, cloying taste. He spat on the floor, something he would never have dreamed of doing back in London, but then people in the city didn't spray each other in the face from a goat's udder. As a rule. Amy bleated again as another spray hit Sebastian, accompanied by more laughter from Neil, who sounded like he'd not enjoyed himself this much in ages.

'That's the only shower you're going to get around here!' he said.

Sebastian wiped the milk from his eyes with his sleeve and blinked at Neil. 'It's not fair,' he said. 'Show me how your doing that.'

8
LONG ODDS

'What in the world have you boys been up to?' Virginia stood in the kitchen, hands on her hips, staring at the two damp figures in the doorway.

Having completed the milking, with Neil stepping in to finish Amy to ensure, as he put it, "the milk doesn't turn into cheese before we get it home", they ushered the goats back into their shed and Neil poured the contents of the two buckets into a metal churn and fastened on the lid. What they had failed to do was clean themselves up before returning to the house, and Sebastian was unsure what to say about the state they had turned up in, their clothes and bodies sticky from their milk fight.

'Nothing,' said Neil, dumping the churn on the kitchen table.

Virginia narrowed her eyes at him. 'There's milk in your moustache. Have you two been playing silly buggers down there?'

Neil gave Sebastian a guilty look, then clapped his hands together. 'Well, I can't stand around chatting all day. Got to get back down and clean up the milking equipment.'

'And I've got to get to the shop,' said Sebastian quickly, wiping a sleeve across his face in case there were any incriminating milk stains. His sleeve was wet. 'Emma said I could use her internet.'

Virginia glanced up at the clock as she swung the churn into the fridge and closed the door. 'Shall we aim to start making the cheese at, say, six o'clock?'

'Sure,' said Sebastian, inching back towards the door.

'Sounds good,' added Neil, joining him as they backed away from the suspicious glare of his wife. 'Close one!' he said, as the door clicked shut behind them. Swinging his leg over the quad bike, he gave Sebastian an exaggerated wink. 'Let's never speak of it again, eh?'

Sebastian smiled. 'Quite.'

'Except of course, to say that I clearly won!' He powered up the quad bike, drowning out any possible response.

Sebastian was relieved to see the butcher's shop was dark and empty as he made his way up Holders Hill. He paused, looking around to check the coast was clear of huge, hulking men, and hurriedly scratched off the dried egg yolk from the bottom of the large window.

The bell danced to announce his arrival at the Village Store, and Emma appeared in the opposite doorway.

'Hello, you,' she said. Sebastian opened his mouth to say… something, but the words died before he even knew what they were as he noticed she had changed her clothes. Instead of the shapeless dresses she'd worn at church and the previous day, she was now wearing a light, white skirt, decorated with small blue flowers, and a close-fitting T-shirt to match. Her long red hair hung loose over her shoulders, reaching down past her…

'Have you had a stroke or something?' asked

Emma. Sebastian shut his mouth quickly, shifting his eyes up to her face. She was giving him the *gotcha* look, and he could feel his cheeks flushing. 'I think you're supposed to say, "Hello". That's how we do things in the country anyway.'

He cleared his throat, worried he might croak a response. 'Er, sure,' he croaked. 'Hello.' There was a pause as they stood staring at each other, long enough that Sebastian wondered if there was something he was supposed to do. Was she expecting him to make a "move"? It wasn't something he'd ever been any good at, a failing he blamed on ten years at an all-boys boarding school and a lack of any sisters growing up. He hadn't really known what girls were until he hit sixteen, and by then it was too late. That was eight years ago, and to date the sum total of his experience had been a furtive, drunken fumbling in the dark at a university party with a girl who had passed out mid-kiss. In short, he had no idea what to do and so it was almost a relief when Emma grabbed his arm.

'Come through to the house,' she said, pulling him towards the rear door. 'The computer's in the lounge.' She let go and turned to look at him. 'What have you got on your shirt? It's all damp.'

'It's not just my shirt,' said Sebastian, gesturing to his body in general. 'My trousers got wet too and it soaked through to my... my underwear.'

Emma rubbed her fingers across the palm of her hand. 'But what is it? It feels sticky.'

'It's milk. Neil took me to milk the goats this afternoon and I spilt a load in my lap.'

'And your shirt?'

Sebastian hesitated, slightly embarrassed to admit what he'd been up to. 'Neil and I had a... a milk fight.'

'*A milk fight?*' Emma frowned, her mouth creasing into a lopsided smile. 'What exactly is a milk fight?'

'We were squirting each other. With milk,' said Sebastian, his eyes sliding to her feet, embarrassed.

'From their udders?'

Sebastian nodded, distracted by Emma's shapely, bare feet.

'You know that's disgusting, right?'

He cleared his throat again. 'So, where's this computer?'

'Through here,' said Emma airily, turning back and heading into the living area of the shop. She ducked through a door on the right and Sebastian followed, finding himself in what he guessed was the lounge. 'This is the lounge.'

It was a small room, it's walls covered on three sides with the kind of wallpaper that had graced, or rather *dis*graced, his gran's living room, the other bare brickwork surrounding an open fireplace. The floorboards were mostly hidden by a large rug that had seen better days, probably when Henry VIII was on the throne, and the furniture consisted of an old-fashioned keyboard instrument standing against the wall and three ancient armchairs gathered around a coffee table, laden with books and knitting equipment. In one of the armchairs sat the middle-aged lady who had been with Emma at church and in the Green Man.

'Oh,' said Sebastian, surprised at finding her here. 'Hi.'

'Afternoon,' she replied, nodding her head stiffly.

Emma gestured towards her. 'This is my mother.'

He stepped towards her, holding out a hand. 'I'm Sebastian. I'm staying with the Symeses.'

'So I hear,' she replied, touching his hand for the

briefest of moments with three fingers, before folding her hands back in her lap. 'You may call me Mrs Standfield.' Sebastian was slightly taken aback by this pronouncement. It sounded like something from a Jane Austen novel; not that he'd ever read one, but it was the kind of thing he imagined people in them saying. Having been somewhat blinkered by Emma's presence to properly notice Mrs Standfield in either the church or the pub, Sebastian took a moment to do so now. He wondered if her hair had once been red like Emma's, but it was now a light grey and gathered up in an austere bun. With the exception of her hands, a dark-purple dress covered everything from the neck down, and she sat upright in the chair as though held up by an invisible board.

Seemingly conscious of this scrutiny, Mrs Standfield looked up at him. 'Well? I'm sure you both have better things to do than to stand around making the place untidy. Don't mind me.' And with that, she swept up a bundle of needle-skewered wool and began knitting.

Sebastian turned to look at the computer, which was perched on a small desk in the corner. It looked old, the once-white plastic around the screen and keyboard now faded to a dirty-cream.

'Does that really have access to the internet?' asked Sebastian, staring at the machine. 'It's even got a CRT monitor. I didn't realise any of those still existed. Thought they'd all been replaced with flat screens.'

Emma frowned at him. 'What's a monitor? And yes, of course it has the internet. It's got a modem.' She pointed to a mess of leads under the desk. 'I put it in myself,' she added, with more than a note of pride.

'Well done, you,' he said, and pointed to the

screen. '*That's* a monitor. So, are you going to boot it up?'

Emma gave him a look of bewildered concern. 'Boot it up?'

'Yeah. You know, switch it on.'

'Ah.' Emma bent down to reach behind the machine and Sebastian tried not to let his eyes wander as she did so. Tried, and failed. 'It takes forever to... *boot*,' she said, her voice muffled slightly as she backed out from beneath the desk. 'Why don't you use the shower while you're waiting and I'll fix us all a nice cup of tea?'

Sebastian stared at her, eyes wide. 'You have a shower?'

The shower in question turned out to be a frosted glass cubicle in the corner of a bedroom; with its antique-looking bedspread and Victorian-style décor, Sebastian reckoned it must belong to Mrs Standfield. Despite having neither clean clothes to get dressed in nor his usual array of washing products, Sebastian was delighted with the shower, which was a luxury after the struggle of trying to spray himself clean in a bathtub, and the water was hot, the jets strong. Emma had given him a towel, which he hung over the top of the cubicle and, after lingering in the steamy spray for over ten minutes, he dragged it on and stepped out of the shower. As he stood there, dripping onto the cork mat, he noticed two things had changed about the room. Firstly, there was a cup of tea sitting on the bedside table. And secondly, his clothes had gone.

'Er... Hello?' he called, sticking his head out into the empty hallway. 'Hello-o?'

Emma appeared through the lounge door. 'Yes?

What's up?'

'*What's up?* My clothes have gone!'

'Of course they have,' she said, as though it would have been foolish to expect anything else. 'I've put them in the tumble drier for a bit. Won't be long.'

He emerged further into the hallway, before remembering how skimpy his towel was and retreated again. 'But I was in the shower. I was undressed.'

Emma nodded. 'Well, obviously. Would you rather I took your clothes when you were still wearing them? Finish up your tea and I'll check to see if they're dry. The computer's nearly done, too.'

Back in the room, Sebastian towelled himself dry then perched on the edge of the bed to sip at his tea. As he picked up the cup, he noticed a small picture frame standing behind it and he bent closer to have a look. It contained a portrait photograph of a young man in a suit that could only have dated from the Seventies. He sported a pencil-thin moustache and a side-parting, both of hair so red it looked as though it had been digitally altered.

'That's my dad,' said a voice from the doorway. Startled, Sebastian breathed in some of the tea and started choking.

'Don't you ever knock?' he said, between coughs. 'I could have been naked!'

'I'll take that as a "thank you",' said Emma, dumping the clothes on the bed. 'They're not completely dry, but they'll do. He died, in case you're wondering.'

'Sorry?' Sebastian frowned, still coughing. 'Who died?'

'My dad. He died when I was eight. Lived here all his life. Born in this room, actually, same as me.

Probably in that very bed.' Sebastian pulled a face that suggested he wasn't entirely taken with the idea of people being born in the bed he was sitting on. 'Don't worry,' said Emma, raising a single eyebrow. 'The sheets have been washed.'

'So, you've lived in this house all your life? Did you go away to university or anything?'

She perched on the other end of the bed. 'I was going to. All my school friends did... but then my mum fell ill and I had to stay and look after the shop. I've been helping run it ever since.'

'Your mother's still ill?'

'Oh no. It's just... I don't know.' She shrugged and fiddled with the corner of the bedspread. 'I guess I got so into the habit of being here, I forgot about leaving. Steepleford's all I've ever known.'

Sebastian nodded. 'Sounds like me and London.'

'Talking of which,' said Emma, dropping the bedspread and looking him in the face, business-like again, 'you'll be wanting to find out what's going on back in the big city. You get those clothes on and I'll make sure the computer's ready.'

Five minutes later, wearing his warm, milk-smelling clothes, Sebastian joined her in the lounge, where the clicking sound of Mrs Standfield's knitting mingled with the loud springs and scrunches of a modem trying to connect to the internet.

'Old school,' he said. 'No fibre broadband here, then, I take it.'

Emma narrowed her eyes at him. 'I guess that's something to do with computers, is it? We've got what you see and that's it. Sounds like it's connected, though. Only three attempts - must be your lucky day.'

'We'll see,' said Sebastian. 'About the computer, I

mean,' he added, realising his comment might be misconstrued. Emma just smiled, skipped over to the armchair opposite her mum and snatched up an ancient-looking book. It was by Jane Austen.

Sebastian sat down in the creaky wooden chair at the desk and peered at the computer. Dragging the mouse across the screen, he clicked on the icon for the internet browser. It took over a minute to run, and a further two minutes to load up his personal webmail. He had eight messages. Two of them were from banks he had never used, alerting him to suspicious activity on accounts he didn't have with links to sites where he could sign in and check. He deleted these and looked at the others. The first was from his father, reminding him that it was his gran's 88th birthday in two weeks and that he was expected to join them for a celebratory meal. Boring.

There were two messages from Brillig, one sent on Saturday morning asking how the journey had gone and how he was finding life on the smallholding, and the second from two hours ago, which simply said, 'Are you dead already?'

He hit the reply button and started typing, quickly realising that the S and N keys didn't work properly.

'Mot dead yet,' he wrote, 'but I was almodt eatem by a dwarm of pigd yedterday and attacked by a psycho chickem. It wadn't fummy! Everythimg id old amd dirty, like livimg im medieval timed. Amd there'd mo mobile metwork amywhere. Cam't wait to come home. Debadtiam.' He sent it without bothering to see if he could fix the stuck keys or make it more readable. Brillig would just have to decipher the message herself.

There was a email from Little Pete and DeVere, copied to everyone who had been at his birthday party, plus a number of others from his office, in which they had opened a book on which day Sebastian would return and whether he would actually survive the ordeal of his week in the country. He scowled as he read it, though he was slightly mollified by the long odds they'd placed on him already being dead. Not *that* long though; it was still 48 to 1. The odds suggested they thought it most likely he would either be home by Tuesday afternoon. Or dead by Thursday morning. He didn't grace their message with a response.

The last email was from Diesel entitled 'Photos from Friday', which had nine attachments totalling twenty megabytes. He clicked on the first image and sat watching the progress bar for several minutes before deciding it wasn't actually moving.

He rolled his eyes at the screen. '*Lack of progress* bar, more like!' he muttered.

'Speak up, young man,' said Mrs Standfield. 'If you've got something to say, say it properly. Can't be doing with mumbling.'

Sebastian swivelled to look at her. 'Sorry,' he said. 'I was just talking to myself. I'm just waiting for an image to download.' He paused, realising this probably meant nothing to her. 'It's a photograph, you see, and the computer can only get it through the telephone wires here,' he gestured to the jumble of wires beneath the desk, 'which is taking quite a long time.'

Mrs Standfield paused mid-stitch and shook her head. 'If it's anything above one meg, you'll have a wait on your hands. That old dial-up barely hits four kilobytes a second.'

Sebastian opened his mouth, but couldn't think of a suitable response. He looked across at Emma, who was grinning at her book, before closing his mouth and turning back to the computer to watch the glacial movement of the progress bar. Behind him the rattling of the knitting needles resumed, seeming to grow to an almost deafening volume as he stared at the screen.

Hours seemed to pass and he felt sure Mrs Standfield must have knitted not only the world's longest scarf, but a hat, gloves and a full set of winter clothing to go with it. A small laugh escaped at the thought of someone wearing an entirely knitted wardrobe.

'Something funny?' asked Emma, tossing her book onto the coffee table and jumping to her feet. At the same moment a group photograph of Friday evening at the pub flickered onto the screen. In the middle of the image, clutching a pair of green wellies on his lap, sat Sebastian, a slightly drunk, but unmistakably miserable expression on his face. As he looked at himself and his friends, a wave of homesickness swept over him. He wished he was there right now, sitting in the pub with a pint in his hand, looking forward to a week in the city and the comforts of his apartment and his own bed and the view from his window. Back home he would be assured of a decent night's sleep. Back home he could wash properly and put on clean, freshly ironed clothes. Back home he could feel safe and secure, knowing he was surrounded by people and places, by busyness and familiarity.

He wanted to go home. The desire in that moment was like a physical force, and if he'd had transport he would have left right then, got on the train and not looked back.

Emma laughed and pointed at the photo. 'You look like you're about to be taken away and shot!'

'They'd just told me I had to spend a week in this

village.'

'Oh.' She looked taken aback. 'Really? It's not *that* bad here, is it?'

Sebastian shrugged. 'Isn't it?' He stared at the picture. His friends smirked back at him, even Sandra, who tended to hide behind other people in photos. Smug gits, the lot of them! They'd tricked him into coming here, and now they were making bets on how long he'd last. He wondered what odds Little Pete and DeVere had put on him coming home tonight and decided not to check. No matter how much he wanted to go home, he wasn't going to give them the satisfaction. He would show them all!

'You look like you're about to burst,' said Emma, placing a hand on his shoulder. 'Are you okay?'

9
LITTLE MISS MUFFET

'Are you okay, dear?' asked Virginia, as Sebastian entered the farmhouse kitchen twenty minutes later.

He sighed. 'Yeah, I'm fine.'

'You don't look it. You look like you're about to be taken away and shot!'

Sebastian almost smiled at this. 'So I'm told. I guess it's just my look.' He peered across at the lounge area, where the back of Neil's head was poking up above the armchair, today's newspaper opened out in front of him. 'How's the milking room?' he asked.

'The milking *parlour*?' said Neil, not turning round. 'Yes, all good. Damned idiots!' This last comment was clearly directed at something he was reading in the newspaper. Neil huffed, rustling the page over in annoyance.

'Are you ready to make this cheese then?' Sebastian turned to see Virginia giving him the kind of look you might give to a child who had fallen over or a friend who, after a serious two-year relationship, had just been dumped via text message.

Sebastian glanced from her to the warm comfort of the sofa and back again, checking the clock as he did so. It wasn't even six; probably still too early to excuse himself and head off to bed.

'Er, sure. I guess.'

'Won't take long, anyhow,' said Virginia. 'It's the

waiting between each stage that's the killer. But I've already got a couple of batches underway so we can get straight through the full process in one go.'

'Great.' He knew it sounded insincere, but nowhere near as much as he felt. Why on earth would he care about horrible goat cheese?

As with the bread-making session, Virginia had gathered the equipment on the kitchen table. There was the milk churn from earlier, a large stainless steel pan with a cloth covering it, a folded up piece of what looked like net curtain, a couple of ceramic bowls, a load of plastic containers with lids, a sieve, a spoon, a thermometer and a small plastic bottle half-filled with a suspicious yellow liquid.

Their first task, after washing their hands, was to warm the milk before adding half a teaspoon of the yellow liquid. The bottle declared it to be "Rennet".

'What is this stuff?' he asked, sniffing at it. 'What's rennet?'

'A special cheese-making enzyme,' said Virginia. 'It's extracted from calves' stomachs.'

Sebastian jerked it away from his face in disgust. 'Calves' stomachs? We're putting *this* in to the milk?'

'We sure are. There's nothing better for making cheese. That little splash you've added will eat its way through that milk in a couple of hours, gathering up all the proteins into curd and leaving behind the whey.'

'Leaving it in it's wake,' called Neil's voice from the lounge. He turned to peer at them over the back of the armchair. 'Get it?' he said, 'In it's *whey*-ke.'

Sebastian and Virginia both shook their heads. 'Nope,' said Sebastian and directed his attention to Virginia. 'So what's next?'

'Give it a good stir to get the rennet-'

'Calf juice.'

'-yes, the calf juice mixed in, then we can leave it to do its job, while we take a look at one I started off while you were at the shop.'

This turned out to be what was hiding beneath the cloth in the large stainless-steel pan. When Virginia whipped the cloth away, it looked pretty much like another pan full of milk.

'Where's the cheese, then?' he asked, peering at the surface to see if there was any bobbing around in there.

'You're looking at it. Or rather you're looking at it in embryonic form. This here is the curds and whey.'

'Like in the nursery rhyme,' said Sebastian, almost sounding excited for a moment.

A voice piped up from the lounge. 'Little Bo Peep, wasn't it?'

Sebastian and Virginia exchanged a "look". 'I think it was Little Miss Muffet,' said Sebastian.

'You sure?' The back of Neil's head tilted slightly. 'Wasn't she that sissy who was afraid of spiders? Reminds me of someone else I know.'

'Here,' said Virginia, pressing a spoon down onto the surface of the pan's contents. To Sebastian's surprise it filled, not with milk, but with a slightly-cloudy liquid. 'This is the whey. The curds are the bit we want, though. We'll give the whey to the pigs.'

Sebastian pulled a face. The whey did not look appetising. 'Lucky old pigs!' he said.

'What we need to do is get as much of the whey out as possible, and for this, we need to use the cheesecloth.' Virginia unfolded the net curtain material and flattened it into the sieve, which she placed over the ceramic bowl. She handed Sebastian the spoon. 'There you go, spoon it in.'

Sebastian did not look thrilled by the prospect, but he did it anyway, the large spoon slipping easily into the curds as he cut them out and dumped them into the cheesecloth.

'It's a bit like one of those set yoghurts,' he said. 'Is that what it is?'

'Yoghurt's made with bacteria rather than rennet, but you're right, it feels similar. Want to taste a bit?'

Sebastian's un-thrilled look returned, though this time it had an extra layer of revulsion. 'Taste a bit?' he said, his voice mirroring his face. 'But it's made out of goat's milk.'

'Nothing wrong with goat's milk,' said Virginia. 'Most people can't tell it from cow's milk.'

Sebastian raised an eyebrow at this. '*I* could!'

'Really? Have you ever tried it?'

'Cow's milk? All the time.'

Virginia raised an eyebrow in return. 'You know what I mean.'

'No,' said Sebastian, pausing in the act of cutting into the curds. 'I've never tried goat's milk.' He was distracted by a chuckle from the armchair and glanced across to see Neil looking round again.

'What do you think you've been drinking since you got here?' asked Neil. 'The milk in your tea and on your cornflakes?'

'I...' Sebastian began and turned to Virginia for assurance. But her face only confirmed Neil's words. 'No. Not goat's milk. Really?' She nodded her confirmation. Neil chuckled his. Sebastian returned to spooning out the curds, with a little more violence than was necessary. 'So what do you do with all this cheese?'

'I take it to the farmers market in Barnstaple.'

Sebastian frowned. 'You sell it to other farmers?'

'No. The farmers market is where farmers go to sell their produce to the public. I sell goat cheese, bread, bacon, sausages, chicken, soups, preserves, cordials - all kinds of stuff.'

'And how often do you do that?' he asked, tipping the pan as he scraped out the last of the curds and dumped in them with the rest.

'Every Thursday.'

'*Every* Thursday?' Sebastian placed the spoon on the table and looked at his hostess. 'You must spend all your time making stuff to sell!' And now that he thought about it, he realised that the only times he'd seen her outside this kitchen were at church and the pub the previous day.

She nodded as she gathered together the edges of the cheesecloth and lifted it up so the curds inside balled together, the whey dripping through the bottom. 'Pretty much. That's how it's been since, well, since we got married and I moved in with Neil, fifteen years ago.'

Sebastian was stunned. Although it might feel as though he'd been stuck here for weeks, it was only two days ago that he'd boarded the train and headed out of the shining city into the dark wilds beyond. The idea of being here for fifteen years - *fifteen whole years* - was too extreme to comprehend. Instead, it gave him an almost palpable feeling of despair, like the thought of a life sentence of hard labour, of being a Roman galley slave or of getting transported back in time to a world before humanity existed with no way to return. 'That's awful!' he said, the words tripping out of him before he could stop them.

Virginia paused only briefly as she tied a knot in

the top of the cheesecloth and carried it and the pan across to the fridge. 'What do you mean, awful?' she said at last, her face hidden as she opened the door.

'I mean... No, when I say "awful", I don't actually mean *awful*,' he replied, back-pedalling as fast as his brain would allow. 'It's just, I couldn't imagine living like that.'

'Living like what?' Virginia had hung the curd-filled cloth on a hook in the fridge, leaving it to drip into a tray beneath, and now leant with her arm on the open door, giving Sebastian her full attention.

He held up his hands at though bracing himself for an impact. 'I'm not saying there's anything wrong with... with this.' He waved his hands at the kitchen as though summing up the full extent of Virginia's world. 'Only, living in the city, I spend most of my time out and about. I couldn't imagine being shut away in here cooking and stuff all day. It'd drive me crazy.'

There was a long pause during which Virginia stood in front of the open fridge, hands on hips, and Sebastian backed up against the table, wondering if he should just make a run for it.

'It'd drive me bloody crazy, too!' called Neil from his armchair, breaking the awkward silence. 'If I had to be cooped up in the kitchen all day, I'd stick my head in the oven and turn on the gas. Better that than baking!'

'The oven's electric, you daft sod,' said Virginia. 'Which just goes to show how little time you spend in here.' And to Sebastian's relief, she started laughing and stepped forward to pat him on the shoulder. 'Don't worry. It's not the life I'd choose now either, but back when I made that decision, it was marry this old git,' she nodded at Neil, who waved a hand over his head, 'or be stuck in the pub with Donny for the rest of my life.'

'Donny?' Sebastian frowned for a moment, trying to work out what she was saying. 'You mean you were going to marry Donald at the Green Man.'

'Mister Master Chef himself!' said Neil.

'No.' Virginia shook her head, turning her attention back to the fridge contents. 'Donny's my brother. I grew up at the Green Man. I hated it! And when Neil came a-wooing, with the promise of a life of horse-riding and freedom, I jumped at the chance to get out.'

Neil coughed loudly from the armchair. 'It was that and my overpowering charm.'

'Charm, was it?' said Virginia, lifting out a second cheesecloth that had already been hanging in the fridge. 'Lies, more like.' She edged over to Sebastian and half-whispered. 'You know what he told me?'

Sebastian leaned in conspiratorially. 'What?'

'He told me I was a princess and that I should be treated like one. He promised me the luxurious life of a country lady, but instead I ended up here in this scruffy old kitchen, with hands like a bricklayer's and clothes you'd think were stolen from a scarecrow.'

'The kitchen ain't scruffy!' said Neil over the back of the armchair. 'And anyways, you said you were going to make yourself a dress for summer, remember? But I haven't seen much sign of it.'

'In case you hadn't noticed,' said Virginia, the filled cheesecloth swinging like a pendulum in her hand, 'I've not had much time to be fiddling about with dresses. And it *is* scruffy.'

'It was only *one* dress,' said Neil, turning back to his paper with a huffing sound.

Virginia dumped the cheesecloth into a bowl with a dull thud. 'Right,' she said, all businesslike. 'Now that we've dealt with that nonsense, let's have a look at how the curds end up after most of the whey's been drained off.' She peeled the cloth open to reveal the white ball inside.

Sebastian peered at it. 'It looks like Mozzarella.'

'Not quite. It's more like a soft, spreadable sort of cheese at the moment.' From somewhere she produced two spoons and held one out to Sebastian. 'Come on. Let's give it a try.'

He looked at the proffered cutlery, but made no move to take it. The only movement he made, in fact, was on his face, which morphed from mild interest to slightly-less-mild disgust.

'What's the matter?' asked Virginia. 'It's lovely, I promise.' As if to prove her point, she cut into the cheese with the other spoon, scooping out a generous helping, and slipped it into her mouth. She closed her eyes, smiling with pleasure. 'Now that is divine!'

'I'll take your word for it,' said Sebastian, still ignoring the spoon held out to him. 'Its just… I'm not a big fan of goat cheese. I had some once before and it left a horrible taste in my mouth for hours.'

Virginia moved the spoon closer to him. 'Well, this won't. I promise. It's clean and fresh, just like it should be.'

Sebastian looked at the spoon, but still made no move to take it. Virginia waggled it in front of his face, a silent challenge.

'Right!' he said, giving in and snatching the spoon from her. He dipped it into the cheese, teasing out a tiny morsel on the tip. He raised it to his mouth, sniffing warily, but it didn't smell of anything.

Frowning, he put the spoon in his mouth and, screwing up his face, placed the cheese onto his tongue. He paused, waiting for that stomach-turning goaty taste. But it never came. It tasted... like cheese. Like normal, soft cheese. Only it was better. It was just like Virginia had said, clean and fresh. His eyes widened in surprise and were matched by Virginia's broad smile.

'What did I tell you?' she said.

'That's actually really nice,' said Sebastian. 'Not at all like the one I tried before. It's like... I don't know. I can't describe it. It's just really nice.'

'Well, I'm glad we got *that* settled. Now all we need to do is decant it into these pots,' she pointed to the plastic containers with lids, 'and get them back in the fridge ready for taking to the market.'

'How much do you charge for one of these?' asked Sebastian as he measured out the last four ounces of the cheese into a pot, sneaking a little out for himself in the process.

Virginia looked up from where she was labelling the pots. 'Three pounds fifty,' she said, 'and they're one of my best sellers. But I only take them along once a month, since it takes that long to get enough milk stored up. I freeze it, see, and then I tend to make it all in one day to save time. I don't usually do it in three goes - that was just so you wouldn't have to hang around for ages. Talking of which, shall we have a look and see how that rennet's getting on?'

Half an hour later, Sebastian hung up the "nude lady chef" apron on the back of a chair, flopped onto the sofa and closed his eyes.

He sighed loudly. 'I am shattered.'

'You'd best get yourself a good night's sleep then,' said Neil, dropping his paper to look up at clock. 'I've been going easy on you so far, but tomorrow your week is really going to begin!'

Sebastian opened his eyes, just a fraction, and peered at his host. 'Seriously?' But Neil just smiled and disappeared back behind his paper.

There was something strange about the ceiling. At first Sebastian couldn't work out what it was, but it definitely wasn't right. It was the wrong shade of white, for starters, more a dirty light grey with cracks in the paintwork that he was sure weren't there usually. And where had that dreadful lampshade come from? There's no way he would have hung such a monstrosity on his own ceiling.

And then he remembered. This wasn't his ceiling. For the briefest of moments he thought he was back in London, a bright Monday morning and a promising week ahead. But no, he was still in Steepleford. And the week ahead promised nothing but hard work, mud, barely-domesticated animals and more mud. And manure.

'Great,' he muttered, dragging himself out of bed and yawning hugely. 'Could it be any worse than this?'

It could.

There was no hot water.

'Sorry about that,' said Virginia, as Sebastian emerged into the kitchen, still shivering a little from the cold shower, his face unshaved. 'The boiler conked out in the night. Neil out getting a new thermistor, so it should be sorted for later.'

Sebastian nodded, idly wondering what a thermistor was, and offered to help with the breakfast things. It was a proper fry up, something he rarely treated himself to back in London, despite the greasy café being less than fifty metres from the entrance to his apartment block.

'Thanks,' he said, as Virginia slid the fully laden plate in front of him.

She turned back to the stove, where the kettle was steaming away. 'It'll help get your strength up for the day. You're going to need it. Tea?'

Once he had finished, Sebastian headed out to the chickens, armed with gloves and boxes, ready for the daily tussle with the Psycho Hen.

'There you are, you horrible bird!' he said as he shut the enclosure door behind him and spotted the chicken in question watching him, no, glaring at him, as it sat on the hen house roof. He knew it was the Psycho Hen, because it had distinctive black markings on its neck and its wings. 'How did you get up there?'

The chicken made no reply, but kept its eye fixed on Sebastian as he approached the nesting boxes. Carefully, so as not to upset the crazed bird, he lifted the long lid, placed the boxes in one of the compartments and began collecting the eggs.

He was five eggs in, when the bird stood up suddenly and began walking along the ridge of the roof as though on a tightrope. Sebastian paused as the hen drew level with him.

'I'm not falling for any of your tricks today,' he said, tensing himself for the expected attack. But the Psycho Hen sat down and began preening itself, pecking at the feathers on its tail as though oblivious of Sebastian's presence, so he returned to collecting the eggs.

Another five eggs were safely in the boxes, when the chicken's head snapped back round to face him again, as though he'd done something to offend it.

Again Sebastian paused, his eyes narrowed at the bird, and again it started preening itself, this time pecking at the feathers on the front of its neck, as high up as it could manage. It was such a ridiculous display it made Sebastian laugh, causing the bird to stop and glare at him again.

The action of reaching in to collect the eggs had exposed a few inches of forearm between his shirt cuff and the rubber glove, and a tickling sensation on this area caused him to look down. Sebastian stopped breathing, his heart froze. There creeping up his arm was a spider. A large spider. The kind of spider that scurries across the living room carpet in the light of the television, making a dash from one piece of furniture to another. It had a fat body, rat brown and shiny-eyed, with thick, hairy legs that looked as though they could puncture your flesh. Sebastian took all this in in a single, terrifying instant. And then he screamed.

It wasn't a manly scream. In fact it was more of a shriek, and he leapt up shaking his arm as though it had caught fire, thrashing at it with his other hand. The chicken, whose existence he had forgotten in his panic, jerked to its feet, startled by all this sudden movement. With a piercing squawk, almost as loud as the shriek that was still bursting from Sebastian, the bird launched itself off the roof, straight at Sebastian. It touched down on his head, its claws, or maybe they were talons, scrabbling at his scalp.

'Get off!' he yelled, flapping his now spider-free hands at the chicken. He made contact and, with another loud squawk, it dropped to the ground, pecked up the spider and hurried away across the enclosure. Grabbing the nearest missile to hand, Sebastian launched it at the Psycho Hen. It was an egg, and though it missed the hen by a couple of metres, it struck one of the fence post squarely in the middle and burst in a shower of shell and yolk.

'A double-yolker, I reckon,' said a voice, and Sebastian turned to see Neil standing at the gate of the chicken run. 'Another "accidental breakage", is it?'

'I…' he pointed at his feathered nemesis, now watching him from behind a water trough. 'That wretched chicken attacked me. Again.'

'So you thought you'd try and kill it with an egg?'

'If only!' said Sebastian, glaring at the chicken which was now idly scratching away in the corner as though nothing had happened. 'There was a massive spider on me, as well! It was terrifying.' He bent forwards, hands on his knees, trying to catch his breath. He could hear his heart thumping in his ears and it sounded upset. 'Sorry. I'm not doing too well at this egg collecting, am I?'

'Well, things might go a little smoother tomorrow,' said Neil, and nodded towards the Psycho Hen, 'since you won't have that pesky bird to worry about.'

Sebastian raised his eyebrows. 'Really? How's that?'

'Because, after you've dropped the eggs up at the shop - and I don't literally mean "dropped" - you're going to get your wish and kill that chicken.'

MURDER MOST FOWL

He took the hill at a run, an egg box clutched in each hand, his mind buzzing as it tried to process what he was being asked - *expected!* - to do. Except for a few spiders, which obviously didn't count as real lifeforms, Sebastian had never killed anything in his life. Sure, as a child, he'd had a couple of pets that died, a hamster and a guinea pig, but he hadn't actually killed them himself. The guinea pig had died of old age, as far as he could recall, while the hamster had escaped and hidden itself in one of his father's shoes, where it met its unfortunate demise when he got himself ready for work the next day. And now, out of nowhere, he was expected to terminate the life of a hen.

It didn't matter that it was the Psycho Hen, the evil bird that had terrorised him on each of his three forays into the enclosure to collect eggs; it was still a living, breathing creature. More than that, this was an animal that had looked him in the eye, that had tackled him bird-to-man. It was a respected foe. And while Sebastian might have been happy to take it out in the heat of battle, he felt stunned, sickened even, by the idea of murdering it in cold blood.

He had to talk with Emma. She would understand. She would know what to do. And so he hurried up the hill to see her.

As he approached the crossroads, he saw the

butcher emerge from his shop, his massive shoulders brushing the doorframe as he squeezed through. He was carrying a blackboard with chalk writing across it. Sebastian didn't see what the sign said, but, as he caught the butcher's eye, the man grunted at him, so he fixed his gaze back on the road and scurried around the corner towards the shop.

The bell announced his arrival in the usual fashion, but unlike the previous times, it was not Emma he found standing behind the counter, but her mother.

'Oh,' said Sebastian, taken aback, 'Er… Hi. I mean, good morning, Mrs Standfield. Is… is Emma round?' He peered around the shopkeeper, but the door to the living area was closed.

'She's out,' came the curt response. 'I take it you've come to deliver those eggs.' She held out a hand towards the boxes and Sebastian handed them over. Mrs Standfield placed them on the counter and opened them, examining the contents, before nodding what Sebastian presumed was her approval. 'So what exactly did you want my daughter for, young man?'

'I… well, it's just I was hoping for a quick chat, that's all.' Sebastian tried to gather his thoughts, aware he might be sounding like some kind of stalker, or a teenager with a crush, which is pretty much the same thing. 'It was about a chicken.'

'A *chicken*?' said Mrs Standfield, in much the way Lady Bracknell is portrayed as saying, 'A *handbag*?'

Sebastian soldiered on. 'Yes, that's right, a chicken. Only, apparently I'm supposed to be killing one later. An actual, live chicken.'

The shopkeeper picked up the two egg boxes and lifted the flap in the counter. As she approached Sebastian she paused. 'And you want Emma to help you?'

'Not *help* as such,' he said, stepping aside so she could get past him to the shop window. 'It was more for support. You know, *moral* support.'

'For you,' she asked, 'or the chicken?'

Sebastian blinked. Was that a joke? From the "We are not amused" Mrs Standfield? He turned to look at her, but she was bending over, placing the eggs in the window with her back to him. 'It's just...' he began, 'I've never killed anything before.'

'Well, Emma's out doing the Monday morning deliveries.' The shopkeeper delivered this pronouncement, as though this was obvious and Sebastian should really have thought about that before he came in demanding to see her daughter. 'As for the killing...' she said, standing up and smoothing the folds of her dress. She turned to face Sebastian, smiling at him in a way that was more disconcerting than anything else. 'First, you have to accept that the bird's got to be killed. Then get it over with as quickly as possible. A good, clean death is as much as any of us can wish for.'

Sebastian opened his mouth. Then he closed it again, while he thought of something to say. 'Well, I can probably think of a few other things I'd wish for *first*,' he said at last, 'but thanks for the...'

'Moral support?' she suggested, heading back to the counter.

'Quite.' Sebastian turned to leave.

'And one other thing,' said Mrs Standfield, as he turned the door handle. 'I find it helps to imagine it's someone I don't like, instead of a bird, I'm holding. Always helps to add a bit of potency as you're breaking the creature's neck! There's really nothing to it.'

Sebastian hurried from the shop and, for the second time, he was sure he heard the tinkle of laughter behind the voice of the dancing bell.

'There's really nothing to it,' said Neil, walking across the poultry field towards Sebastian, who was standing in the covered straw storage area that jutted out from the side of the goat shed. In one large hand, Neil was clutching a hen - though not the 'Psycho' one - upside down by its feet, and while the bird did not seem to be especially fazed by this, Sebastian felt he might be sick at any moment.

The sky was overcast, and a gentle breeze added an extra layer of coolness to the morning, rustling the leaves in the trees above, but Sebastian could still feel the cold sweat trickling down his spine and when he wiped the back of his gloved hand across his forehead and it came away damp. 'Goodness, lad, you're white as a sheet. Are you feeling okay?'

'It's just nerves, I think,' he said, fanning his face with a hand. 'It's just, I've never killed anything before.'

'So you've told me... about twenty times.' Neil smiled, but it made no difference to Sebastian's feeling of anxiety.

'It's not just that though,' he said. 'I've not even *seen* a chicken being killed before. I saw a cat get run over once when I was a kid and that was bad enough.'

'I thought you didn't like cats.'

'I don't, but it was still horrific. I remember watching it feebly trying to scrabble to the pavement with its back legs all...' He shook his head, in an attempt to dispel the mental image.

'Well, this'll be nothing like that,' said Neil, placing

his free hand on Sebastian's shoulder. 'We've got much swifter ways to dispatch them than running them over with a car! It'll be quick and painless... for *you* as well as the chickens.'

'I suppose they do *have* to die, do they?' asked Sebastian, remembering Mrs Standfield's comment about accepting that the chicken had to be killed.

Neil turned and gestured about the smallholding with the dangling chicken. 'Take a look around,' he said. Sebastian did so, taking in the various breeds of poultry scratching at the ground and, lazing nearby, the goats peering at him from the entrance to their shed, the masked horses standing motionless in the next field and the pigs milling about in the dirt beyond. 'The fact is, none of these creatures would be here if we didn't kill them and eat them. The same is true for all such farm animals. This is their purpose, it's why we breed them and raise them. They exist only as part of our food chain, and in order to fulfil their reason for living, we have to kill them. It's as simple as that. Except for the horses, of course. And the dogs. We don't eat them... unless of course we're really hungry!'

Sebastian smiled at this and nodded his understanding, though he still felt anxious at the thought of the chicken, still hanging in Neil's grip and peering around without concern, being killed at any moment. And indeed, it seemed that moment had arrived.

'Right then,' said Neil. 'This is how it's going to be done. I'm going to take hold of the chicken's neck, with the skin that join's my thumb and index finger,' he held up his free hand, the two digits in question forming an L-shape, 'in the ridge between the skull and the top vertebra, and my other finger's around the underside of its beak.' He demonstrated, wrapping his hand around the chicken's neck, its comb pressed against his palm, its head hidden inside. Sebastian bent closer to look as Neil continued. 'With the other hand, make sure you've got a firm hold on the legs. Then you simply twist the bird's head backwards, rolling your knuckle towards it's neck, while pulling downwards firmly. It'll resist for a moment, but keep going and you'll feel the break.'

Sebastian looked up. 'The break?'

'Like this.' With a swift, practised motion Neil jerked down on the chicken's head. Almost immediately the bird began flapping wildly, catching Sebastian on the cheek. He leapt backwards, tripping over his own foot and landed across a bale of straw, his eyes locked on the chicken's violent death throws. 'Don't worry,' said Neil. 'It's just nerves, is all. It's quite dead.' To demonstrate, he released the head, letting it flop around as the creature writhed, beating at the air. The eyes were closed, the neck clearly broken.

Sebastian own eyes were wide open and he hardly blinked as he stared at the flapping bird. It seemed to take an eternity before the wings began to still. In truth, it couldn't have been much more than sixty seconds, but it was the longest minute of his life. The longest so far, at least. He still had his own chicken to kill.

'Easy, see,' said Neil, as Sebastian clambered to his feet. 'Pass me a piece of that baler twine, would you? The orange string, there.' Sebastian did so, moving as if in a trance, and watched, numbed, as Neil tied a slip knot with one hand and looped it round the chicken's feet before attaching the other end to a handy nail, sticking out of one of the overhead beams. 'Good weight on that bird,' he said, feeling the chicken's breast. It let out another couple of lazy flaps, then hung still again, twisting slightly in the breeze. Neil stooped to pick up a small cardboard box. 'Right. Ready for yours, then?'

Sebastian shook his head, and leant against the wooden post that held up the roof. 'Not really,' he said, staring at the box. 'I don't feel so good.'

'What's up? You saw what I did, right? There's nothing to it, lad.' Neil began to open the flaps of the cardboard box, but Sebastian put a hand on it.

'Just... just give me a moment.'

Neil sighed. 'Alright, but we can't wait long or it'll be a misery plucking this thing.' He jabbed a thumb at the dangling chicken, which let out a final, feeble flap.

Sebastian wandered off across the field towards the river. They had known, of course, his friends from the office. He could remember someone mentioning it at his birthday celebration, some offhand comment dropped into a barrage of abuse about things that proved he wasn't a real man.

'Bastards!' he muttered. 'Sending me off here without any information, with no real clue what I was going to end up doing. What'll be next? Gunning down a horse, perhaps, or dog fighting?' He looked at his watch, which said it was ten-fifteen already. Sebastian imagined Brillig and the others all gathered at their desks, sipping coffee and chatting away about nothing in particular. No doubt DeVere and Little Pete were busy taking bets on when Sebastian would be home. He wondered whether murdering this chicken was in the book, and what sort of odds they'd placed on him not doing it, on him "chickening out". 'Bastards!' he said again. 'I'll show them!' And he turned back to where Neil was watching him, still holding the cardboard box under one arm.

'I'm ready,' Sebastian called, startling the goats. 'Let's get it over with.'

The next few minutes seemed to pass like a kind of dream, and not one of the good ones either. But despite the other-worldliness, every second of it became etched into Sebastian's mind as though carved into granite, lodged with crystal clarity in his memory.

Neil opened the box, slipping in a hand to take hold of the chicken's legs, before drawing it out upside down, like a conjurer pulling a rabbit out of an empty hat. The difference, though, was that they did it by magic, while Sebastian had seen the Psycho Hen being shoved into this box back at the farmhouse. As Neil held it out for him to take, the bird fixed one eye on Sebastian's face as though it knew what was coming.

'That's it,' said Neil. 'Slip your index finger between the legs so you can get a firm grip with your thumb and third finger.'

Sebastian did so and, as Neil relinquished his hold, he was surprised at how heavy the chicken was. He began to comment on this, but found his mouth was too dry to speak. All his bodily fluids seemed to be used up in producing the sweat that was still running down his back and prickling his face.

'Stop looking at me,' he croaked at the bird.

Neil stepped round to get a better look at the chicken. 'Now, remember what I said. Palm down, base of the skull nestled between thumb and index finger. That's right. Now, wrap the other fingers under the beak. Not *too* hard - just enough to hold it in place.' Neil bent down to check, then straightened up, taking a step backwards. 'When you're ready, just hold the legs still, while you twist and pull downwards on the head.

You'll feel it come away from the neck.'

Sebastian looked down and was relieved he could no longer see the beady eye boring into at him. But his relief was barely a flash. It was time. There was no going back now. He was going to have to kill this creature, this bird that had done nothing to him. Alright, it had spooked him a few times, but that was hardly reason enough to end its life.

Again he had a flash of his friends, all busy gossiping away back in London, and at the thought he felt the anger rising up in him. This was all *their* fault! This, right now, this ordeal he was going through, this chicken murder, was all because of *them*. And he remembered Mrs Standfield's rather creepy words about imagining it was someone else, and not the bird, whose neck you were breaking.

He took a deep breath and pulled. Hard. Hard enough that, when he met the resistance of whatever was keeping the chicken's skull attached to the rest of its body, he felt it rip away - a clean break. Then he felt the bird's head dropping from his hand on the ground and realised he had pulled it right off. The flapping began and the creature writhed around, the legs tugging to be free from his grip, the neck twitching from side to side like a crazed serpent, blood jerking across his boots and up his trousers.

Sebastian stared at it in horror, wondering how the creature was managing to scream. Then he realised the sound was coming from him.

'It's alright, lad,' said Neil, placing a hand on his shoulder. 'It's done. It's dead. *Very* dead. Get away, Tank!' This last comment was directed at the dog, which had sprung to life and was busily licking at the blood on the ground. 'Go on, get away!' Tank ignored him and set about chewing on the chicken's head.

Sebastian did not move, but continued staring, open-mouthed, though now silent, as the headless bird's flapping began to slow. He still didn't move as Neil tied a length of baler twine around its feet and teased it from his grip. He just stood and stared at the blood, spattered across his trousers and boots. So much blood.

And then he vomited on the dog.

'Well, that wasn't entirely unexpected,' said Neil, chuckling from somewhere behind him. 'Feeling any better?'

Sebastian turned round, bleary-eyed. 'A bit.' He looked back at Tank, who hadn't reacted at all, but continued chewing on the chicken head as sick dripped off his coat. 'Sorry about your dog.'

'Ah, he won't mind any. I'll take him for a dip in the river in a bit. But first, we've got to get these girls plucked.'

'But I need a shower,' said Sebastian, gesturing to the general mess of his clothes and noticing for the first time that he had blood on his right glove and his sleeve, and on the small patch of skin that lay between them. 'Look at me. I'm a mess!'

Neil shook his head. 'All in good time, lad. But if we let these birds get cold, the job'll take twice as long. Come on. It won't take fifteen minutes.'

It didn't.

It took forty.

Most of this was taken up with Neil trying to correct Sebastian's technique of picking out only one or two feathers at a time.

'But it feels like I'm hurting it,' Sebastian kept explaining, a feeling that was heightened at one point, when the bird twitched suddenly mid-pluck. To Neil's great amusement Sebastian screamed again when this happened and jumped back into the straw bales.

Neil's assurance that, 'When you get into your stride, it's actually quite therapeutic', never quite matched up with Sebastian's experience. As far as he was concerned, the whole ordeal was nothing short of horrific.

'That was nothing short of horrific,' said Sebastian, as the two men entered the farmhouse, each holding a mostly naked chicken, their hair and clothes covered in small feathers.

'You got the job done though, eh?' said Virginia, who was drying up at the sink.

Neil dumped his chicken on the table, so Sebastian did the same. 'I pulled its head off by mistake,' he told her. 'And I was sick on your dog.'

Virginia tried to look understanding. Tried. And failed. Instead she burst out laughing and had to cover her face with the drying-up cloth. 'Sorry, love,' she said, as her giggles subsided. 'Why don't you go get yourself cleaned up and bring me those clothes? Then we'll get these birds drawn and ready for the oven.'

Sebastian made to move towards the stairs, then stopped. 'Drawn?' he said. 'What's that?'

A large hand landed on his shoulder. 'It means you've still got to get the guts out, lad.'

'*The guts?*' Sebastian turned to face him, looking as though he was about to be sick again.

'Uh oh!' said Neil, with a chuckle. 'Quick. Get the poor dog out of the way!'

THE VEGETARIAN OPTION

People often assumed that Sebastian was a vegetarian, possibly even a vegan, though he could never work out why. He wasn't especially thin or pasty or ill-looking, three symptoms which he associated with people who chose to live their life without meat. And yet, on those rare occasions when he was invited to a friend's house for dinner, his hosts would invariably present him with nut cutlets, veggie burgers, salads and other drab, meat-free excuses for food. Any suggestion from Sebastian that he was not, in fact, vegetarian would be met with incredulity, as though it was just his little joke.

At such times, Sebastian would chew on the tasteless mouthfuls, and think back with longing to the meals his mother used to make, every one of which had some animal product as the main attraction. He could even recall the occasional Sunday roast that included several different meats, though the mainstay was usually a chicken.

He had helped her once, as she prepared the Sunday bird, and had been surprised to find there was a plastic bag tucked away inside the chicken, like the hidden prize in a macabre treasure hunt. His mother had pulled it out to reveal a number of brown and purple items just visible through the blood-stained bag.

'Yuck!' he'd said, with feeling. 'What're these

horrid things?'

His mother had smiled as she took up a knife from the draining board. 'They're the chicken's giblets,' she said, slipping the blade through the plastic. 'Heart, liver, gizzard and neck.' She tipped up the bag, the gruesome contents flopping out into a bowl. Sebastian pulled a face at the alien-shaped meat. 'It might not look like much,' his mother said, 'but it makes the best gravy!'

Since that day, Sebastian had never touched gravy again. Nor had he bought a chicken to roast in the five years he'd lived in the flat, all thanks to the grotesque bag of innards hidden in that chicken.

That experience, however, had been nothing compared with drawing the Psycho Hen, as he still couldn't help thinking of it. Evil in life, evil in death - he wished he'd never laid eyes on the wretched bird. It didn't even have the decency to keep its guts in a nice, handy plastic bag, but just left them lolling around inside its body with no thought for the person who had to take them out.

And now that person turned out to be him.

'Do I really need to do this?' These were his first words as he emerged from the stairwell after his shower.

Virginia looked up from the table, where she had arranged the weapons for this latest crusade. 'Well, the poor chicken's not going to draw itself, is it?'

'I guess that's a yes,' said Sebastian. As he headed to join Virginia in the kitchen, he glanced across at Neil, slumped in his usual place in the lounge, paper spread in front of him like a shield. 'Not doing yours, Neil?'

'I don't keep a dog and bark myself!' came the reply, and a dishcloth flew past Sebastian's face, landing with a damp slap on the back of Neil's head. He chuckled away to himself, making no attempt to remove the cloth.

'Ignore him,' said Virginia, turning her attention to the two plucked chickens that lay, breast upwards, on the table. 'Let's get cracking, shall we? It won't take fifteen minutes.'

Sebastian, pulling on a new pair of yellow gloves, edged round the table to stand in front of his chicken. 'I've heard *that* before.'

The next thirty minutes were some of the least pleasant of his life so far, even out-grossing the murder he had committed that morning, though he managed not to throw up this time. Most of the drawing session was taken up with Virginia's encouragements, cajoling and, at times, parade ground style commands - military in their delivery, and gory in their content.

The process began with cutting the gizzard away from the skin of the neck, which Virginia demonstrated after nipping off her bird's head, with a swift chop from the heel of her knife.

'I didn't realise gizzards actually existed,' said Sebastian, trying not to look at what his gloved hands were doing. 'I thought they were just something pirates talked about in films. What do they do?'

'They goes around stealing treasure,' called Neil from behind the armchair, still wearing the dishcloth, 'and then burying it again on desert islands.'

'Gizzards,' said Virginia, rolling her eyes at her husband's comments, 'are where chicken's crush up their food. It's a bit like us with our teeth, only the gizzard is just a muscle which the chicken fill with small stones, that act like teeth.'

'Really?' Sebastian looked down at the saggy, pink

pouch with distaste. It didn't look like much of a muscle.

'Here, look.' Virginia took her knife and cut into the gizzard of her bird, then pushed a few grains of half-chewed corn out through the hole. 'Clever, eh?' Sebastian pulled an involuntary face that didn't suggest he found it that clever. Disgusting, yes, but not clever.

Next, they removed the legs, pulling out the tendons with far more effort than Sebastian had expected, before opening up the bird's cavity, which Sebastian couldn't help thinking of as "making an incision", as though he was a coroner performing an autopsy.

It certainly smelled like it, or as he imagined it might, though he'd never actually been in a morgue. He hoped he never would either after this - the smell was dreadful, something like a mixture of sewer and citrus, and he had to take small gulps of air over his shoulder in an effort to avoid it.

'You need to slip your hand in,' said Virginia, as she did so, showing no sign of even noticing the odour of inside-a-chicken, 'keeping your fingers up, away from the intestines.' Sebastian pulled another face, even more nauseous than the last. 'Then, after pushing through the diaphragm into the chest cavity, keep sliding your hand up the inside of the ribs until you feel its heart.'

'Its *heart*?' Sebastian's voice was little more than a croak, and he took a deep breath to clear his head, regretting it as he caught a fresh waft from one of the chickens; Virginia's, he reckoned, since she was the one with her hand inside it. She was saying something, tapping the bird's chest, but he wasn't really listening. He was thinking back to that giblet bag again and wishing he wasn't here. He looked up at Neil, still sitting in his chair, rustling the paper.

'Fancy a go?' he asked in the same croaky voice.

'Me?' said Neil, half-turning. 'Can't. Hands are too big.' he raised one so Sebastian could get a good look. It certainly was a large hand, much broader than his own. 'If I tried to get inside one of them chicken's with this hulking fist, I'd end up ripping it in half.' He turned fully now, eyes meeting Sebastian's. 'Still, I reckon you'll be fine with those dainty little mitts of yours. I see you've got your trusty gloves on again!'

'Of course I have!' he said. 'These are a new pair.' He held them up for Neil to see, noticing for the first time the red-brown streaks marring the yellow rubber. 'Gross! These'll be going straight in the bin when we're done.'

'How many of those things have you got?' asked Neil.

'Nowhere near enough.'

'Any chance of us finishing this some time today?' said Virginia, her hand still deep inside the chicken. 'Right. Once you've got your fingers around the heart, you can pull everything straight out.' She demonstrated and Sebastian found himself having to swallow hard at the sight of the innards. Everything was bright and glistening, a mass of greys, purples, pinks and reds, flopping in a wobbly mass onto the chopping board. 'I'll save the liver. Neil goes crazy for them on a thick slice of toast.'

To his own surprise, Sebastian started to giggle, which grew into involuntary, slightly manic, laughter. He pointed at the pile of organs and, between breaths, managed to say, 'Why is… it so col-…colourful?' He felt a tear forming in his eye and wiped it away. 'It was such... such a dull-looking... chicken.' At last his laughter began to fade.

'Are you okay?' asked Virginia, sounding so concerned that it started him off all over again. Even Neil had swivelled round to see what was going on.

'The lad's lost it!' he said, shaking his head at the sight. 'I can't believe we broke him so soon. Give him a slap, Virg.'

Virginia looked torn for a moment, half-raising one ooze-covered hand, but Sebastian held up a gloved one in response, gathering himself together.

'Sorry,' he said. 'It's just nerves. Tension at everything that's happened.' He looked down at the waiting-to-be-drawn chicken and corrected himself: 'Everything that's *happening*.'

'Well?' said Virginia, as Sebastian continued to stare at the bird. 'The sooner you get stuck in, the sooner it'll all be over and I can get it ready for dinner. You've, er... you've smeared blood under your eye, by the way.'

There was nothing pleasant about any of the next few of minutes; no redeeming features whatsoever, unless one counted the fact that it was eventually over. And for Sebastian that was a big deal. That, and the fact he still wasn't sick. Not even when he was tugging on the chicken's innards and, with a loud belching sound, they surged out up his arm, part of the long, grey intestines slipping into the top of his glove. Virginia stepped in to whip out the liver, before consigning the rest of the innards to a bag.

'You can give those to the pigs in the morning,' she said, as if this was the most normal suggestion in the world. 'Nice and clean,' she added, bending to peer inside the chicken. 'Good work.' She went to pat him on the shoulder, but thought better of it; she was still holding the liver in her hand.

'So, we're done here, yes?' asked Sebastian, his voice full of pleading. 'Can I go back upstairs and wash again?'

Virginia nodded. 'Of course, dear.'

'Don't be too long, though,' said Neil, folding up his paper and tossing it onto the coffee table. 'I've got a little treat for you when you're done. A *real* treat,' he added, seeing the look of suspicion on Sebastian's face. 'Trust me.'

There was a loud crack as the rifle fired followed, a moment later, by the sound of the lead shot punching into wood.

Neil looked up from the rife sights and pointed to where the pellet had struck. 'I meant *that* tree!'

'Oh, right,' said Sebastian, as though some deep truth was suddenly dawning on him. 'I thought you meant some other tree. Over there.' He flapped a hand, now ungloved, to indicate the wooded area in general. He was actually starting to enjoy himself, the last few hours of his life if not exactly forgotten, at least ignored for the moment as Neil took him out on this little treat.

They'd travelled down to the smallholding on the quad bike, a journey that was not improving with experience, and they were now leaning against its trailer, facing the tree-covered hill, each clutching a .22 air rifle.

'Well, since you didn't manage to hit *any* of the trees "over there",' Neil mimicked the hand flapping, 'it makes no odds which one you thought I meant. Now see if you can hit *that* one.' He pointed again to the target.

Sebastian broke the barrel of the air rifle with some difficulty, slipped in a pellet and snapped it shut.

'Here goes,' he said, jamming the stock into his right shoulder, as Neil had taught him, and peered down the length of the barrel. He pulled the trigger and felt the rifle jerk backwards against his shoulder. Somewhere, a few fallen leaves jumped as the pellet buried itself among them.

'You can see the tree, can't you?' asked Neil, jabbing his own gun towards it. 'It's that big one, just there, about twenty yards away.'

Sebastian lowered the weapon. 'Well, it's alright for you,' he said. 'No doubt you come out here popping off a few rounds each day, catching - what? - foxes and wolves and stuff. The only time I've ever fired a gun was at a stag do. We went paintballing and I shot the father-of-the-bride in the backside. It was a far wider target than that scrawny tree over there. And besides,' he pointed to Neil's rifle, 'you've got that telescope... thing on top. All I've just got is this little notch here,' he indicated the rear sight, 'and a sticky-up bit at the other end. That's hardly fair!'

'Okay then.' Neil held out his air rifle to Sebastian. 'Give this one a go.'

Sebastian swapped the weapon with his own, reloaded it and placed the stock in his shoulder, his eye against the telescopic sight.

'Remember which tree you're aiming for?' asked Neil.

'Yes, thanks,' said Sebastian, his voice slightly muffled as the rifle pressed into his cheek.

'Oh! And make sure your eye isn't-'

The rifle fired and something hit Sebastian so hard in the face it jerked his head backwards, making him stagger to the side. He yelled in pain, clamping a hand over his right eye.

'- touching the scope,' Neil finished. 'Else it'll kick back into your face, like that. That's got to smart a bit.'

Sebastian glared at him with his uncovered eye. 'Smart? A bit? It feels like a horse kicked me in the face.'

Neil nodded, evidently trying his best not to grin. 'Aye. It'll most likely black up like it, too. Still,' he held out an arm towards the tree, 'you did manage to hit the tree, well, *graze* it, at least.' He cleared his throat, half-masking a chuckle. 'So, you want another go at it, or shall we have a crack at something a bit more... challenging?'

'Like what?' asked Sebastian, a hand still gripping his face. He could feel his eye watering as it throbbed painfully.

'There's usually some rabbits scattered across the fields,' Neil began, but Sebastian interrupted him.

'No more killing. Not today. Please.'

'Fair enough,' said Neil, allowing a chuckle to escape at last. 'You'd probably end up shooting one of the goats anyway. Even if we weren't in their field. We'll just do a little more target practice, then. See if we can sharpen up your skills.'

'*My skills?*' Sebastian let out a harsh laugh at the idea. 'I'm not sure I've demonstrated any skills since I got here. I couldn't even put a tent up. Damn, my eye hurts!'

'Sit down a mo,' said Neil, taking the rifle from Sebastian and guiding him towards the quad bike seat. 'Let's have a look.' Sebastian clamped his hand harder against his face, a small protest escaping his lips, but Neil eased the hand away without discernible effort.

'Help!' Sebastian wailed as his right eye was exposed, his vision blurred. 'I've gone blind!'

Neil grinned, but Sebastian didn't see. 'Don't talk such rot, lad. It's just watering is all. No doubt you've got a tissue hidden about your person some place. Give it a wipe and good blink and it'll be sorted in no time.'

As expected, Sebastian produced a clean, white handkerchief and dabbed at his eye, wincing as he did so. Neil wandered off to set up a few targets and, by the time he returned, Sebastian's sight was back to normal, though his eye was still sore.

Neil peered at it. 'You'll live,' he declared. 'Looks like it caught you between your nose and eye. Sensitive, but pretty tough! So which one do you want?' He presented the two rifles and, without hesitation, Sebastian grabbed the one without the telescopic sight. 'Fine choice. Let's go shoot some stuff!'

It was quarter to six when they bowled into the farmhouse, air rifles in hand, voices raised like schoolboys in a playground.

'It's beginner's luck, is all,' said Neil, kicking off his boots on the doormat.

Sebastian leant against the wall as he eased his off, placing them carefully on the shoe rack. 'Call it whatever you like, it still means that I won. And you lost. Making *you* the loser.'

'I was going easy on you, after your attempts at hitting that tree.'

'Anything else you want to add to keep proving my point?' asked Sebastian, handing over the gun. 'And let's not forget you had the one with the half-binoculars on the top.'

Neil tutted. 'It's called a scope, as well you know.

How's that eye doing by the way?'

'Still sore.'

'Listen to you two,' said Virginia, as they bundled into the kitchen. 'You're like a couple of drunk teenagers. How did it go with the shooting?'

Neil shrugged and went to store the guns in their cabinet in the lounge. 'So-so.'

'Speak for yourself,' said Sebastian. 'After all, it wasn't you that won. Guess what?' Virginia shrugged. 'I hit a two pence piece at thirty yards. Two pence.' He held up his hand, thumb and forefinger forming a circle roughly the relevant size. 'At thirty yards.'

Virginia looked impressed. 'Not bad.'

'Lucky shot,' mumbled Neil, striding back into the kitchen.

'I hit it *twice.*'

'Two lucky shots, then!'

'Which makes me the winner.' Sebastian folded his arms, a broad smile nailed to his face.

'Is that why he punched you?' asked Virginia, gesturing towards Sebastian's face with her eyebrows.

Sebastian touched his swollen eye and winced. 'Is it that obvious? It was that wretched eyeglass attached to his rifle. It kicked back into my face when I was shooting at a tree.'

'*Missing* a tree, more like,' said Neil. He sniffed at the air in the kitchen. 'Something smells nice, and I don't reckon it's either of us two. Well, not me anyways. And it doesn't smell like a tart's handbag, neither, so it probably ain't you, lad.'

'That,' said Virginia, turning to open the oven, 'is dinner. Why don't you two grab a seat for a bit, while I get it finished up and ready. You must be worn out after all your excitement!' And although her voice was laced with irony, they scurried off into the lounge, Sebastian dropping onto the sofa next to Tank and Neil slumping into his armchair, where they spent the next twenty-five minutes tackling the crossword. It was the easy one, but in that time they only managed to answer eight clues. And two of those they weren't *that* confident about.

'Of course it's "Suzuki",' said Neil, jabbing his pen at the page, 'because forty-six down, "given shoes" has to be "shod".'

'Yes, but it could be "Subaru". That's a make of car as well.' He leant over to peep at the puzzle. 'What's thirty-nine down? That'll help.'

'"Concretion of nacre". Thirteen letters.'

'What?' Sebastian frowned in incredulity. 'What's that supposed to mean? What paper is this?'

'Are you two coming in here or am I slaving away at this stove for nothing?'

They both turned to see Virginia in the kitchen, enveloped in swirls of steam as she carried a large dish to the table.

'Coming, dear,' said Neil, tossing the paper onto the coffee table with a sigh. 'We can finish that later.'

Sebastian pushed himself up out of the sofa. 'You mean we can *start* it later. There's still over forty clues to get through.'

They took their places at the table, Sebastian at one end, Neil at the other, Virginia's chair sitting empty between them.

Sebastian looked thoughtful, still lost in the crossword. 'I've never even heard of nacre,' he said. 'Have you?'

'Nope,' said Neil, snatching up the carving knife in his fist, and resting it on the table, pointing at the ceiling. 'It's a new one on me.'

Virginia, who had been fiddling around by the stove, turned round, holding a carving board in oven-gloved hands. 'Nacre?' she said. 'That's mother-of-pearl, isn't it?'

Neil and Sebastian stared at her, both adding up the letters in their heads. Neil got there first. 'How in blue blazes did you know that?'

'Oh, I came across it in a magazine. Surprising the things you can pick up.' She dumped the board on the table in front of Neil, revealing the former Psycho Hen, its skin now crispy and brown, the meat beneath no doubt cooked to perfection.

'Well, I guess it was "Subaru" after all,' said Neil. 'Leg or breast?' He pointed to the two areas in question with the carving knife, and looked up at Sebastian. 'Lad?'

Sebastian was staring at the chicken, his mouth open, breathing loudly, his face drained of its colour. He looked as though he was going to be sick again, but then he blinked, swallowed and his eyes flicked up to his hosts.

'I'm sorry,' he said, his voice little more than a whisper. 'I just don't think I can do it.'

'Do what?' asked Virginia.

'Eat it. The chicken. Only... just this morning, it was sitting on the roof of its house and running around the place - it even jumped on my head! And now... now it's dead, and I did it.' He jabbed a finger into his chest, as though clearing up any doubt as to who he felt was to blame. 'I killed it. And then I pulled out its feathers and its... inside bits. But I can't eat it, I just can't.'

He looked from Neil to Virginia and back again,

the silence stretching out between them.

'Well,' said Neil, breaking it at last. 'Luckily for you, there's plenty of vegetables.' He swept the knife in front of him, indicating the steaming bowls of potatoes, kale, carrots and other non-chicken items. 'Help yourself to whatever you fancy. It's all good stuff. I grew most of them in the patch out front. And if you change your mind…' He left the sentence hanging as he began to carve the chicken for himself and Virginia, who had returned to the stove.

'Thanks,' said Sebastian, spooning vegetables onto his plate. 'I really am sorry about the chicken.'

Neil paused in the act of cutting off a leg, and pointed at Sebastian with the carving knife. 'You know what, though? The moment I caught sight of you, standing on the pavement out front of Barnstaple station, I marked you down as a veggie. Funny thing, eh?'

'Not really,' said Sebastian. 'It's a common enough mistake, for some reason.'

Virginia returned from the stove, carrying a small ceramic jug and offered it to Sebastian. 'Here you go,' she said. 'Lovely bit of gravy, to go with all that veg.'

12
PEEPING TOM

The old railway clock in the Green Man saloon bar struck five o'clock as Neil and Sebastian walked through the door at a little after eight-thirty. The place seemed oddly quiet, reminding Sebastian of old Western films, where the noise would drop away as the villain or the tough-looking stranger entered, the saloon doors swinging behind him as he swaggered to the bar, all eyes watching. But this wasn't the situation in the Green Man. This wasn't a lull. It was just quiet because there was hardly anyone there.

The two old guys, Sid and Harry - though Sebastian couldn't recall which was which - were sitting on the same stools as the previous day, clutching their pints as though afraid they might be stolen if left unguarded on the bar top, and a middle-aged couple occupied a table by the fire. Donald was leaning against the inside of the bar, peering at a newspaper, a pen poised in one hand. He looked up as the pub door clicked shut, and stirred himself into action, lifting a handled pint glass from a hook above his head. Without a word, he began to fill it.

'Well, if it ain't the London gourmet, himself,' said one of the old men, smiling toothlessly at Sebastian. 'Come for a second helping of rabbit stew, is it?'

'Course he ain't, Harry!' said the other, who must be Sid, before Sebastian could respond. 'Why would he come here to eat, when he's already tasted the food? Less, of course, he's a crazy. You ain't a crazy are you, boy?'

'Time was when you could get decent vittles in 'ere,' continued Harry, 'back in the old man's day. And at the right price. Ah, it was a proper pub back then. With real food.' He held up his glass, his face twisted to show his distaste. 'And real beer.'

'Had a blacksmith, an all,' added Sid.

'In the pub? Don't talk rot, man.'

Their conversation continued as Donald clattered the full pint glass on the beermat, spilling it down his hand in the process. 'Neil,' he said, with a curt nod.

'Donald,' came the response, accompanied by another equally-curt nod.

'And for yourself?' said Donald, switching his not-overly-warm attention to Sebastian.

He eyed the beer engines. Three commercial lagers, similar in strength, colour and lack of flavour; not much of a selection for an old English pub. He shrugged and pointed at one.

Neil paid, and, as Donald took up his pen and bent back over the paper, he and Sebastian carried their beers to the same table as the previous day.

'Cheers,' said Neil, raising his glass and clinking it dully against Sebastian's. 'You did well today, lad.'

Sebastian frowned slightly. He had always been uncomfortable with praise, never quite knowing how to accept it, out of fear of either coming across arrogant - "Yes, I know. *Of course* I'm good at it. Why are you even telling me?" - or that it was a prelude to being knocked down - "Yes, you are good at it, no one's denying that. It's just a pity you're so useless at everything else. And ugly." He went for a cautious,

'What do you mean?'

'With the chicken and that. I wasn't sure you had it in you. Thought I'd have to get the job done myself.'

Sebastian's frown matured and he sipped at his pint. 'Wait a minute,' he said, setting the glass back on the table with a thump. 'Are you saying that you'd have been prepared to kill it instead of me?'

'Instead of you?' said Neil, a smile stretching his moustache. 'Why on earth would I want to kill you?'

'You know exactly what I mean.'

'Oh, I'd have done it alright. Course I would. But I didn't have to, did I? Because you stepped up.' His smile faded and he fixed Sebastian with his dark, brown eyes. 'I'm proud of you, lad.'

Sebastian coughed, trying to mask his discomfort. 'I did puke on your dog, though.'

'Yeah, there was that,' said Neil, picking up his beer and taking a sip. 'Let's pretend it didn't happen. That, and your little fluke with the rifle.'

'You mean when I hit that tiny, little two pence piece.'

'It was *normal* sized.'

Sebastian leaned back in his chair, his voice raised. 'And then I hit it again, after you missed. And then... remind me, did you hit it after that? The *normal* sized coin?' Whatever Neil mumbled in response was lost somewhere in his moustache. 'Sorry what was that?'

'No.'

'No,' said Sebastian, shaking his head with exaggerated condescension. 'No, you didn't. You missed it, and I hit it. Twice.'

'How far away was it?' came a voice from the bar, and Sebastian turned to see Sid and Harry eying him from across the room.

'Thirty yards,' said Neil, 'give or take. And don't you know it's rude to eavesdrop on other people's conversations.'

'Shouldn't talk so loud, should you,' said Harry. 'Thirty yards, eh? Did you hear that, Sid? Ain't much of a distance, is it? Not for something what ain't moving.'

'Remember Rupert?' said Sid, turning to face his companion. 'Rupert Shaftesbury? Lived over Buckland way?'

Harry thumped his empty beer glass on the bar top, earning a disapproving look from Donald. 'Old Ropey Shafter? Course I remember him. Got run over by the drayman, didn't he?'

'That's the one. Now there was a guy who could aim, a real artist. You know, he could hit a rabbit on the run across the field with nothing more than his old catty-polt, what he'd made himself. Remember?'

'I do indeed,' said Harry. 'I do indeed. And I remember something else an all, Sid.'

'What's that, then?'

'It's your round.' He slid the glass towards Donald. 'Get them in!'

'Anyway,' said Neil, the distraction over for now, 'I reckon you did pretty well, all told. With the shooting as well as the slaughter and everything that went with it. Not bad for a...' He looked up, as though trying to recall something, then looked back to Sebastian. 'I've just realised I have no idea what you actually do in London.'

Sebastian, who had forgotten all about the city for a moment, blinked in surprise. 'Oh, er, yes. I work for an IT firm. Not as a programmer or anything - no way! Leave that to the geeks. I work in marketing.'

'What's IT, exactly?'

'Computing stuff. The company produces bespoke software. We've got some fairly major clients, too. Even a couple of the large banks use us for some of their in-house IT.'

'Right,' said Neil, the word drawn out in an "I didn't understand the half of that" kind of way. 'And this "IT" stuff is Greek, you say?'

'Greek?' Sebastian drained the last of his pint as he tried to work out where this had come from. 'Oh,' he said, 'you mean *geek*. The geeks. Yes, that's what we call the guys who actually write the software. I have as little involvement with that bunch as possible. My job is to raise awareness of the company and what we do. I get the name out there! It's just marketing.'

'Well,' said Neil, easing himself out of his seat, 'you did pretty well for a marketing guy. Deserves another drink!' He reached for the empties, but Sebastian beat him to it.

'No, no,' he said, snatching them away from Neil. 'I'll get these.'

'Same again, is it?' said Donald, dropping the pen onto his paper and shuffling across to the beer engines.

'Yes, please.'

As the landlord did the business, Sebastian peered at his newspaper and the crossword he'd been doing. There were a few scribbled answers, some of which he recognised. It was the same one he and Neil had been struggling with earlier. 'It's not "Suzuki",' he said, pointing at the offending word. 'Forty-six down,' he added, in response to Donald's confused frown. 'It's not "Suzuki".'

'Of course it's "Suzuki",' said the landlord, placing the first full pint on the bar and lifting down another glass, 'because forty-six down, "given shoes" has to be "shod".'

'Yes, but thirty-nine down, "Concretion of nacre", is "mother of pearl", which means that's an "R",' he pointed at the puzzle again, 'making this "Subaru".'

Donald peered at him from beneath his frown. 'Concretion of nacre, eh? And how does a young lad from the city, like yourself, know what that means? They always do that, you know,' he continued, before Sebastian could respond. 'They always slip in a clue that no one can get - well, no one except city folk, I guess. They must get some sort of perverse pleasure out of it. Concretion of nacre! I thought it had something to do with the Crusades, some secret weapon from the middle-Eastern Middle Ages. Mother of pearl!' He shook his head, spilling lager as he placed the second, now *almost* full, pint on the bar. 'So you're in marketing, I hear.'

'Er… yeah,' said Sebastian, caught off-guard by the sudden change of topic. 'That's right.'

'Don't you know it's rude to eavesdrop?' said Sid, wagging a mock-stern finger at the landlord.

Donald ignored him. 'Answer me this then: how would you go about marketing this place.' He spread out his arms to indicate the Green Man, banging his elbow on a plastic, dog-shaped collection box and knocking it off the bar. It was saved by a length of chain securing it to the wooden surface.

Sebastian looked around, taking in the worn carpet and the mismatched furniture, the filthy windows and the stained ceiling. He even peered through the archway into the public bar, which was much the same as the saloon bar, though lacking a carpet. A single bulb cast a dim light across the empty space.

He turned back to Donald. 'It's not really my area

of expertise, to be honest. My work's based around computer software promotion.'

'Humour me,' said the landlord. 'Just tell me what you think?'

'Bloody awful, ain't it!' said Sid. 'The old place's gone down the pan in the last twenty years. That's why no bugger comes here no more.'

'Excepting us,' added Harry, pointing at himself and Sid. 'Couple of old fools that we are. Best thing Donald could do for this pub is to give it away to someone as knows what they're doing!'

Donald gripped the edge of the bar, but managed to ignore the jibes, his eyes fixed on Sebastian.

'I wouldn't say *that*!'

'I would,' said Sid.

'But they do have something of a point.' He paused, bracing himself for the landlord's ire.

'Go on,' said Donald.

'Well, the pub itself is charming. From the outside, it's a lovely old building, full of character. But when you come in, it looks like it hasn't been decorated in years. It's all nicotine yellows and worn out fittings. If you could spruce things up a bit in here - get a new carpet, re-paint the walls, smarten up the furniture... even clean the windows - it'd make a world of difference.'

Donald looked unconvinced. 'You reckon a bit of tarting up's gonna drag people in here?' He *sounded* unconvinced, too. 'The people in this village would hardly notice if I painted the whole place bright pink and filled it up with bean bags. They don't care about a little grime and gristle. What they care about is their own pockets. They'd rather travel up the supermarket in Barnstaple to get bottles of cheap beer to drink on their own, than come in here and spend a few more pennies and drink together.'

'Sounds like good sense to me,' said Harry, with a toothless grin.

'You've got to spread your net a little wider, then,' Sebastian continued, ignoring the interruption. 'People in Steepleford already know you're here. What you need to do is promote the Green Man to the other villages and towns nearby. But before you do, you have got to put some money into this place. Otherwise they'll come and check it out once, and never come back again. You know: speculate to accumulate.' He gave Donald a knowing look.

'I don't know what that means,' said the landlord, raising derisive laughter from the two old men.

'It means you need to spend money if you're going to turn this place into somewhere people want to come.'

'On decorations?'

'On *everything*.' Sebastian paused, gathering his thoughts as he considered the pub from a customer's perspective. 'First thing you need to do is recruit a chef.'

'A chef?' Donald looked stunned by the suggestion.

'Don't know what that means, either?' asked Sid. 'It's a cook. Someone what can actually make stuff people want to eat, rather than that muck you shovel out to poison your non-existent customers.'

'But *I'm* the chef.'

'And the beer,' said Sebastian, soldiering on, despite feeling a bit sorry for Donald. 'All you have is these three lagers. In a pub like this people expect proper, hand-drawn real ale.'

'But it don't keep,' said Donald, releasing his grip on the bar to hold up his hands in despair. 'No one drinks the damned stuff!'

'Not here, they don't,' said Harry, 'on account of there being none on offer. Haven't had any decent beer in here for years, have we Sid? Not in years!'

Sebastian picked up the two pints of lager, hoping it would help him escape. 'Decorate, recruit, update the menu, get in some real ale. Then, and *only* then, do you start promoting the pub. Get out posters, put ads in the local paper, set up a website and suchlike. Then, have a grand reopening, with discounted beer and a selection of free tasters from the new menu. Before you know it, the place will be teaming with customers from all over.' He hurried away to the table, dumping down the beers.

'Thanks,' said Neil, clearly amused by the conversation.

Sebastian returned to the bar, drawing out his wallet. The expression on the landlord's face was of a man deep in thought, the kind of glazed-over look a person makes when trying to catch the words of a distant conversation.

'You really reckon that'll work?' he asked, blinking his eyes into focus again.

'Well, as I said, it's not really my field, but I don't see why it wouldn't - it's pretty solid sales and marketing sense. How much do I owe you for the beers?'

Donald pushed the wallet away. 'Them two's on the house,' he said. Sid, or maybe it was Harry, started choking into his pint.

'Well,' said Neil, when Sebastian had returned to the table and Donald to his crossword, 'that's something I've never seen before. Free beer in this place. You reckon he'll do it?'

Sebastian shrugged, yawning hugely as he did so. 'Tired!' he said.

'I'm not surprised. You've been through the wringer today, sure enough. Come on. Let's drink up and head on back. Hopefully we'll have got out of doing any chores by the time we get home.'

When they had finished, Sebastian took their empty glasses back to the bar.

'Just the man,' said the landlord, hurrying over. 'Mind if I pick your brains for a moment?'

Sebastian turned to look at Neil, already framed in the open doorway. 'You go on ahead. I can find my own way back. How can I help?' he asked Donald, as the door clicked shut behind Neil.

The landlord smiled. 'Can you tell me a bit more about getting one of these webbed sites?'

Twenty minutes later, Sebastian emerged from the Green Man and headed towards the crossroads. There were no street lights in Steepleford, which wasn't much of a surprise. It was more of a shock to find they had access to electricity and running water. He stopped in the middle of the road and pulled out his mobile. Even if there was no reception here, it could at least come in handy as a flashlight. He switched it on and the road ahead was bathed in light. For a moment, he thought it was the mobile, but the glow was far too bright. Someone had switched on the light in the village shop and, looking up, he made out the figure of Emma, swathed in a light blue dressing gown, fiddling around with something on the counter, while her mother stood in the doorway to their living area.

Suddenly feeling exposed in the light, Sebastian

ducked to the left, hiding in the shadow of the house next door. He peered round the edge, drawn back to the brightly lit room and the red-haired girl he hadn't seen all day. Evidently unaware of his surveillance, she strode across to the shelves on the far side of the store, climbing the small ladder to tease down a couple of brown cardboard boxes.

As he watched her, reaching up on tip toes, the hem of her dressing gown lifted to reveal slender calves, the skin white and flawless. His breathing became shallow, his heart racing, and he felt like he shouldn't be looking, as though he was some sort of pervert, peeping in at her from the shadows. But still he stared, unable to drag himself away. She really was beautiful, and he had the vaguest suspicion that she liked him, though he had no real evidence to back this feeling up - he wasn't aware of any signs or even how to spot them if there were.

Emma skipped off the ladder and carried the boxes across to the till. As she set them down, she paused as though struck by a sudden thought or sensation. Then her head snapped round towards Sebastian.

He was sure she couldn't see him out here in the dark, but the shock was enough to send him ducking back around the edge of the building, breathing heavily, his heart thumping like he'd been in a race. After a few moments, and with infinite caution, he eased his eye around the corner. Emma was no longer looking in his direction, but was scribbling something on a piece of paper. She laid the pen on the counter and, without glancing back, walked past her mother into the house.

Mrs Standfield peered around the shop, staring for a moment at the window, though not in his direction, then she raised a hand to the wall and the light winked out. Sebastian started breathing again.

'What're you doing?'

He stopped breathing again. The voice was deep and dark, heavy with accusation, and appeared to come from the darkness itself. But even more startling was the menacing East End accent, at once so familiar and yet so out of place in this village far from the streets of Whitechapel and Wapping. He swallowed and took a step backwards.

'Who's that?' he said, his voice sounding thin and frightened.

The shadow on the other side of the shop stirred and settled into the shape of a man. A large man. A man Sebastian recognised.

'I asked what you're doing,' said the butcher, stepping forwards to tower over Sebastian. 'What you doing skulking around in the dark?'

'I…' Sebastian looked up at the butcher's face, noticing for the first time the large scar where his cheek met his left ear. The man was evidently a murderer, he could see that now. He took another step backwards, flashing a glance over his shoulder towards the lights of the Green Man. It wasn't that far away, he could make it. He was sure he could outrun this lumbering man-ogre. In fact, it sounded as though he'd already been running, his breathing was as laboured as Sebastian's had been when… 'Hang on,' said Sebastian, peering up at the butcher again. 'What were *you* doing skulking around in the dark?'

The change was immediate. Where before there had been a hulking monster, towering over Sebastian with wrath in his eyes and judgement in his fists, there was simply a man. Still a big man, admittedly, but just a man. A man who looked a bit awkward.

'Well...' the butcher began, pulling at his shirt collar as though it had suddenly become too tight. 'I was, you know.' He jabbed a finger the size of a child's shoe in the direction of the crossroads. 'I was just passing. Out for a stroll.' He fixed Sebastian with a look that was somewhere between a challenge and an entreaty, leaning slightly towards the latter.

Sebastian nodded. 'Yeah,' he said, 'me too.' He also pointed towards the crossroads. 'I should probably... you know.'

'Sure,' said the butcher. He redirected his own pointing finger in the opposite direction and set off to follow it. 'Er... night.'

'Yeah,' said Sebastian, letting out his breath at last. 'Good night.'

He felt shaken as he hurried down Holders Hill, his head filled with wondering about the butcher's sudden awkwardness. He, Sebastian, had felt guilty, because he'd been spying on Emma. Is that why the butcher was there? Is that why he had been hiding in the shadows, so he could peer in at her as well? He thought back to the church service, when the butcher had seemed to be glaring at him, but now he wondered if he'd simply been looking at Emma. The thought made him feel a sense of protective jealousy for her - one that was entirely unreasonable, considering he was a mere visitor to this strange place, and he had no claim to the girl. Still, he didn't like the idea that someone else liked her as well, especially someone clearly much tougher than him, someone with his own arsenal of weapons. Someone who had access to her every day.

He shook his head in an attempt to clear it as he headed up towards the lights of the farmhouse. Just a few more days and he'd be out of here, that's what he really needed to focus on, not this village girl from the dark side of the country.

'I'll just keep my distance,' he said to himself, as he opened the door. 'I'll avoid her as much as possible, then go home and forget all about her. Easy!'

'Morning, stranger,' said Emma, as the bell danced above his head. 'Thought you were avoiding me. Brought my eggs, have you?'

Sebastian looked down at the two egg boxes as though surprised to find them clutched in his hands. There had been only twelve eggs to collect this morning, which had tinged the experience with a shadow of melancholy. That, and the lack of interest shown by the remaining chickens, none of which demonstrated a discernible personality. Not like the poor Psycho Hen.

He cleared his throat. 'Yeah,' he said, walking forward to place the boxes on the counter.

'You had a run in with someone?' asked Emma, and Sebastian could feel the flush spread across his cheeks. Surely the butcher hadn't grassed him up, not after he'd looked so shifty himself! How was he going to explain what he was doing, peeping in at her from the dark street ?

'What?' he said, trying for carefree, but sounding like he was being throttled instead.

'What the hell happened to your face?' She took hold of his chin and tilted his head towards her. 'Did someone take a dislike to you?'

Sebastian began to pull away, but her touch seemed to have hypnotised him and he was powerless to resist. 'It was a gun,' he said.

'A gun?' She looked shocked. 'Who shot you?'

'*I* did. Or rather, I shot the gun and it kicked back into my face.'

Emma run a finger along the line of the bruise, sending a shiver down Sebastian's neck. He hoped she didn't notice, but her eyes had a sparkle that suggested she did. 'It's almost a perfect circle,' she said. 'What was it? The scope?'

'Yeah. Stupid, huh?'

'A bit,' she said, 'but it does look rather manly.' She released his chin and took a step backwards. 'So, are you looking forward to today's adventures?'

He shrugged in response, silently wondering why she'd taken her hand away - he could still feel the ghost of her fingers on his face. 'I'm not sure,' he said. 'Something awful, no doubt.'

Emma laughed at his pessimism. 'A day with Mac shouldn't be so bad.'

'What?' Sebastian looked put out by this revelation. 'How come *you* know what I'm doing, when *I* don't? And who's Mac, anyway?'

'Mac?' said Emma. 'Mac's the butcher.'

Sebastian sighed. 'Of course he is.'

THE FIRST CUT

Blood. That was the first thing Sebastian smelled as he entered the butcher's shop. Blood. And raw meat. And behind it, just detectable on the edge of his tongue, was the sharp edge of decay. He screwed up his nose and tried breathing through his shirt sleeve. It didn't help. This, he suspected, was why normal people got their meat from the supermarket, where the airtight packaging kept the odours contained. Were there any people who went to an actual butcher's anymore? Or was this simply another dying relic of the Victorian era, like post offices, steam engines and the terror of talking about sex?

The shop even *looked* Victorian with its tiled floor, a chessboard of terracotta and black, giving way to the green, glazed tiles of the walls. Instead of the usual glass display cabinets, there was a single counter, the top of thick wood, the front of white panelling. Around the store were a number of wooden barrows, filled with vaguely recognisable cuts of beef, pork and lamb, interspersed with sausages, bacon, pies and other meat-based items. Hanging from the black beams that ran across the ceiling were a series of vicious-looking hooks from which dangled an assortment of dead animals, whole and not quite so whole. Some of these Sebastian recognised - chickens, pheasants, a leg of pork - but others were unknown to him, such as the smaller birds, of which there were many varieties, and the larger hunks of meat. From somewhere a chill breeze was blowing, though he couldn't quite work out the source. Maybe it was from the back room, which was hidden from view by a curtain of coloured chains that hung in the doorway.

'Hello?' called Virginia, who had accompanied Sebastian to the shop and seemed entirely unfazed by the place. 'Mac? Are you out back?'

For a moment, her voice elicited no response, then the curtain burst apart and the butcher's considerable bulk strode into the room. He had seemed big to Sebastian in the dark last night, but here, on his own territory, as the morning light slanted in through the large, and egg-free, shop window, he was enormous, his bald head glinting with imagined menace, his black beard bristling with much the same. He nodded at Virginia, then his gaze slid to Sebastian and he narrowed his eyes. Sebastian swallowed.

'Come to learn about butchering, is it?' Mac's voice managed to convey the suggestion that, given a thousand years of training, he considered it unlikely Sebastian would ever make a butcher.

'That's right,' said Virginia. 'I don't think you boys have been properly introduced, have you? Mac, this is Sebastian.' She gestured to him with both hands, then swung them the other way. 'Sebastian, this is Mac. His real name's Victor, but all his friends here call him Mac, don't they?' The butcher gave an almost imperceptible nod, but made no move to offer his hand for Sebastian to shake.

Virginia had brought with her a cloth-covered basket and heaved it onto the counter, alongside the ancient till, before pulling a creased envelope from beneath one of its flaps. She straightened it out, the plastic window crackling noisily. The paper was covered in the same, unintelligible scrawl as the note Sebastian had found on his first morning here and, with a shock, he realised that was already three days ago. Time seemed to be moving at last!

'This here is a list of the various cuts I'd like,' she said, handing the note to Mac. 'If you could get them all bagged up for me as usual, that'd be great. I'll pick them up early Thursday before market, okay?' Again the slight nod. 'Excellent.'

She looked from Mac to Sebastian and back again, the only sound the distant whirr of a fan somewhere beyond the curtain. Virginia smiled and shook her head at the two silent men. 'Well, I guess I'll leave you two chatterboxes to get on with it then. Don't have too much excitement!' And with that she turned on her rubber-booted heel and marched out of the shop. The door slammed shut behind her and the silence returned.

Mac let out a long, low breath into his beard and jabbed a thumb towards the doorway behind him.

'Sooner we get on,' he said in his dark, East End tones, 'the sooner we'll be done.' Without waiting for a response, he swept the chains aside and stomped back through.

Sebastian wasn't sure what to expect in the room beyond, probably something like a medieval torture chamber, complete with evil-looking weapons, gore and grime. Certainly nothing like the pristine laboratory that met his gaze as he eased through the curtain. It was like walking into a different world, or rather a different time. Gone was all trace of the Victorian era, the ornate ceramic tiles and woodwork.

In its place was the clinical glare of stainless steal, bright white plastic and space age equipment. Most of it was alien to Sebastian, though he recognised the meat slicer from a similar one in his local delicatessen, and the largest item, taking up half the room, definitely looked like a white-painted shipping container with a couple of refrigeration units attached to it, the source of the whirring noise. The only similarities between this area and the one he had just left, were the hooks in the ceiling, though these were all empty, and the smell. If anything, it was even stronger and the edge of decay more cutting.

'What is that awful stench?' He raised a hand to his nose as he tried to work out where it was coming from.

Mac sniffed at the air, as though he hadn't realised there *was* any smell. At last, grudgingly, he answered.

'Deer. Been hanging for a week or so.' Walking over to the door of the shipping container, he yanked down the lever. As the door opened a fresh wave of the smell washed over Sebastian, the scent of decay almost overpowering.

He tried breathing through his shirt sleeve again, making as little difference as before, and peered into the container. Inside, a harsh light revealed two rows of carcasses hanging from the ceiling. Down each wall stood stainless steel shelves, all loaded with what Sebastian tried to think of as simply "animal products". He looked at the dangling carcasses and noticed only one of them still looked like a real animal, coated with fur, its head still attached.

'Is that it?' he said, pointing with his free hand, the other still holding his sleeve over his nose.

The butcher peered inside. 'That's the one,' he said, his breath clouding in the refrigerated air. He reached in and, to Sebastian's disgust, stroked the creature's fur. 'Good meat on that.'

'Did someone shoot it? Or was it knocked down by a car or something?'

'Shot,' said Mac. 'Up in the woods.'

Sebastian swallowed, trying not to think of Mac wielding a shotgun. 'Did *you* shoot it?'

The butcher looked surprised. 'Me? Nah, I don't shoot. I never touch a gun, me.' He glared at Sebastian, as though daring him to suggest otherwise. 'The vicar shot it.'

'The *vicar*?' Sebastian's shirt sleeve dropped away, forgotten. 'That guy at the church? But... But he's a vicar!'

'So? Vicars is people too,' said Mac, shifting the deer out of the way to lift down another carcass. 'Some of them, anyways.'

Sebastian stepped back to watch as the huge man hefted the carcass onto his shoulder. It can't have weighed much less than Sebastian himself, but Mac performed the movement with no evidence of effort. He stepped out of the fridge, shutting the door behind him with his heel and headed across to one of the large, stainless steal workbenches.

'I shot a two pence piece yesterday,' said Sebastian, in an attempt to make conversation. 'Twice. It was on a tree branch over twenty metres away.'

Mac dumped the carcass onto the workbench and turned to Sebastian, eyeing him as if trying to work something out. 'Ain't much eating on a coin,' he said at last and, although his mouth was hidden by the thick beard, Sebastian thought there was a suggestion of a smile there, the slightest hint of a sparkle in the butcher's eyes.

'I shot a couple of trees as well,' he said.

The carcass turned out to be that of a pig, one of three that the Symeses had taken to the abattoir the previous week. Two of these, together with a lamb, were to be butchered today and this was apparently why Sebastian was here.

Mac hung the first pig from a couple of ceiling hooks, one attached to each leg, then drew a massive cleaver from its place on the wall. Suspecting it was the one he'd seen Mac wielding on his first morning in Steepleford, Sebastian eyed it nervously, flinching as Mac slammed the blade between the pigs hind legs, driving it downwards through the spine. He twisted it free, the metal glinting yet surprisingly bloodless, and slammed it down again.

'Want a go?' asked the butcher, pulling the cleaver free again and turning it towards Sebastian.

He shook his head. 'No, you're alright, thanks. You seem to have it all under control.' The butcher shrugged his broad shoulders and sliced down into the carcass again.

After a few more cuts, including a swift slice with another wickedly-sharp knife to remove the head, the pig hung in two halves, swinging slightly in the breeze from the cooling fans.

'Butcher's perks,' said Mac, holding up the pig's head by an ear. Sebastian eyed it with distaste. There were still a number of hairs around its mouth, and its lips were drawn back to show yellowed teeth.

'If you say so,' he said. 'I probably won't be coming to dinner, though, if it's all the same to you.'

Mac only grunted in response as he placed the head to one side. Grunted, and frowned. Then, with practised ease, he hefted one half of the pig off its hook and laid it across the workbench, business-like.

Thankfully, the next twenty minutes were so focussed on butchering, turning the pig into pork, that there was little need for any other conversation. Not that Mac seemed interested in chatting, and Sebastian had no idea how to break the ice.

The work started with slicing off the back leg, which somehow then stopped looking like a leg and looked like a nice, big ham. Mac then separated the first half into its general cuts - hand, shoulder, loin and belly - before embarking on the more fiddly work of boning out the shoulder and separating the chops with that massive cleaver.

'Going to get involved at some point?' asked Mac, flicking the carved out shoulder blade into a handy bucket, and slid a long knife across the worktop. 'This lot needs dicing up.'

Sebastian looked first at the knife, as though it was some alien weapon, then at Mac, but the butcher was already occupied with heaving the second half of the pig onto the worktop. There was nothing else for it. It was time to man up and get on with yet another unpleasant task this week had dumped on him - either that or lower himself even further in Mac's estimation.

He gripped the knife handle and eyed the huge lump of shoulder meat, trying to work out what exactly to do with it. He'd diced meat before, in his kitchen back in London, but never anything more challenging than a chicken breast.

'Not too small,' said Mac, his attention flickering to Sebastian. 'About an inch or so.' He demonstrated with an enormous thumb and forefinger, before turning back to his work.

Sebastian sighed, stepped up to the chopping board and cut into the meat, gripping it in his washing-up-gloved hand. They were his last pair, and he hoped Emma had some stashed away up on the village shop shelves. He tried not to think about her climbing the ladder in her light blue dressing gown, and focussed instead on the meat. The meat. It was still cold and felt unpleasant even through the rubber gloves. Still, it was nowhere near as bad as the hideous things he'd had to do with that chicken yesterday. He shook his head, trying to get the wobbly, glistening innards out of his mind.

'Easy, boy!' yelled Mac, gripping Sebastian's wrist. 'You nearly had your hand off!'

Sebastian, who hadn't been paying quite as much attention as he should have been, blinked down at the shoulder, cleaved right through, and saw the tiny line of yellow beneath.

'Is that..?' he began, and pulled his hand out from under the meat. There was a perfect line cut through the glove, across the ball of his thumb. Sebastian yanked the glove off, feeling sick at the thought of what he would see. But his hand was okay, with only the slightest mark in the top layers of skin to show for his lapse.

'Another inch and you wouldn't be able to tell where the pork stopped and your hand began!' said Mac. 'Concentrate!'

'Thanks,' said Sebastian, looking up at the butcher in gratitude. 'You saved my hand.' He held it up for inspection, in case there was any confusion over which part of his body had been in jeopardy.

Mac shrugged. 'It's only the left one.' Again there was that suggestion of a smile behind the thick, bushy beard, and Sebastian decided this was as good a time as any to try and make a little small talk. He took a deep breath.

'I take it from your accent you're not from around here?'

The smile, if there had been one, was gone, and the bald expanse above his eyes creased into a frown that glistened in the stark, fluorescent lights. 'Not originally,' he said, in a voice that suggested this might not be the time for small talk after all.

Sebastian soldiered on. 'Let me guess. Shoreditch? Shadwell? Am I close?'

Mac shrugged his huge shoulders. 'Why does it matter? This is my home now.' He swept a hand out at the building around them. 'Has been for nigh on thirty years.' He turned back to the carcass, but Sebastian couldn't leave it there. He was stunned by the idea that Mac had chosen to live in this middle-of-nowhere village, when he had experienced, maybe even grown up in, the busy, vibrant life of the city.

'Don't you miss it?' he asked.

The butcher paused, his knife halfway through the meat. 'If you mean London. No. I haven't missed it for a single day.' Sebastian drew breath to respond, but Mac cut him off. 'Focus on the job, boy. You don't want your hand off, do you?'

Hoping this wasn't a threat, Sebastian dropped it, taking up the knife instead and got on with dicing up the shoulder in silence.

Before long, they had reduced the carcass to various recognisable cuts - chops, ham, roasting joints and the like - and a mound of diced pork, free from human body parts. All the 'bits', such as the skin from the shoulders and the strange plastic-like membrane from inside the ribcage, had ended up in the bucket and Sebastian eyed it suspiciously, hoping these 'bits' weren't going to become ingredients in anything he was ever likely to eat.

'Right,' said Mac, consulting Virginia's scribbled list. 'Let's get this lot back in the fridge for now, and we'll get to work on one of these lambs.'

Sebastian was surprised to find that butchering a lamb was almost exactly the same as butchering a pig. The layout was the same, the cuts were made in the same places, and the stack of meat they were left with at the end was mostly the same. The only real differences were the colour of the flesh and the size of the carcass.

'That took longer than I'd hoped,' said Mac, washing his hands in one of the three large sinks. 'We'll grab something to eat before starting off on the sausages.'

'We've still got to make sausages?' said Sebastian, whose arms were worn out from the morning's work.

'Well, they won't make themselves, will they?'

The two men headed back through the bead curtain to the counter, where Mac lifted one of the flaps on the picnic basket Virginia had left for them. Leaning forwards to have a look, Sebastian made out the shapes of lunch - sandwiches, apples, a jar of something that was undoubtedly homemade. Mac rang up 'No Sale' on the till and tugged out a five pound note.

'Would you grab us a couple of drinks from the shop?' he asked, holding out the money. 'I'm rather partial to a diet Fanta.'

Sebastian took the money.

'Sure,' he said, and set off, wondering why the butcher didn't keep a supply of cans in his ridiculously massive fridge. Health and safety, maybe? Or perhaps he just liked going up to the shop whenever he was thirsty?

As he rounded the bend past the Head Mistress, and the watchful eyes of the dome-headed ladies within, Sebastian's eyes were drawn to his hiding place of the night before. He hadn't really noticed the building on the far side of the Village Store on his previous visits, which wasn't surprising. It was just a normal house. A normal house *for the country*, he corrected himself. You wouldn't find anything like this in the city. It was made out of a network of thick, black timbers, the spaces between filled with smooth, white plaster. Where Sebastian had been hiding, there was a window with a diamond pattern of lead across its small panes, and he hoped no one had been peering out at him, while he'd been peeping in at Emma.

On the other side, between the Village Store and the hairdresser, was a narrow alleyway that Sebastian also hadn't noticed before. Had he been paying *any* attention when walking around this place? He stopped by the alley and looked along it, surprised to see it led to a garden that stretched away behind the shop. This must have been where Mac had been hiding, though why he had been down there was a mystery. He shook his head at the weirdness of country people and headed into the shop.

'Afternoon, Victor,' said a voice as the bell announced Sebastian's arrival. Sebastian's eyes were still adjusting from the bright sunlight to the gloomy indoors, but he recognised the voice.

'Er... it's me, Mrs Standfield,' he said, blinking at the apparently empty shop. 'Sebastian.'

'Oh.' A head appeared from behind the counter to

his left, followed by more of Mrs Standfield, clutching a couple of bags, which Sebastian noticed were labelled *Spelt Flour*. She peered at the door behind him, expectantly. 'Where's Victor? I thought you two were working together today.'

Sebastian nodded. 'Yeah. Victor… Mac sent me to get drinks.' He held up the five pound note as evidence. A look of disappointed flashed across Mrs Standfield's face, but her prim, Victorian visage slotted back in place almost immediately.

She pointed to the fridge that stood against the left wall. 'The diet Fanta's in there. Take one from the back. Victor likes it cold.' As Sebastian chose a couple of cans, she climbed the ladder to the shelf of flour. 'How was yesterday's slaughter?' she asked.

'As awful as expected. But I did it, though. And I took your advice, about imagining the chicken was someone else.'

'Works well, doesn't it?' she said, stepping off the ladder and brushing flour from the front of her dress. 'Best way to get your confidence up for the kill. That'll be two pounds, please. And do pass on my regards to Victor.'

MAKING LINKS

'Mrs Standfield sends her "regards".' Sebastian made speech marks with his fingers, hoping Mac might find the term amusing, but the butcher just squinted into the distance, looking pleased.

He was sitting on the moss-covered, uneven brick patio in front of the shop, leaning back on a wooden chair, which creaked alarmingly under his bulk. He gestured to a second, equally rickety-looking seat, and tossed Sebastian a sandwich from Virginia's basket. 'Thought we'd have lunch outside, since it's such a nice day.'

'Good thinking,' said Sebastian, cautiously seating himself next to the butcher.

Mac took a bite on his sandwich before waving it at Sebastian's face. 'So what happened then? To your eye?'

Sebastian turned to look at his reflection in the large shop window. He had forgotten about the black eye. 'Shooting accident,' he said. 'Got a bit too friendly with the scope.'

'Looks nasty. Still, at least you got that two pence, eh?'

Their lunch, like their morning, was interrupted a few times by customers, but Sebastian enjoyed sitting in the sun, not having to worry or even think about anything in particular. Birdsong, from the hedgerow down the hill, accompanied the meal, and one in particular caught his attention. For the first time in his life, he found himself wondering was sort of bird it was.

'Which bird?' asked Mac.

'The noisy one,' said Sebastian, pausing to listen. 'There! The one that sounds like when you accidentally phone up a fax machine.'

Mac opened his can and took a sip as he tilted his head towards the hedgerow. 'Blackbird,' he said. 'Though I reckon they sound more like that little robot thing from Star Trek.'

The two men sat in silence, both listening to the blackbird as it twittered away, hidden by the foliage. 'You might have a point there,' said Sebastian, turning his head so Mac wouldn't see him grinning, 'but I think you probably mean Star Wars. I wonder what it's singing about.'

'Same two things as any other animal. It's all either "Come and fight me!" or "Come and…" you know… what the birds and the bees do.' The tops of Mac's cheeks flushed with evident embarrassment.

He turned at the sound of footsteps approaching down the hill and Sebastian peered round to see a middle-aged lady, who he vaguely recognised from the church service, marching towards them with a purposeful look about her.

'Ah. Mr McGeenie,' she said, in tones so clipped it could have been topiary. She glanced at the remains of the sandwich clutched in his massive hand. 'Sorry to interrupt your lunch.'

'Not at all, Mrs Farley' said Mac, heaving himself to his feet. He looked grateful for the intrusion. 'How may I help you?'

'As you know, the parish council have placed me in charge of the fayre and, if it's not too much trouble,' she looked from Mac to Sebastian with an expression that implied they obviously they had nothing better to do, 'I would like to inspect the animal for the hog roast.'

'Follow me,' said the butcher, his voice more London gangster than ever, and ushered her into the shop.

Sebastian settled back into his chair, which was not as uncomfortable as it appeared, and relaxed in the sunlight, a grin forming in the butcher's wake. He leant his head back and stared up at a sky that seemed far broader than in the city. Back in London the sky was just a distant thing that you glimpsed between buildings and occasionally invaded the world with rain. Here, it was the backdrop against with everything moved, a living canopy that set the pace of daily life. Today it was blue. Insanely blue, as though it had been digitally enhanced, all traces of cloud edited out. Here and there birds of some description - Sebastian was as inept at identifying them by their form as by their song - flapped and glided far above him, and the sun was directly overhead, burning into his retinas.

He took a deep breath and closed his eyes, savouring the peaceful sounds of the nearby birdsong, coupled with a gentle breeze that rustled the trees down the hill and, somewhere far off, the sound of a lawnmower, or maybe a tractor busy at work. And for the first time since leaving his apartment four days before and watching the metropolis slipping into the distance, he felt content - happy to be just where he was.

'This is no time for falling asleep!' Sebastian jerked

awake and opened his eyes to see Mac leaning over him. 'Don't forget about them sausages.'

'I wasn't asleep,' Sebastian mumbled, though he knew he had been. He wiped the line of dribble from the corner of his mouth, trying to disguise the action as a cough.

Mac pointed at his chin. 'You missed a bit.'

Although Sebastian hadn't been looking forward to an afternoon of further butchering, he found the process of making sausages strangely satisfying; far more so than dicing up meat and whittling out bones. The work was centred around a large stainless-steel contraption with a panel of buttons and winking lights. Sebastian pointed out that it looked like some kind of time machine.

'You mean like a clock?' asked Mac, that glint back in his eyes. He patted the shiny surface. 'This is my grinder. There's nothing she can't turn to mince.'

Their first job was to put the diced pork through the grinder, before splitting it into four batches and mixing it with various herbs, spices and other ingredients, to produce Lincolnshire, Cumberland, Pork and Apple, and Traditional sausages.

That was when things started to get interesting. Mac fitted some kind of funnel attachment to the front of the grinder, threaded with sausage skin. Sebastian was disgusted to learn they were actually sheep intestines, and he was sure Mac had waited until he had been threading them on for several minutes before he made this revolting revelation. They then fed one batch of sausage meat at a time through the machine to fill the skins, a task which Mac made look easy, and which made Sebastian look like a bumbling idiot.

'Try and fill it evenly,' said Mac, his beard failing to conceal his amusement. 'You're gripping it too hard. There's no need to yank at it.'

Sebastian, who was buckling under the pressure, almost yelled at the butcher. 'I am not yanking at it! I'm doing it exactly like you showed me.' The flow of meat sped up suddenly, causing a length of sausage to leap at him, coiling across his arms. 'Help!' he shouted over the noise of the machine. 'It's got me! Turn it off!'

Although Sebastian failed to get the hang of his part of the process, they did at last end up with four lengths of sausage, each several metres long. The final stage of the process was turning those snakelike coils into individual sausages.

'It's real simple,' said Mac, placing one of the sausage-filled containers on a workbench and lifting out the end. 'First you have to make a knot in the end, so it doesn't all come oozing out. Then make a couple of pinches, like this.' He demonstrated, squeezing the skin together between his broad fingers at six-inch intervals. 'And here's the clever bit, where you link them into bunches of three.'

The manoeuvre that followed appeared to be both simple and impossible at the same time, as though, with a couple of twists, he had managed to defy the laws of physics and cause solid objects to move through each other.

'Whoa!' said Sebastian, eyes wide. 'What was that, some kind of magic trick? Show me again.'

Mac did so, pinching the length into two sausages, bending them together and, with a flick and a twist, somehow passed another between them to form a trio of sausages. Pinch, flick, twist and there was another set. Sebastian's eyebrows creased together in concentration as he motioned for Mac to do it again.

'Right,' he said. 'I reckon I've got it. Can I have a go?'

Mac gave him a "This I've got to see" look. 'Sure, but it won't work with them gloves. Too much friction. You'll tear the skins.'

So, with bare hands and only a vague idea of what he was trying to do, Sebastian relieved Mac of the sausages and gave it a go. How hard could it be?

'I give up,' he said less than a minute later, as he handed the jumbled mess he had produced back to the grinning butcher. 'It's clearly some sort of witchcraft and I, for one, want no part in it.'

'So how'd it go?' asked Virginia, as Sebastian kicked off his shoes by the door. As usual, she was in the kitchen, a steaming pot clutched in oven-gloved hands. She tried to blow a stray clump of her long, messy hair from her face without success. 'Did you get it all done?'

Sebastian trudged in and propped himself against the table. 'Most of it, I think. Mac said there's a few bits he'll have to finish up tomorrow.'

'And the sausages?' said Virginia, dumping the pot on the table and lifting the lid to peer inside. 'Did you manage to do that weird twisting thing where you make the links?'

'Nope.' He shook his head, catching a whiff of whatever was in the pot. It smelled delicious. 'Not even close.'

'Me neither,' she said. 'It's clearly some sort of witchcraft. Neil won't be back for a couple of hours yet,' she added, with a quick glance at the lounge clock. It was just after four. 'Why don't you take the weight off your feet for a while? The bathroom's free if you want a bath or anything? You'll find clean clothes on the end of your bed.'

'Thanks,' said Sebastian. The sofa certainly looked inviting after standing up all day, and the thought of a hot shower after the chilled air at the butcher's was equally tempting. 'But I feel like going for a stroll, if that's okay.'

Virginia raised her eyebrows. 'Yes, of course. You do whatever you like, dear. Dinner's going to be early today - six o'clock - so you'll have plenty of time for tonight's brew up at the vicarage.'

Sebastian's eyebrows raised just as much as hers. 'Tea with the vicar?'

'Not exactly,' said Virginia. 'You'll find out later. It'll be fun.'

Sebastian, who had heard this promise now a number of times, decided to withhold judgement. That was something for later. Now was the time for walking.

Living in the city, he was accustomed to having to travel by foot. Only the rich or the foolish had cars in London. And taxi drivers, of course. He'd resisted the trend of riding a bike, mostly because he thought it wasn't safe what with the buses mowing cyclists down at every opportunity, but also because he didn't like the helmets people wore and didn't want his hair getting blown about either. But walking around the city streets was a different game altogether from walking in the countryside. There were no crowds here to weave through, no traffic to drown out all thoughts and clog up the air, and no tall, shiny buildings to block out the horizon.

Sebastian climbed the hill, waving to Mac through the butcher's shop window on his way, and stopped at the crossroads. To the right lay the shops and the pub and straight ahead the small church peeped out between the yew tree branches. He considered taking the road on the left, since it was invitingly named 'High Street', but this appeared to be some sort of country joke as it led to only a handful of houses before becoming a dirt track that disappeared over the hill. He turned back towards the crossroads and headed past the hairdresser and the store - no sign of Emma... not that he was looking, of course. Beyond the Green Man, picturesque cottages lined the road, and they really *were* cottages, he was sure of that. His great aunt Joan, she of the house that smelled of cat, had owned a small collection of pottery models that looked just like these buildings, complete with thatched roofs, wooden frames, and front doors that were surely too short for anyone to walk through without ducking. She had always referred to them as her "dream cottages" and had been most upset when Sebastian knocked one off her dresser when he was six.

Most of the Steepleford cottages were named after flowers, 'Lavender Cottage', 'Bluebells' and so on, but as Sebastian made his way along the gently curving street, he noticed some that had more descriptive names - names from Steepleford's past. 'The Old School' was taller than its neighbouring cottages. It had large, arched windows and a garden to one side, bordering the road. In an alcove above the porch, a brass bell glinted in the sunlight, as silent as the playground and classrooms that must once have been full of life.

Opposite this stood the 'Post Office', though its days of delivering the mail had clearly been over for many years. Still embedded in its wall was a red postbox, the paint now dull and flaking, its mouth sealed closed. There was a stone trough on the pavement in front, filled not with water, but with brightly-coloured pansies, forget-me-nots and the tumbling pink of a soapwort - all of which Sebastian recognised as simply "flowers". Next door was 'Forge Cottage', where no doubt the postal horses would have been shod before motor vehicles drove them out and the post office closed its doors.

Sebastian looked up as an eerie, squeaking sound caught his attention, but it was only an old horseshoe that hung above the door swinging gently on its rusty chain. He turned to look back along the deserted road. Everything was quiet, the old village dozed in the warm afternoon, the busy days of its life now over.

He felt a curious sadness wash over him at the thought that, once upon a time, maybe fifty or sixty years ago, this street would have been as busy as those in London. Not in terms of the volume of people, but in terms of activity. He imagined horses clip-clopping along the street, pulling carriages and wagons behind them. A postman leaning against a cottage wall, sharing gossip with the villagefolk as he did his rounds. The shout and laughter of children playing hopscotch and leapfrog in the school playground, waiting for the bell to call them back to class. The clang of the hammer and the puff of the bellows as the blacksmith worked his craft, repairing a gate or hammering out a set of agricultural implements. Shopkeepers and shoppers, frequenters of the pub, cricketers on the green and farmers bringing in their produce.

As he stood in the road, shielding his eyes from the glare of the sun, the only sounds were the birds singing from their hiding places, and the only movement a discarded paper bag shuffling its way along the gutter, caught by the breeze. No one came or went along the empty street. No cars rolled by, no children played.

Sebastian wasn't sure how long he stood there, gazing into the distance, thinking of nothing, but after what seemed like an age, the sound of a door banging open and jumble of raised voices startled him out of his reverie. Instinctively he ducked around the side of the old Post Office, much as he had hidden the previous night, and peered through the wisteria that grew across the front of the building. Across the street, two houses up from the Old School, a man and a woman emerged from a cottage. The man, Sebastian hadn't seen before, but he recognised the woman standing in the doorway. He couldn't recall her name, but it was the woman who had come to see Mac at lunchtime.

'Well, I don't know what you expect me to do about it at such short notice,' she said, her voice sharpened with irritation, making it sound even more posh than earlier. 'What am I supposed to do now?'

The man, who had an impressive set of side whiskers and was clutching a cloth hat in his hands, addressed his comments to her feet. 'Sorry, Mrs Farley.' Yes, that was her name - Sebastian remembered now. 'But there's nothing to be done about it. I came to tell you as soon as it happened.'

'The children will be most disappointed, to say nothing of the parish council! Is there nothing to be done? The fayre is still three days away.'

The man looked up suddenly. 'I could bring a couple of cows instead. Got some lovely heifers up in the...'

'Don't be preposterous!' she interrupted, astonishing Sebastian with a word he'd never heard spoken out loud before. The man mumbled something which Sebastian couldn't quite make out, but whatever it was it clearly didn't please Mrs Farley. 'And what exactly is Old Geronimo?'

'My Aberdeen Angus bull. He's a big fella, right enough, but he's soft as Simnel cake. He'd be fine with the children to be sure.'

Without comment, Mrs Farley turned back into the cottage, slamming the door behind her, and the man sagged, either in defeat or, more likely, with relief, before hurrying away to duck into the Green Man.

The street was empty once again. Sebastian let out a long sigh and stepped out from the cover of the Old Post Office, wondering what that had been all about.

'You lost or something?' said a voice, so close behind him he nearly jumped into the trough.

DAMSONS IN THE NOSE

'Bloody hell!' said Sebastian, spinning round. 'You scared the life out of me!' He was surprised to find Emma smiling up at him, clearly amused at his reaction. There was something different about her as well. 'Are you… are you wearing make up?'

'Yes,' she said, a defiant look on her face to go with the lipstick and rouge. 'Like it, do you?'

Sebastian did not, and he seized the opportunity to take the upper hand for once. 'Not really,' he said. 'I think you look better with nothing on.' There was a pause, during which Sebastian shut his eyes and sighed at his own rubbishness with women. He peeped out at her with his right eye, and wasn't sure whether her grin was a good sign or not.

'I think I'll probably just take that as a compliment,' she said at last, moving closer to take his hands in hers. He was certain she only did it to see how flustered she could make him. *Very* was the answer. 'Want to come back to mine and check your emails again?'

He did want to - of course he wanted to! - but a quick glance at his watch, without dislodging his hand, confirmed the suspicion that he'd been loitering here for quite a long time. 'Sorry,' he said. 'I've got to get back for dinner soon. We're eating early so Neil and I can go and hang out with the vicar or something.' He shrugged to indicate how daft he thought this sounded.

'Oh, you're going to be there, too?'

Sebastian frowned. 'Eh?'

'I'll be there,' said Emma and, to Sebastian's vague disappointment, she released his hands and started off up the street. 'It'll be fun!'

'So people keep telling me,' said Sebastian, hurrying after her.

And, in the end, it really did turn out to be fun. It was just the hangover that let it down. And the head-butt, but that wasn't until much later.

It was just before seven o'clock when he and Neil arrived at the vicarage, a ludicrously large building, consisting of three storeys in grey stone and grounds that could have housed half the village.

'This place is bigger than the church,' said Sebastian, looking back through the hedge that separated the vicarage from St Bartholomew's. 'A *lot* bigger.'

'Course it is,' said Neil. 'That's because vicars are notorious for having vast quantities of children. And they need space for taking in all the waifs and strays and that.'

'Get many of them around here, do you?'

Neil chuckled. 'Only the ones that come here from the city.' He pulled an old iron handle that protruded from the stone and, somewhere far beyond the door, a bell rang.

'Hey!' said Sebastian, realising what Neil had been inferring. 'What do you...?' But then the door swung open to reveal the chiselled features of their host.

'Excellent,' said the vicar, beaming at his guests and stepping to one side. 'Come on in, Neil.'

Neil stepped inside, followed by Sebastian who peered around the entrance hall, amazed not only by the fact that there *was* such a room, but by its immensity and stately décor. It reminded him of the stag do of an old school friend earlier that year, which had been held in one of the more salubrious gentleman's clubs London has to offer, though it was mostly the oak panelling that gave this grand effect, accentuated by the large staircase with its deep, stair-rodded carpet, and the ancient-looking doors, no doubt hand carved and weighing half a ton. The place smelled old, the mingled odours of long-forgotten meals, tinged with moth balls, though Sebastian suspected the latter had something to do with the many animal heads that were mounted on two of the room's walls.

'And you must be young Sebastian,' said the vicar, who couldn't have been more than a couple of years older that him. 'Didn't get the chance to chat on Sunday, but great to have you join us this evening.' He gripped Sebastian's hand in his powerful fist and pumped it vigorously, before gesturing to one of the many doorways. 'Usual place. Straight through there, second on the left.'

Neil opened the door and strode along the passage beyond. Sebastian trailed behind with a more cautious gait, wondering what exactly was going on. The room, second on the left, was very much in keeping with the entrance hall, with the addition of a large oriental-style rug and a host of antique furniture all lined up against the walls. Above a wide mantelpiece a particularly large stag's head gazed unblinking at the gathering from beneath the expanse of its antlers. The gathering consisted of the trio who had just entered the room and its two current occupants: Emma, as promised, and, to Sebastian's surprise, the man with the impressive side whiskers who had been speaking with Mrs Farley that afternoon. He was bent over, picking up a large bag of what looked to Sebastian like chicken feed, and spotted Neil as he straightened up.

'How do, Nelly,' he said, flashing a smile at Neil and nodding towards Sebastian. 'And who's this then? Not that lad from up city way you was telling us about?'

'The very same,' said Neil, dragging Sebastian forward by the shoulder to show him off. 'This here is Sebastian. Sebastian, this is my good friend and neighbour, Jephthah.'

'Call me Jeph.' The man dumped the sack on an expensive and antique-looking table, and grasped Sebastian's hand. His fingers were so rough and calloused that Sebastian had to check he wasn't wearing an old pair of leather gloves. He wasn't. 'Jephthah's a rubbish name.'

'Nice to meet you,' said Sebastian, feeling in his pocket for some alcohol gel, but he'd evidently left it somewhere. 'Hi Emma,' he added, allowing his eyes, at last, to shift across to her. In response, she glanced round at him from where she was lining up several rows of beer bottles and flicked a loose strand of red hair away from her face. He was pleased to see she was no longer wearing makeup.

'Feel free to call me Vic, by the way,' said the vicar, giving Sebastian a nod.

'Is that short for Victor?' he asked. Across the room Emma let out a snort of laughter.

The vicar smiled, teeth flashing. 'No, no. Nothing like that. It's short for vicar. Ah!' he said, as a bell rang out from the hallway, 'and that must be the last of our number.'

He strode out and, a few seconds later, strode back in again, followed, at a shuffle, by another familiar figure.

'Donald?' said Neil, clearly surprised at the landlord's presence. 'What in the world are you doing here?'

'Come to check out the competition, is it?' asked Jeph with a grin.

'Oh, we're hardly that,' said the vicar, looking awkwardly at the three men. 'Little more than a few artisans honing their craft.'

Donald shook his head. 'It's okay, Vic. I'm used to these two ganging up on me. Been that way since school. But since you ask,' he directed his words towards Jeph and Neil, 'I've not come here as competition. I'm here to learn.'

'To learn?' Neil stared at his brother-in-law in open amazement.

'Indeed,' said Donald, puffing out his large belly. 'It was your young visitor here that gave me the idea.' He swung a hand out to indicate Sebastian. 'Gave me a *few* ideas, in fact. It's high time I got the Green Man back in the business proper. And when I overheard Jeph here,' the hand swung round, 'talking with Sid about this here brewing session in the pub this afternoon, I though I'd come along and see how the whole thing's done.'

'Don't you know it's rude to eavesdrop?' said Jeph, frowning at the landlord and twisting his whiskers in one hand. Donald ignored him.

'Shall we get started then?' asked the vicar. 'I believe everything's ready,' he picked up one of the bottles Emma had been arranging, holding it up to the light, 'including a fine collection of the year's previous efforts to sample on our journey.'

Sebastian turned to look at one of the tables that stood against the wall opposite the fireplace, on which was displayed a number of large, stainless steel containers, lengths of plastic tubing, bottles and other items that he did not immediately recognise. In pride of place was an urn, a red light winking above its black dial, and he wondered if its main role, when not being used for clandestine beer making, was boiling up water for W.I. meetings or the yearly flower show or such parochial activities.

Emma strode across to this table and snatched up a sheet of paper.

'Right,' she said. 'This week we're going with a porter from a recipe I found online.'

Donald nudged Sebastian with his bony elbow and whispered, 'I've been having a look into that myself, after what you said. Apparently the telephone company can get me "on the line" using some sort of golem.'

'It's called a *modem*,' Sebastian whispered back.

'Excuse me?' said Emma loudly, fixing them with a stern look. 'Do you want to hear about this recipe or not?' Sebastian and Donald both nodded apologetically. 'Good. Well, the guy on the forum said it will produce a dark, full-bodied beer, bitter-sweet with…' she consulted the piece of paper, 'with liquorice notes, whatever that's supposed to mean.'

'I can taste it already,' said Jeph.

'Well, perhaps you and Vic could sort out the grain? It's mostly pale malt, but there's a little roast barley and chocolate malt in there too. Donald and

Neil, could you handle the other dry ingredients? Everything you need is on the table. Sebastian and I will get the water ready in the mash tun.'

'So are you the leader then?' asked Sebastian, as the team got to work. His task was to set up the mash tun, which looked to him exactly like a plastic picnic box with a tap on the front, while Emma measured the temperature of water in a large urn, perched on a beautiful, antique chair.

'Don't be silly,' said Emma, her attention focussed on the thermometer. 'I just happen to be the one who comes up with the recipes, thanks to being the only person here with access to the internet. That's seventy-two degrees! Let's get a couple of gallons in the mash tun. Where are we at with the malt and that?' she added, calling towards the others over her shoulder.

'Just coming,' said Neil, 'only Donald here got a little mixed up weighing out the hops.'

The landlord straightened up, looking indignant. 'It's hardly my fault. How was I to know it wasn't ounces?'

'The word "grams" after the number there?' said Neil, flicking a finger at the sheet of paper. 'Not enough of a clue for you?'

'Well, we're up to temperature here,' interrupted Emma as Donald was gearing up to respond. 'Let's get what you've got in the mash tun and we'll get this brew going.'

As the grain and water was mixed together, making something that looked to Sebastian unpleasantly like porridge - something he had avoided since being forced to eat a bowl of the gritty mess by his gran when he was eight - he sidled over to Donald.

'So, you've never done this before either?'

Donald shook his head. 'Never really seen the need. I put in my order to the beer company and they send out a dray to delivery the barrels. All I have to do is connect them up to the pumps and give it to customers, well, I mostly give it to those two old gits, Sid and Harry, but on those rare occasions when another customer does happen to stray in and order a pint, that's what they get. I've never really been much for all this real ale lark, myself - always struck me as a bit full of itself, if you catch my drift, a bit too much like the old wine-tasting weirdoes you gets on the telly, all "Clear notes of coriander and oak leaves on a crisp, autumn morning" or "I'm getting damsons in the nose". Give me a cold pint of lager instead, any day of the week, but it ain't *my* taste what matters, that's what you said. I got to give people what they want instead, and that's what this here's all about.'

Sebastian, who couldn't recall saying anything of the sort, decided to deflect the conversation back to the current proceedings. 'So, do you know what they're up to here?'

'Not a bloody clue.'

'This is the mash,' said Emma, clearly taking Donald's profession of ignorance as an opportunity to show off her insight. 'It's where the sugars and starch in the grains get turned into something the yeast can make into alcohol.'

'By heating it up?' asked Sebastian, unconvinced.

'Exactly. That's why we needed to get that temperature just right. The malt's got these enzyme things in it that do the work, but only when its hot. And we've got to keep it at that temperature for almost two hours.'

'Blessings be on this brew!' intoned the vicar. 'How

about we crack out a few bottles of that IPA we made in February?'

'Sounds good to me!' said Neil, already advancing on the bottled-filled table.

'Alright,' said Donald. 'Let's see what all the fuss is about.'

'Damned fine stuff,' said the landlord, as he led the group across the green a few hours later. They had completed the brewing process for the evening, most of which Sebastian hadn't understood - the terminology was confusing enough, with words like sparging, wort and amylase being thrown around as though they were normal conversation material - and each step had been followed by the sampling of their previous efforts from earlier in the year, including two strong ales and a stout that almost needed to be chewed before swallowing. Now they were heading to the Green Man for a final tipple to "round off the evening", as Jeph had put it.

Sebastian had felt quite sober throughout the proceedings, but as the fresh night air hit his lungs, he found his feet were not quite as certain as expected and he staggered slightly on the drive.

'Oops!' he said, grabbing at someone for support. 'Bit of uneven ground there.'

'Don't pull on me!' said Emma, whose arm he was clinging on to. 'You'll have us both over.'

After a brief battle with himself, in which the idea of sprawling on the ground with her had the upper hand for a moment, he let go. 'Sorry,' he said, noting a slight slur to his voice. 'Didn't see you there.'

'You're slurring.'

'No, I'm not!' he insisted, wishing the words hadn't come out as, "Narm a not" - it seemed to undermine his point somewhat.

The six brewers traipsed together across the village green, lit by stars peeking through the clustered clouds and a handful of lighted windows from the nearby cottages. Donald arrived first at the pub, tripping over the step as he tugged out his keys.

'I hate that stupid step,' he mumbled, scratching the key around on the door until it slotted into the keyhole, more by accident than design. The door banged open and he flicked on the lights before heading off behind the bar.

'After you,' said Sebastian, waving Emma in first and rapping his knuckles on the door frame as he did so.

'What'll you have?' called Donald as the others bumbled in and arranged themselves on barstools. 'I'm for a whiskey, myself.'

'Same for me,' said Jeff, taking up position at the end of the bar. 'You joining us, Nelly?

Neil squinted at him. 'Whiskey, eh? Yes, thanks.'

'What about you, Vic?' asked Donald, peering past the two men.

The vicar shook his head. 'Not whiskey, thank you. I'm afraid it doesn't agree with me. Not at all. Perhaps a little port?'

'I didn't realise vicars were allowed to drink,' said Sebastian, dragging a barstool towards the clergyman while trying to perch on it. 'But then I thought you weren't allowed to marry either.'

The vicar smiled, and his perfect, white teeth glinted in the light. 'Heavens no. That's the Catholics, dear fellow. No, it's not the case at all in the Anglican church, thank goodness. Wouldn't have signed up otherwise. Not that I'm married yet, of course, but there's plenty of time for that, eh?'

'And the alcohol?' asked Sebastian, finding the word "alcohol" particularly tricky to pronounce without slurring. 'I thought that was frowned upon or something.'

Vic nodded as he considered this. 'We would certainly discourage drunkenness, or at least being *a drunk* - it can be such a destructive idol, you see, one of the worst. But let's not forget that our Saviour's first miracle was to provide a group of wedding guests with the equivalent of something like eight baths filled with wine. And that, when they had already drunk the place dry!'

'Really?' said Sebastian, unconvinced. 'Where did you hear that?'

'The Bible, dear chap. It's all in there.'

'Found it!' said Donald, jamming a bottle of port onto the bar top. He jerked out the cork and slid it across to the vicar. 'Fill your boots, Vic! It's on the house. And what can I get for you two?' he added, focussing blurrily on Sebastian and Emma.

When the party eventually broke up, with Donald wishing them all farewell from the open pub door, the vicar pronounced a parting blessing and jogged back to his palatial home, seemingly unaffected by the evening's alcohol intake. Somewhat less soberly, the others headed in the vague direction of the crossroads, with Jeph and Neil in the lead, deep in conversation about something which Sebastian thought had to do with the coming village fayre. He lagged behind with Emma, angling towards the Village Store.

'Here we are then,' he said, flapping a hand towards the door.

Emma turned to look at him, her face mostly hidden in shadow. 'Thanks for walking me *all* the way home,' she said, though her voice lacked its usual mocking edge.

'A pleasure, my lady.' He had decided to produce a dramatic bow at this point, but instead, his left knee gave way for a moment and he nearly collided with her. Emma placed a hand on his chest to help steady him.

'Have you been drinking?' she asked.

He held up a hand, his forefinger and thumb forming a slightly broken "O". 'I might have had a teensy little tipple earlier, officer, but I assure you, I'm quite safe to drive.'

'Drive?' Emma frowned. 'Not leaving just yet are you?'

'Nope.' He shook his head, but stopped quickly - it was a bad idea. He looked down at her and the moon chose this point to emerge from among the clouds, etching their surroundings in its ghostly light.

'Good,' she said, looking up at him, her face serious. Through his alcho-haze, he was suddenly very aware of how close she was. And how beautiful she looked in the moonlight, her eyes huge, her hair almost silver. He also realised he was shaking, just a little, his breath quivering in his chest, despite the warmth of the night air. Was this it? Was this the moment he was supposed to kiss her? Once again, his schooling and his experience to date had in no way prepared him for this. What if he leant in and she didn't want him to kiss her? That would be awful. And yet she wasn't moving away. If anything she seemed to be drifting closer, though that could be the alcohol - even the buildings seemed to be drawing slowly in. He looked up at the shop for a moment, attempting to catch his breath, and decided to just go for it. Now. Before she vanished away inside and he never got to the opportunity again. What's the worst that could happen?

He screwed up his eyes, formed his mouth into an approximation of kissing lips… and head-butted her in the nose with his cheek. Hard.

On reflection, closing his eyes had probably been a mistake.

16
HANGOVER CURES

'I am *so* sorry!' said Sebastian, as he stood in the Village Store the next morning, egg boxes clutched under one arm, the other hand on his forehead. He felt terrible, and not just for colliding with Emma, though the recollection of it made him shudder. Mostly it had to do with his hangover, one of the worst he could recall since downing two litres of cheap cider at his own sixteenth birthday party. On that occasion he had been enormously and noisily sick behind his dad's van. At least this time he wasn't physically sick, but he wasn't far from it - he certainly hadn't felt up to eating breakfast at the farmhouse. Everything hurt - his arms, his legs, his back, his neck and, of course, his head. It felt as though a family of travellers had decided to settle in it, dragging with them their dogs, horses and a full complement of wagons. Walking hurt. Talking hurt. Moving his eyes hurt. Even thinking hurt, and all he could think about was how disastrously he had muffed things up last night. 'Sorry,' he repeated, chewing his lip. That also hurt.

Emma narrowed her eyes. Between them the swelling of her nose after its clash with Sebastian's cheek was slight, but enough to be noticeable. 'Those my eggs, are they?' she asked, taking them before he had a chance to answer and turning to place them on the counter.

He watched her as she worked in silence, shrouded once again in one of the shapeless dresses she seemed to like wearing, and tried desperately to think of something to say, something that would put last night behind them, something more than just, 'Sorry'. His eyes alighted on the picture of a large, bearded man displayed on the front of a bag of oats, and it gave him an idea.

'Do you reckon Mac was a gangster?' he said, his voice conspiratorial.

'Mac?' said Emma, her voice incredulous. 'A gangster?'

'Sure. Why else would he have come and hidden himself away in the middle of nowhere, instead of staying in London?'

'Mac?'

'He told me yesterday that he doesn't touch guns.' He gave her a meaningful look, but she just frowned back at him, her mouth a lop-sided smile. 'Maybe he got caught up in some sort of turf war. Or grassed up the boss and had to enter one of those witness protection things and take on a new identity.'

'Mac?'

'Yes, of course Mac.'

'A gangster?'

'He's pretty handy with a knife,' he added, as though presenting damning evidence before a jury.

Emma laughed. 'You don't half come out with some rubbish!' It was her turn to lower her voice to a whisper. 'He left,' she said, 'because his best friend stole his childhood sweetheart.'

'Mac?' Sebastian took on the incredulous role. 'A childhood sweetheart? Now who's talking rubbish?'

'That's what my mother told me, anyway. And

she'd know. She's the only person in the village who's *really* talked with Mac about his old life. She likes him.'

Sebastian was only half listening, still trying to take in the idea of the massive butcher fleeing because of a girl. 'It doesn't make sense,' he said. 'Why would he leave the city? London's massive! If he wanted to avoid them, he could've just moved up the river, not across the country.' He paused and looked at Emma, noticing the swollen nose again and trying to ignore it. 'What do you mean you mum likes Mac? What sort of *like*?'

She glanced over her shoulder into the corridor beyond, then whispered. 'I mean she *likes* him. And I'm pretty sure he likes her too, since he comes in here almost every lunchtime when mum's running the shop.'

Sebastian considered this, picking up a wooden spoon from the counter and fiddling with it, unconsciously. Could it be true? Is *that* what Mac had been doing in the dark the other night, watching Mrs Standfield, while Sebastian was busy watching Emma? He considered this huge man, who was still so hurt by a thirty-year-old love affair that he refused to even speak about London and, Sebastian suspected, even begrudged the presence of a fellow Londoner in Steepleford. He thought back to the cold cans that were noticeably absent from the butchery refrigerator, an excuse to visit the shop each day, and to Mac staring across the church aisle, not at Sebastian or even at Emma, but at someone sitting a little further along the pew. He dropped the spoon with a clatter.

'You know what,' he said, stooping to pick it up. 'I think you might be right. You don't think Mac and your mum… you know…?' He raised one eyebrow suggestively, unable to complete the question.

'Fat chance!' said Emma, striding behind the counter and letting down the hatch. 'Mother's been interested in him for ages, but she'd never do anything about it. Not *the done thing*, a woman asking a man out. That's what she says, anyway. Load of rubbish, if you ask me. As for Mac, he's probably still too cut up about whoever-she-was in London to ask her out either. So what makes *you* think he's interested?'

Sebastian paused, mouth open, not wanting to mention his night time meeting with the butcher, in case it led to questions about his own shadowy reasons for being there. Emma stared at him in silence. 'Just a feeling,' he said, the hangover flush of his cheeks hiding his embarrassment. 'And you could well be right about Mac. I know I'd be put off asking someone out if I'd been rejected.'

She titled her head at him and grinned. 'And who would reject a lovely man like you?' She paused, and Sebastian could feel the sweat breaking out on his forehead - he desperately needed to get out in the fresh air. Emma straightened up. 'I think we might be able to do something about their situation,' she continued. 'We…' She stopped and held up a hand, evidently alerted by something in the living quarters behind her. 'My mother's coming,' she whispered, leaning towards Sebastian. 'This needs thinking about, though. Are you free this evening?'

'I should be asking you! Everyone else seems to know more about my daily schedule here than I do.'

'Good,' whispered Emma, as though this settled it. 'I'll meet you at the front of the church at ten o'clock tonight.'

'Good morning, Mrs Standfield,' said Sebastian, as Emma's mother emerged through the doorway into the shop. He tried to rustle up an ingratiating smile, but it hurt too much.

'That's as maybe,' she said. 'Though by the look of you, my morning might well be better than yours. Did you fall down a hole or something?'

He managed half a smile. 'I ache like it! But you're right, I need to go and freshen up. See you later, Emma. And sorry again about the nose.'

He trudged his way back to the farmhouse, dragging his hangover with him. The morning sun had risen above the tree-line and fired bright needles of pain into his eyes. His mouth was dry, his tongue swollen and seemingly in need of a shave, and there was an insistent nagging in his head that everyone hated him. In short, it was a fairly standard hangover. Perhaps he didn't really look as bad as all that.

'What the hell happened to you?' said Neil, looking up from the breakfast table as Sebastian opened the door. 'You look like you died and someone dug you up again.'

'However terrible I look, it's nothing compared to how I feel.' He raised a hand to his head as Neil dragged a chair out for him, scraping it noisily across the tiled kitchen floor. He perched on it, as though poised to depart at any moment. 'What was in that beer we were drinking? I feel like I downed a bottle of meths.'

'Just good old homebrew, lad,' said Neil, reaching out a hand to slap him on the shoulder, but thought better of it as Sebastian flinched away. 'Bad, is it?'

'You have no idea.'

'Maybe not. But I've got the perfect cure. Or rather Virg has.' Sebastian turned to look at his hostess, who was busy working at the stove, her back towards them.

'How's it coming, love?' asked Neil.

'Almost ready!'

The 'cure' turned out to be a breakfast of the Full English variety. It was easily the largest such breakfast Sebastian had ever seen, his plate loaded high with sausages, bacon, black pudding and eggs, beneath which were hidden slices of fried bread, tomatoes, mushrooms and no doubt other delights fresh from the frying pan. He made no move towards it, but sat eyeing the food as though deciding whether to eat it or report it to the Environmental Agency.

'Don't just stare at it,' said Virginia, dumping a large mug of tea in front of him. 'Get that down you, you'll feel ready for anything.'

Sebastian wasn't convinced, suspecting the only thing he'd be ready for after such a breakfast was to cower in bed clutching a sick bowl. And maybe having a little cry. 'This is the cure?' he said, with a sideways glance at Neil.

'Well, it's half of it, at least.'

Sebastian picked up his fork and considered where best to begin. 'And what's the other half?' he asked.

The other half of the cure turned out to be hard labour. Or at least what passed for hard labour in Sebastian's world, where even loading up the dishwasher was considered a burdensome chore. He had been surprised at how much better he felt once he had worked his way through the breakfast, assisted by Neil occasionally skewering stray bits of bacon or mushrooms the moment he decided Sebastian was starting to flag.

Then, bumping their way to the smallholding on the quad bike, which had only grown slightly less distressing over the last few days, they had headed to the stable block armed with a broom, something that looked like a large plastic shovel on a stick, two pitchforks and a wheelbarrow.

'Don't look at it like that,' said Neil, correctly reading Sebastian's expression as he took in the size of the stable. 'We'll have this done in no time.'

This was clearly nonsense, but Sebastian got grudgingly to work, copying Neil's technique of sliding the pitchfork into the straw and muck covered floor, and lifting out a load to dump into the wheelbarrow. It wasn't as easy as Neil made it look, and Sebastian kept banging the unwieldy pitchfork against the barrow or the doorway, dislodging its cargo back onto the floor. In time, though, he got into a kind of rhythm and the work began to lift him out of the last clutches of his hangover.

'My headache's gone,' he said, wiping a gloveless hand across his forehead, where his fringe, usually kept until firm control, had collapsed into his eyes.

'See,' said Neil. 'I told you we'd get you cured. Better than hiding away in bed all day, feeling sorry for yourself. Decent bit of grub and some work in the fresh air cures just about anything.'

Sebastian, who wouldn't describe the atmosphere in the stable as "fresh air", wondered if there was something to this. 'Do you get ill much?' he asked.

'Me? No, never. Too much to be getting on with to have time for being ill.'

'It's not like people *choose* to get sick,' said Sebastian, swinging his loaded pitchfork over the barrow. 'It just, you know... happens.'

Neil paused and leant on his pitchfork, like a sage propped up against a staff. 'There's a farm over Brayford way,' he thumbed over his shoulder as if

Sebastian might glimpse this far-off village through the stable wall, 'that rears pigs for the supermarkets. They've got thousands of the things, all jammed up in barns so tight you can't hardly see the floor between the poor creatures. *Intensive* farming, they call it, and Ted - he's the farmer - he has to keep them pumped full of all kinds of vitamins and antibiotics and Lord knows what. As you can imagine, the end product gets affected - tasteless, medicine-laced pork that's not fit for a dog to chew on,' outside, stretched out in the sunshine, Tank's ears pricked, 'but if Ted don't keep them pigs dosed up, disease'll spread through them like a plague.' He gave Sebastian a meaningful look. '*A plague!*'

'Sorry,' said Sebastian, when no concluding remarks seemed to be coming. 'Why are you telling about this? Is that about going organic or something? Coz I do buy it, you know, if it's reduced.'

'Nah,' Neil continued, still leaning on the pitchfork. 'I mean, them pigs is like you city folks. It can't be good for you all being packed up together so tight, gulping in exhaust fumes and spending most of your life huddled up in some concrete cocoon. Out here in the country, it's different.'

'You're telling *me*?' said Sebastian, feeling he, at least, had a fair comparison of them both.

'Big open spaces, clean air, the earth beneath your feet and good, hard work to be done. It keeps everyone healthy.' Neil set down his fork and began wheeling the barrow out to the muck heap in the corner of the field, Sebastian wandering behind. 'Poor old Doctor Timmons has to cover five parishes, because so few people ever need his services.'

'You really love it here, don't you?' said Sebastian,

looking around at the smallholding as it basked in the mid-morning sunlight.

Neil upended the barrow and wheeled it round to join him. 'What's not to love?' he said. 'It's all so glorious - the sights, the sounds, the smells. Look at it - the sunlight sparkling on the Bray, everything so still and peaceful, while also stirring, alive. The birds are in fine voice, the trees are whispering to each other on the breeze, and beneath them the low murmur of the water as it winds its way south.' He patted Sebastian on the back. 'Breathe it in, lad, the smell of the earth and the nettles baking in the sun. Glorious, I tell you. The space, the freedom, the beauty of nature and the wonder of life itself. It makes me feel like singing!'

Sebastian laughed, the last of the hangover slipping away. 'You did sound like you were gearing up for a song.'

'Well, I'll save you from that particular torture. For now.' He took up the wheelbarrow again. 'Let's get back to it.'

'I have to admit,' said Sebastian, following him back into the stable, 'it is much nicer than I thought it would be. And far less threatening. But it's not much of a life, is it?'

'How do you mean?' asked Neil, setting down the barrow and snatching up the pitchfork.

'Back in London, I work eight hours a day, five days a week. In at nine, out at five - that's it. I don't take anything home with me, I don't worry about the business when I'm not there. I do my job and the rest of the time is my own. But here,' he gestured to the fields beyond the doorway, 'weeds and the like are always trying to take over, animals fall sick or escape or get up to who knows what, and you're at the mercy of

England's famously unpredictable weather. You don't have a job, so much, as a never-ending battle with nature twenty-four hours a day, seven days a week. And I bet there's no day off for Christmas. When did you last go for a holiday, for instance?'

Neil frowned in thought, as he switched his fork for the brush and started sweeping straw against one wall. 'Me and Virg went for a weekend in Torquay a few years back,' he said, smiling at the memory. 'Good time it was, too. Jeph, who you met last night, looked after things here while we were away.'

'*A few years ago?*' Sebastian was stunned, not only by the length of time, but by the fact that Neil seemed quite okay with this situation. 'One weekend off in a few years? That's terrible. It's... it's like slavery.'

'It's ecstasy. It's all I've ever wanted, to work on the land, living in harmony with the seasons. It's not slavery, lad, it's freedom. If anyone's a slave, it's you, locked away in your dingy office while the sun shines and the birds sing, then trudging through the grey streets to some flat or suchlike, where you lock yourself away again like a catty-pillar in its cocoon. The problem is, you never get the chance to be a butterfly, unless you count slapping on a bit of hair gel and dressing up in sharp suits.'

'I use wax actually,' said Sebastian. 'It tends to produce a more natural hold - less shiny and rigid than gel.' He lifted a self-conscious hand to his fringe, which had flopped down in front of his face again to cover his blackened eye. 'Admittedly, I didn't use any this morning. I *do* have some sharp suits, though. Sharp as a razor!'

'See,' said Neil, as though his point had been proven. 'That's what the city does to you. Makes you a catty-pillar dressed up in butterfly wings. But look what a difference the country has made already. Like you say, you haven't bothered with your hair today. You've stopped wearing those ridiculous yellow gloves and that alcoholic's hand gel stuff. And, between you and me, you clothes are looking a bit... well, scruffy. And your flies is undone.'

Sebastian looked down and quickly adjusted his zip. 'So, what you're saying is that, thanks to my few days in the country, I've become a dirty tramp. Hardly a butterfly, is it? More like a moth!'

'Forget the damn butterfly,' said Neil, sweeping the last of the straw into a corner with more vigour than was really necessary. 'All I'm saying is you're emerging from your shell...'

'You mean, "cocoon", surely?'

'I mean, you're emerging from... whatever it was you were locked up in. You're being liberated.' He leant on the broom and jabbed a finger at Sebastian. 'And *that* is what the countryside does, my lad.'

'You have some hay in your moustache,' said Sebastian.

Neil pulled the strand from the bush of hair with a grunt. 'It ain't hay, it's straw,' he said, and pointed to the shovel-on-a-stick implement leaning against the wall. 'Grab that scoop and let's get these last bits swept up, then we can start on the other stable.'

'The *other* stable?'

THE NATIVITY

Sebastian had not really warmed to any of the animals encountered so far on the smallholding, with the possible exception of the late Psycho Hen, but he felt there was something particularly sinister about the horses. Though he had seen similar creatures in the city, while walking past the crowds of tourists watching the Changing of the Guard or spotting the occasional mounted policeman bobbing along in the distance, he had never really got close to one before, so as Neil led the first of the two masked creatures in from the field to its nice, clean stable, he found himself backing away in alarm.

'Why is it so big?' he said, his voice raising in pitch with each words as he almost tripped over his booted feet. 'It's obscene.'

Neil brought the horse to a halt and patted it affectionately on the neck. 'She needs be big, if she's going to carry someone like me around.'

'She?' Sebastian made to point at the horse, but nodded instead, not wishing to get any part of him closer to it than was absolutely necessary. 'That *thing's* a girl. And what ridiculous name have you given her?'

'This here's Belle.'

Sebastian thought for a moment. 'Okay, that's actually not a bad name for it, but I still don't see how you can be around something like this without wearing armour or something. Look at its eyes. They're the eyes of a serial killer. What if it takes a dislike to me?'

'*She!*' corrected Neil. 'And in that case, I suggest you run!'

Sebastian took another step back and found himself collapsing somewhat abruptly into the wheelbarrow. He yawned in an attempt to make it look as though he was just having a little sit down. 'Just get *her* in the damn stable, would you?' he said. 'And keep that lethal backend away from me. Bloody hell!' This last outcry was in response to a noise behind him which, when he looked round, turned out to be the other horse, who had wandered over to see what all the excitement was about. Sebastian jumped up, knocking the wheelbarrow towards the newcomer as he did so, causing it to lurch away with an indignant snort. To his horror, Sebastian found himself caught between two pairs of hind legs, any of which might whip out without warning and dash him to the ground like a rag doll, tossed by an angry child.

Instinctively, he dropped to the floor, hands over his head, his eyes tight shut.

'Please don't kick me!' he said, his voice a whispered shout, afraid he might startle the horses.

He felt Neil's strong hand gripping his arm, pulling him back to his feet. 'Come on, lad,' he said. 'They're safe enough.'

Sebastian opened one eye and was met by the sight of Belle's rump barely a foot or two away. He watched, terrified, as Neil gave it a smack, raising a cloud of dust. But instead of lashing out with a hoof, as seemed inevitable to Sebastian, the massive creature skittered away from them.

'See,' said Neil, gesturing to the horses. 'They'll not

hurt you. Couple of old softies, these two.'

Sebastian watched as Belle wandered into the stable, her flank shimmering in the sunlight, her muscles moving easily like well-oiled pistons shifting beneath its skin. 'It doesn't look that soft to me.'

'Not as much as some around here,' said Neil, chuckling once again. 'Come on. Let's head back for some lunch before we get on to mucking out the goats.'

That evening, Sebastian returned to the farmhouse tired and filthy, his hands, which hadn't felt the soft inside of a pair of gloves all day, nursing blisters and his arms aching from the constant forking, sweeping and shovelling. Though the idea of a proper shower at the Village Store was extremely appealing, he wasn't sure his legs would get him up the hill, so he settled for washing in the farmhouse bath beneath the dubious flow of the shower attachment, and although it went cold after only a couple of minutes, he was just glad to be clean again and to no longer feel like a walking manure heap.

'Hot water's out,' called Virginia from the kitchen, where she was busy boiling up potatoes and frying some of the sausages Sebastian had made the previous day, and when he came downstairs a short while later to join the Symeses for dinner, he was delighted at how well they had come out.

'I reckon this was one of yours!' said Neil, jabbing with his fork at a sausage so long it hung over the edges of his plate.

Sebastian just nodded, his mouth too full and his appetite too intense to permit any conversation.

For the rest of the evening, as he and Neil tackled another crossword and Virginia set about preparing to go to market in the morning, Sebastian kept one eye on the time. Ten o'clock, Emma had said, and, although it was lumbering towards that time at a tedious pace, each glance at the slowly advancing hands felt like someone punching him in the chest. He tried to ignore it, but couldn't help how excited he felt at the idea of meeting up with her. *In the dark.*

'You alright, lad?' asked Neil, giving him a quizzical look. 'You look like you're about to be sick again. Shall I go get the dog?'

Sebastian swallowed. 'Yes,' he squawked, and quickly cleared his throat. 'I mean, no. I'm fine.' His eyes flicked up to the clock again. It was only quarter to nine. 'Actually, I might go and have a read upstairs. Thought I might go out for a stroll a bit later.'

'Right you are,' said Neil, folding up the newspaper. 'Got to nip out myself , anyway, and check on the sheep.'

Although Sebastian hadn't brought anything to read from London, there was a small bookshelf in his bedroom that was mostly filled with an obscene amount of well-thumbed romance novels. Among their ranks, he found a copy of *Great Expectations* and settled down on the bed to read it. The book was not his sort of thing at all, but since he wasn't really taking any of it in, just scanning blankly over the words, it didn't really matter. His watch was of far more interest and, after its slow start, ten o'clock seemed to approaching at a decent pace at last.

At nine-fifty, he could take it no longer and, closing the book, having got little more from it than the vague idea that it had something to do with a boy in a graveyard, he got up, pulled on his coat and headed downstairs.

He was just pulling on his shoes, when the back door slammed open and Neil burst in. Kicking the door shut behind him, he leaned against it, breathing heavily. He had clearly been running.

'Thank goodness I caught you,' he said and pointed at Sebastian's shoes. 'Don't bother with those dainty little things, it's your boots you'll be needing.'

Sebastian stared at him in confusion. 'Eh?'

'Come on! They're lambing. You don't want to miss this.'

'But I was just going out,' said Sebastian, a half-on shoe dangling from his foot. 'For that walk, remember?'

Neil grabbed a sack from the corner of the small room. 'That's okay,' he said. 'You're still going out.' Sebastian continued to stare at him, unmoving. 'Boots!' said Neil, kicking the wellingtons across the floor at him. 'Let's go.'

Sebastian gave in. There was no point arguing with Neil - he was clearly excited about this "lambing" business, whatever that was, and was determined for Sebastian to join him. But what about Emma? In a few minutes, she'd be there, waiting in the shadow of the church for him. He imagined her standing there, a delicate dress barely concealing her figure as it shimmered in the breeze, arms open to welcome him, to hold him, to draw him in and...

'Wipe that stupid look off your face, lad,' said Neil, yanking the door open. 'We don't have all night.'

Sebastian, kitted out in his wellies, followed Neil as he strode up the hill towards the centre of the village. Just before the butcher's shop, however, he turned left to fiddle with the latch on a small gate.

'Where are we going?' asked Sebastian, staring

longingly up at the crossroads and the yew trees that concealed the small church where, even now, Emma was no doubt waiting for him in the gathering dusk. He turned at the sound of whining hinges as the gate swung open.

'This is our top field,' said Neil, gesturing through to the grassy expansive that swept steeply away downhill. 'The sheep are in that barn there.'

The building in question was not what Sebastian thought of as a barn; not that it was a concept he had spent much time considering, but as he peered at the structure that huddled on the hillside, it was more what he would call a shack; a few short walls that looked like a hastily piled jumble of grey stones, topped off with a roof that looked like the tiles had been Frisbeed on, rather than set in place in the usual way. The only break in the stone walls was a single, lop-sided doorway and Neil dragged back the metal gate that was blocking the way in. Beyond, the straw-covered floor and spider-covered walls were lit by the glow of a couple of oil lamps.

'Is this where Jesus was born?' asked Sebastian, leaning against the doorway. 'It's like a nativity scene.'

Neil crouched down next to one of the two sheep that were slumped in the straw. 'It's about to *be* a nativity scene!' said Neil. 'Lisa here's getting very close.'

'Lisa?'

'That's right,' said Neil, looking up at him over his shoulder.

'You shouldn't be allowed to name the animals.' Sebastian inched forwards to have a look at the sheep in question. Although he was no expert, Lisa certainly seemed to be bulging and was panting in a way that gave even Sebastian the impression that *something*, at least, was about to happen. Something he wasn't especially keen on watching. 'So this is what you mean by "lambing", is it?' he said, and jabbed a thumb towards the entrance, or rather the exit as he was now thinking of it. 'Shall I, er, wait outside?'

'Outside?' Neil looked at him as though he'd suggested eating his way through the wall. 'What do you think you're going to see from out there?'

The image of Emma standing by the church filled Sebastian's head again and he glanced at his watch. Ten past ten... she would still be there. He blinked and realised Neil was looking at him through narrowed eyes. 'Nothing?' he said.

'That's right.' Neil turned back to Lisa, running a huge hand over her swollen flank. 'There ain't anything to be squeamish about, lad. Certainly nothing worse than you've been through already this week.'

'Who said anything about being squeamish?'

'The look on your face was yelling it loud enough. I'm surprised the whole village didn't hear. Easy, girl,' he added as Lisa shifted slightly, her breath rasping through her nose.

As Neil continued to stroke her side, Sebastian looked around the small barn, at the other sheep panting in the straw, at the buckets of water standing by the entrance, and at a small wooden stool leaning in a corner. He shuffled across to it and, despite the fact it looked so ancient that the old stone walls might well have been built around it, he sat down. It creaked alarmingly, but held his weight.

How long he sat there, Sebastian wasn't sure, maybe minutes, maybe hours; the combined effect of the warm night air, the flickering glow from the oil lamps, the rhythmic panting of the sheep and Neil's gentle murmurings sent him into some kind of trancelike state, his mind blank, his mouth lolling open. Something he couldn't discern, some change in the air or unseen movement, brought him, blinking, out of the stupor, consciousness flooding over him like a rush of cold water. He cleared his throat.

'Did you say something?' he asked, wiping the back of his hand across his chin, just in case he'd been dribbling. He had.

'I said it's time,' said Neil, easing himself round in the straw to look at Sebastian, his eyes sparkling in the lamplight. 'Her lambs are coming.'

'How can you tell?'

In response, Neil pointed towards the rear of the sheep, leaning to the side so Sebastian could see. There, just below the dirty stump that passed for Lisa's tail, something was glistening. It was round and dark red, about the size of Neil's fist, and even in the half-light Sebastian could see it was translucent. A stab of nausea forced him to his feet, one hand over his mouth as though afraid of breathing in air that might have touched this hideous protrusion.

'What the hell's that?' he said, trying to keep his voice calm as he spoke through his fingers. 'She's given birth to a bloody cricket ball!'

'That's part of the sack,' said Neil, his voice full of concealed amusement. 'It's what the lambs are grown in.'

'What? Like some big, floppy egg? That's horrific!'

Neil chuckled, clearly enjoying Sebastian's reaction. 'It's perfectly normal,' he said. 'In fact, it's very similar to the sack you would have grown in before you was born.'

'There's no way!' he said. 'I was never born. They created me in a sterile lab, vacuum-packed and pristine.'

'That wouldn't surprise me,' said Neil.

Against his will, Sebastian's gaze dragged itself back to the bulging water sack just in time to see it rupture, gushing a pinkish stream of fluid across the straw. Sebastian span away and supported himself on the wall with one hand, concentrating on breathing in an effort not to throw up.

'Thar she blows!' said Neil, still stroking Lisa's flank. He glanced up at Sebastian. 'Oh, come on, lad. You're missing it. One of nature's most glorious moments, this is.'

'One of it's most *goriest* moments, you mean,' said Sebastian, definitely not turning round. 'What you going to do now, put your hand in there or something?'

'No, no. Lisa doesn't need my help. This is her third lambing - she's a pro!'

Sebastian continued leaning against the wall as Neil kept up a running commentary: "Here come the nose and feet", "Look, the head's out" and "Just one more push!" Having finally got control of his insides, Sebastian turned at Neil's cry of, "And it's out!" to see what looked just like a small, sticky lamb, still half-shrouded in the water sack.

'It's not moving,' he said. 'Is it… dead?'

'No,' said Neil, slipping a hand under the lamb and dragging it across to Lisa's head. 'Watch this.' Sure enough, as it's mother nudged it and licked at it, the lamb twitched suddenly, then started shifting around as though trying to get away from all this unexpected attention. Sebastian inched forwards to watch as the tiny creature struggled in the straw and within a couple of minutes, it had managed to heave itself up onto its legs, wobbling like someone trying to walk with stilts for the first time.

'That's unbelievable,' he said. 'It's standing up.'

Neil beamed up at him. 'Course it is. Course *he* is.'

'How do you know it's a he?' asked Sebastian, then immediately regretted it. 'Forget that. Dumb question. But standing up just minutes after being born? My cousin, Emily, had a baby and it didn't start walking until it was almost a year old!'

'*It?*'

'He,' corrected Sebastian. 'He's called Leif.'

Neil raised his eyebrows. 'And you think the names I choose are odd! Hold on,' he added, peering across at the other sheep. 'Looks like Doris is about to pop too.'

Outside the barn, the last of the light had slipped from the sky as Sebastian and Neil emerged, leaving behind them Lisa and Doris with their four healthy and amazingly energetic lambs. Except for another brief moment of stomach-squeezing nausea, when his hand brushed the straw soaked with amniotic fluid, Sebastian had found the whole experience exhilarating. Through his fingers, he had watched the birth of Doris' twins, and had even lifted one of the lambs so she could nudge and lick it into life.

'I can't believe how quick the whole process was,' he said, peering at the luminous hands on his watch as they made their way down the road towards the farmhouse. It was twenty past midnight. 'Just over two hours and you've got three times as many sheep as you had before, all running around and everything. I am going to need to wash my hands fairly soon, though.'

'I can hardly believe didn't bring those wretched yellow gloves of yours. It's a bleeding miracle, lad.'

'Not exactly. I ran out and failed to buy more from the Village Store.' At the mention of the shop, Sebastian couldn't help gazing back over his shoulder towards the place where Emma had arranged to meet him. For a moment he wondered if she was still there, but it was over two hours since he had failed to show up and, though their surroundings were silver-etched by the almost-full-moonlight, it had become bitterly cold.

'Easy, lad!' said Neil, as Sebastian tripped over a pothole in the road.

When they entered the farmhouse, Sebastian was surprised to see Virginia still standing at the kitchen sink as though she hadn't moved since he left. The table, however, which had been piled high with plastic containers, was now completely empty.

'How was it?' she asked, setting down her drying up cloth and collapsing into a chair. 'How many lambs?'

'Four,' said Sebastian. 'Half boys, half girls.'

Virginia raised her eyebrows. 'Really? Must be pretty funny looking!'

'Not at all,' said Sebastian, who hadn't noticed the amused look on her face. 'They look just like normal lambs, trotting about and everything. Or is it *gambolling* that lambs do?'

'Only if they can get hold of the cash,' said Neil, edging round the table. 'And how've you got on, love? All set for market?'

Virginia sighed and swept her unruly hair out of her face with a hand, looking genuinely surprised to find it holding a large knife. 'I think I'm just about there,' she said, laying it down on the table. 'I'm done in.'

'Best get to bed, then. And so should you,' he added, patting Sebastian on the shoulder. Sebastian tried not to think about what nastiness was on Neil's hand. 'We've got to be up in five hours.'

'Five hours?' Sebastian stared wide-eyed at his hosts. 'Why only five hours?'

'You're leaving for market at half six,' said Neil. 'And before that, we've got to castrate the boy lambs.'

Sebastian opened his mouth to comment, but couldn't come up with any words. Instead, he shrugged wearily, bid them goodnight and trudged up the stairs, trying not to think about the horrors tomorrow had in store.

Ten minutes later, after multiple hand washings, he sank into bed, nestling into the warm sheets and the soft pillows. But despite being shattered after the long day, he spent what felt like an age battling with the insomnia that comes from knowing you have to get up in a few hours. He was just drifting off at last when the sound of something hitting the window startled him back to consciousness. For a moment he wasn't sure if it had really happened or if it was one of those weird dreams that jolt you awake, but then something else hit the window. Hard. With a tinkle of glass a small pebble landed on the carpet by his bed.

18
MASS PRODUCTION

'What are you doing?' said Sebastian, whispering as loudly as he dared. He was leaning out of the now-open window and below, ghostlike in the moonlight, was the unmistakable figure of Emma. He couldn't quite make out her face, but he reckoned she seemed a bit cross. 'You just chucked a stone through my window!'

'Course I did!' she called up, her voice defiant. 'But I'd rather throw them at your head! A whole hour I waited up at the church. An hour! Where the hell were you?' She pulled back her arm as if she was about to launch another stone through the window.

Sebastian ducked back into the room, narrowly avoiding stepping on broken glass, but when, after several seconds, no missile whirred in from the night, he peered out again. 'Hold on! Please, don't throw anything. I'm coming down.'

Virginia and Neil had already headed off to bed and the sound of his door groaning open seemed horribly loud in the stillness of the house. Not wishing to alert his hosts to his late night visitor, he tried to creep silently across the landing, but every slight movement elicited creaks and squeals from the floorboards which he was certain had not made a sound during the daytime. He took the stairs two-at-a-time, the wooden treads complaining all the way, before tip-toeing across the lounge, through the kitchen and to the backdoor. He was pleased to find the unfeasibly large key hanging on a piece of orange string from the handle. The lock graunched like a driver trying to find the right gear, but the door itself swung open without so much as a whisper, to reveal Emma's face. There was more of Emma below this and Sebastian was vaguely aware of glowing, white lace, but he tried to keep his eyes trained only on her face. It was scowling.

'Well?' she said, jabbing him in the shoulder with a finger. 'Let's hear it then. Where were you? And it had better be good.'

Sebastian started to explain, but a wave of exhausted anger washed over him and he suddenly didn't want to apologise. It wasn't *his* fault, after all. He hadn't deliberately stood her up. 'To be fair,' he said, mirroring Emma's scowl, 'I never actually agreed to meet you. Your mum interrupted us, remember? You just assumed I'd come and meet you.'

'Oh, so it's *my* fault now?' Her voice was laced with sarcasm. 'How foolish of me. I should have known that you'd just not bother showing up when you *knew* I would be there, alone and vulnerable, in the dark church yard.'

'I'd hardly call you vulnerable.'

'Really? So what would you call me then?' She narrowed her eyes at him, daring him to say something insulting, or at least something she could interpret as being an insult.

He sighed, the fight draining out of him as the tiredness took hold again. 'Beautiful,' he suggested, the word hardly a whisper. 'I'd call you beautiful.' Emma made no response, though her scowl softened in surprise, so he soldiered on. 'Look, I'm sorry about this evening. I did mean to come and see you, really, I did. But then lambs were being born and Neil took me to see and, before I knew it, it was gone midnight and it was too late. And I did want to see you. Honestly. I'm sorry.'

Emma opened her mouth, and closed it again, clearly lost for words for the first time in her dealings with Sebastian. Instead, she took Sebastian's hands in her own, smiling at last. 'Okay,' she said in a far softer voice. 'How about we try again tomorrow, when you're back from the market?'

'How did you-' he began, but stopped. Of course she knew he was going to market. Everyone in the village probably knew. 'Sure. That'd be great.' He couldn't help smiling as she looked up at him, her right thumb stroking the back of his hand. Her eyes looked much bigger than usual and her long red hair glinted in the moonlight. She really was beautiful.

'If it's all the same to you two lovebirds,' came a voice from the farmhouse. Sebastian dropped of Emma's hands and span round guiltily to see Neil framed in the open doorway, 'some of us have to be up in a couple of hours, so maybe you could continue your lovemaking tomorrow, yes?'

'We weren't lovemaking!' Sebastian blurted out, thankful that the darkness concealed most of his embarrassment. 'We were just talking. That's all. Honestly. Talking.'

Neil's teeth sparkled beneath his moustache and he chuckled quietly. 'Pardon me,' he said. 'My mistake.' And he disappeared back into the house.

'Tomorrow then,' said Emma. 'After market. I'll be up at the shop.'

Sebastian nodded. 'Great.'

'And you'd better not stand me up, this time!' Before Sebastian could reply, she lifted herself up on tiptoes and kissed him on the cheek. Her lips barely brushed him for an instant, but it left him stunned, his mind blank, his mouth half-open. He lifted a hand to his cheek as if to catch hold of the kiss, to keep it and store it away for later use.

'Oh, and Miss Standfield,' said Neil, appearing in the doorway again and causing Sebastian to almost leap away from Emma. 'I believe you owe me for a broken window.'

The fitful few hours' sleep that followed mostly consisted of Sebastian looking at his watch every thirty minutes or so to see how long was left before he had to get up. When at last five-thirty arrived, he felt even more weary than when he'd clambered into bed, but he dragged himself out of the warm covers and staggered to the bathroom, performing the minimum requirements to get himself looking at least vaguely presentable. Downstairs, Virginia and Neil had already finished their breakfast so, grabbing a couple of hastily buttered slices of toast, he followed Neil back up the road to the small sheep barn, his eyes drawn to a strange-looking tool in Neil's hand.

'What is that?' he asked mid-yawn, as Neil pulled the gate away from the barn entrance. 'Is that what you use to... you know?' He nodded vaguely downwards.

Neil tossed it to him and chuckled as it bounced off Sebastian's arm and fell to the ground. 'See if you can work it out,' he said and pulled a metal tin from his wax jacket pocket. 'Goes with these things.'

Sebastian took the tin and bent to pick up the tool.

It had handles such as you might get on a pair of pliers, but instead of jaws, it had four prongs that pulled apart when he squeezed the handles together. The tin offered few clues, as the scratched writing on the lid declared the contents to be pipe tobacco, so he tucked the tool under his arm and wrestled to get the lid off. With a jolt, it burst open, spilling tiny rubber rings across the grass.

'I don't get it,' he said as he scrabbled around trying to pick them up. 'What are these things? I was expecting a knife or a pair of scissors or something.'

'A pair of scissors?' said Neil, clearly taken aback. 'What kind of barbarians do you think we are?'

Sebastian, who was now kneeling on the floor in his quest for stray rubber rings, peered up, eyebrows raised. 'Well, it may come as a surprise, but I've not been involved in a whole lot of castrations back in the city. Our lambs tend to come vacuum packed and ready for the oven.'

'Well, we don't use scissors, I can assure you,' said Neil, bending down to pick up one of the rings, holding it up between a large thumb and forefinger. 'We use these little fellows. Come on, I'll show you.'

In the barn, things were much as they had been the night before, with Lisa and Doris sitting in the straw while their four lambs chased each other around making little, high-pitched bleating sounds.

'Lively, aren't they,' said Sebastian, smiling despite himself as one of the lambs jumped on his foot. 'Which are the boys?'

With a single, swift action, Neil scooped up one of the lambs and turned it belly up. 'Here's one. Have you got one of them rubber rings?'

'Er, yes.' Sebastian opened his hand to reveal fifty

or so of them.

Neil perched on the seat by the wall. 'Slip one of them on the end of the applicator, would you? Over the four prongs.'

Sebastian stuffed the rings into his pocket, keeping hold of one, which he tried to stretch over the prongs. 'Damn it!' he said, as he dropped it into the straw.

'Want me to do it?' asked Neil. 'You can sit here and hold this little fellow.'

'No thanks.' Sebastian fumbled around for the ring, one hand fending off a lamb who had taken an interest in what he was doing. 'And anyway, I thought you said *you* were going to show *me* how this was done. This is getting a bit hands-on for my liking.'

'Best way of showing. There's no better way to learn than getting involved, I always say. You got that ring on yet?'

'Yes,' said Sebastian, straightening up and holding out the applicator, the small ring in place. 'And I think I've sussed out how it works.'

'Oh yes?' Neil looked at him expectantly, but made no move to take the proffered tool. 'Let's hear it then.'

With some effort, Sebastian squeezed the handles together and the ring stretched out. 'You open up the ring and then you put it over the lamb's... you know, its bits.'

Neil shook his head. 'Nope.'

'Oh.' Sebastian frowned. He'd been almost certain he was right. 'What then?'

'*I* don't do anything,' said Neil, the corners of his moustache turning up in a grin. '*You're* the one who's going to ring his balls.'

Ten minutes later, Sebastian emerged unsteadily from the barn. His wobbly legs were due less to tiredness that to the trauma of the rings. The first had gone quite smoothly, once Neil had cajoled him into doing it, and having squeezed the handles to stretch open the ring, he had slipped it over the small, fluffy pouch that hung between the lamb's hind legs and let go, leaving the ring firmly in place. The second lamb, however, had jerked at the vital moment, and the ring ended up trapping only a single testicle. Although the creature showed no discomfort, just the thought of it was enough to make Sebastian weak at the knees, much to Neil's amusement.

'Should've brought the scissors, after all,' he said, easing the applicator from Sebastian's limp fingers and finishing off the job. 'There we go, all done.'

'And… what? The rings cut off the blood supply and they just shrivel up?'

'Exactly,' said Neil, setting the lamb back down and watching it skip away with the others as though nothing had happened. 'They'll just slough off in a week or so.'

Sebastian tried not to think about the phrase "slough off" as they made their way back to the house, walking with his feet wide apart to ensure he didn't accidentally cut off his *own* blood supply.

Virginia was busy loading the last of her containers into the back of the Landrover. She turned to look at them as they walked up the drive, her eyebrows raised at Sebastian's curious gait.

'All okay?' she asked.

'Except for one little balls up,' said Neil, chuckling. 'You all set, love?'

'Ready to go! Have you got everything Sebastian?' Uncertain what "everything" might be required for going to the market, Sebastian shrugged and made for the passenger door. As he opened it, he paused as he considered grabbing his mobile from upstairs, but couldn't face the stream of text and email messages that were no doubt queuing up for his virtual attention, so he climbed into the front seat of the car, being careful not to sit in a way that might cause any intimate constriction. 'Grab this, would you?' said Virginia, dumping a large box on his lap, heedless of the possible damage that might be caused to his future child-producing prospects. 'Right, let's get to market!'

Sebastian was not a complete stranger to farmers markets, or at least *one* in particular, tucked away in a car park behind Notting Hill Gate tube station. He'd stumbled across the market by accident one Saturday morning and though he preferred his food in pre-sealed packaging, complete with lists of ingredients and the security of brand names, rather than dished out to order and wrapped in brown paper, he had returned on a number of occasions simply to enjoy the busy atmosphere and the quaint feel of the place, rather than to buy any of the produce on offer. And after five longs days in the isolation of Steepleford, he was looking forward to getting out in public again and soaking up the busy surroundings and the jostling of the crowds.

'Well, you look happy,' said Virginia as she steered the Landrover along the road to Barnstaple. 'Anything to do with your "late night visitor"?'

'Eh?' Sebastian blinked, confused for a moment. 'Oh. No, nothing to do with that. Honestly. Just thinking about the market, that's all.'

Virginia raised disbelieving eyebrows, but didn't comment and they lapsed back into silence, each lost in their own thoughts. Sebastian was only slightly peeved that his were now focussed on Emma. Emma in her lace nightclothes and, though he hadn't seen what lay beneath, his mind was happy to furnish him with various suggestions, some of which were decidedly scanty.

'Sorry what?' he said, vaguely aware that Virginia had spoken and hoping it was nothing to do with the "late night visitor".

'I was just wondering...' she began, but trailed off into what seemed to be a slightly embarrassed silence.

'Yes?' For a moment Sebastian thought she wasn't going to say anything else.

'Well...' she said, pausing again as though uncertain how to continue. 'It's my hair.'

Again the embarrassed silence.

'Yes?' he said again.

'Well, look at it.' Virginia grabbed at a lock of her hair and held it out towards Sebastian, like exhibit A at a murder trial. 'It's awful, ain't it?'

Uncertain how to respond to this Sebastian eventually opted for, 'I wouldn't say that.' He certainly *thought* it, though.

'Well it is. I know it is.' She let go of her hair and turned to look at him. 'A woman's hair is supposed to be the fount of her beauty, but mine's just plain ugly. It looks like it was woven from the hair of a dead camel.'

'Road,' said Sebastian, gesturing out of the window as the Landrover slewed into the right hand lane.

'It's a scratchy, brown cloud,' she continued, eyes back on the road. 'A wiry, dry mess, and I hate it!' Another pause, and this time Sebastian try to fill it with the sound of tapping his fingers on the box that still nestled in his lap. 'Anyway, ever since I noticed all those lotions and stuff-'

'Products.'

'Yes, ever since I noticed the *products* you brought with you, I've wanted to ask if you knew anything that could make my hair less...' She trailed off, clearly searching for the right words.

'Less like a scratchy, brown cloud?' he suggested.

'Exactly!' Virginia turned to look at him, an eager smile on her face. 'There are plenty of shops in Barnstaple.'

'Road,' said Sebastian, pointing again. 'I've got a few ideas. I'll have a look around when we're in town and see what I can do.'

The rest of the journey passed without incident, or accident, and ended in a narrow street by a building which declared itself to be the Pannier Market.

'The market's in there?' asked Sebastian, pointing towards one of the doors that stood at intervals along the wall, its old brickwork reminding him of the view from his window back in London. 'It's *indoors?*'

'Course it is,' she said, opening her door and stepping out into the street. 'Give us a quick hand getting this stuff out, would you?'

The hand in question was not all that quick; Virginia had brought a vast amount of produce with her and it was almost eight o'clock before they had everything set up on the couple of trestle tables that were apparently her weekly area.

'Perfect,' she said, placing the last loaf of bread on the pile and stepping back to survey the stand. 'Just perfect.' Sebastian joined her, looking at the products on offer. In addition to the loaves, sausages and goat cheese that he had helped to make, there were various other cuts of meat, mostly pork and lamb, together with jars of pickle, chutney and other preserves, containers of soups and sauces, eggs of various sizes, pies, cakes and other baked goods, all priced up and ready. He nodded, impressed by both the quantity and variety.

'That's a whole lot of food. How much of it do you reckon you'll sell today?'

'Oh, everything, I should think,' said Virginia.

'All of it?' he asked, turning to look at her in surprise.

She shrugged, as though this was perfectly normal. 'You'll see. Come two o'clock, we'll have nothing left but empty boxes to load back in the car. Here come the hoards,' she added, as the main doors to the market hall burst open and people started spilling in.

No longer needed, Sebastian decided to wander around, looking at the other stalls lined up between the pillars of the long hall, but soon the place was heaving with other people doing just the same. To his surprise, he found the jostling of the crowd and the din of people talking over one another annoying, even oppressive, so he pushed his way between the old ladies shuffling along with their shopping trolleys, the large men pausing in the middle of aisles for no discernible reason and the mums dragging small, unhappy children behind them, back to Virginia's stall.

'I'm off to the shops,' he called, trying to make himself heard over the clamour. 'Going to look out some products for you.'

Virginia, who was holding out a loaded paper bag to one of the old ladies, and taking a five pound note with the other, glanced across at Sebastian and gave him a quick nod.

Once out on the relatively uncrowded street, he took a deep breath, relieved to be out of the crush and noise of the market. It was worse than London in there!

'What do you mean, "Worse than London"?' Virginia asked as they hurtled along the road back to Steepleford. It was only just after two, thanks to her selling the last of her produce earlier than predicted. 'I thought you loved London. "Always something going on," you said, unlike our lifeless, medieval little village.'

'It was all a bit too busy for my liking,' said Sebastian, staring out of the passenger window as the trees and fields swept past. 'Maybe I've just got used to the quiet or something. The town itself was alright, though, and I at least managed to find a few products to help with your "dry, wiry mess".'

As soon as they were back at the farmhouse, Sebastian scurried off up the road to the Village Store, pausing briefly outside to catch his breath before pushing open the door.

'Well, that makes a nice change,' said Emma, as the bell jangled above his head. 'Thought you were going to stand me up again.'

'I told you-' he began, but she cut him off.

'I'm only teasing,' she said, then turned to call into the house. 'I'm off out, mum. Back in a bit.' And without waiting for a reply, she swung the counter up and walked over to Sebastian. 'Beautiful day, isn't it?' she said, as they emerged into the street.

Sebastian, who hadn't really taken any notice of the weather, looked around at the village basking in the afternoon sun. Unseen birds were singing out their demands and bees buzzed industriously around the hanging baskets and wallflowers. A short distance along the road the unmistakable figures of Sid and

Harry were perched on the bench in front of the Green Man, chattering away about something he couldn't quite make out. A few people were on the village green, following around the figure of Mrs Farley, who was gesturing at areas of grass as though conducting the world's dullest sight-seeing tour. It really was a beautiful day; warm, peaceful and so much more pleasant than being jostled around in that noisy market.

'It certainly is,' he said, turning to look at her. He was pleased to see she was wearing a light summer dress again, instead of one of her shapeless frocks.

'Perfect day for it,' she said, taking his hand in hers and pulling him away from the shop.

Sebastian frowned, confused, but allowed her to lead him along the road. 'Perfect day for what?' he asked.

'For taking a dip in the river.'

19
MAN WITH A PLAN

Despite the warmth of the day and the bright sunshine sparkling off the Bray, the water was cold. Ice cold.

'What did you expect?' asked Emma, already knee-deep, her dress gathered up in one hand. 'No colder than the Thames, is it?'

Sebastian, hovering barefoot on the bank after a long struggle to roll the tight legs of his jeans up above his knees, shrugged. 'I wouldn't know. Only people who want to catch some hideous disease go paddling in the Thames. Anyway, I thought we were going to talk about Mac. And your mum.'

'We are. I've got it all planned out, how we're going to get them together.'

'A plan?' said Sebastian

'A plan!' She smiled at him, beckoning him forward with a nod. 'Come on in, I'll tell you.'

'Are we even supposed to be here?' he asked, peering up the hill towards the grassy track that led back to the High Street to see if anyone was around. Through a nearby hedge and the low hanging branches of a weeping willow, he could see the end field of the smallholding, the pigs with their faces buried in the ground, industriously churning up the earth in their desperate search for who knew what. Turning back to the river, he dipped a cautious toe into the swift-flowing water, withdrawing it again almost immediately. It was already numb. 'Aren't your legs freezing?'

'Don't be such a wimp,' said Emma, splashing him with her free hand. 'Get in and prove you're a real man.'

Sebastian stopped in mid-retreat from her watery attack, stunned. That was how this whole thing had started, back on his birthday last Thursday, with his friends accusing him of not being a real man. None of them had believed he would make it through the week. They thought he'd be home by Tuesday. And dead by today! Hadn't he already proved himself? What did he have to do to show everyone he *was* a real man?

'Fine!' he said, and strode out into the river. He strode, rather than copy the dainty tiptoeing action Emma had used to pick her way across, partly because he thought it might counter the chill of the water, but mostly out of bravado. Unfortunately he had misjudged both the speed of the Bray and the fact that its bed consisted mostly of large stones and rocks, many of which were coated with a slimy layer of algae. He wasn't entirely certain, later, if he had stubbed his toe first or slipped, nor did it seem that important. The main event was the elegant pirouette he performed that landed him on his back in the water. The ice-cold, fast-flowing water, full of rocks. At least it wasn't deep, and as he disappeared, thrashing, under the surface, he felt strong hands gripping his shirt, hauling him back to his feet.

'Bloody hell, it's cold!' he said, trying to shout between gritted teeth as he straightened up. He looked at Emma. 'You're surprisingly strong!'

'And don't you forget it,' she said, grinning at him through a curtain of red hair. She flicked it away with a toss of her head. 'Well, I know I said we should go for a *dip* in the river, but I didn't necessarily mean your whole body.'

'Just proving I'm a real man,' said Sebastian, who had started to shiver.

'Huh. A real *idiot*, more like.'

'An idiot?'

'No,' she said. 'A *real* idiot! You need to get yourself dry. Get off!' This last was in response to Sebastian lunging forwards and wrapping his arms around her, his wet shirt pressed against her dress, his hair dripping into her eyes.

'Not so strong now, are you?' he said, though he could tell she wasn't struggling all that hard. 'I can feel myself drying off nicely. You're like a human towel.'

'Nice weather for it,' said a voice behind him and Sebastian almost lost his footing a second time as he jerked away from Emma to look, guiltily, towards the bank. Through his sodden fringe, which had flopped over his eyes, he made out the figure of Jeph, leaning against the weeping willow that stood between his land and the Symeses, eating an apple. 'Whatever *it* might be.'

'We, er... we were just going for a dip,' said Sebastian, gesturing to the water flowing around his knees.

Jeph nodded, chewing on a mouthful of apple. 'I can see that, alright.'

'You don't mind, do you, Jeph?' said Emma, in a tone that suggested she was sure he didn't.

'No. Plenty of river for everyone. Surprised the water ain't a bit on the cold side, though.'

'It is actually,' said Sebastian, who had started shivering again. 'I think I'll probably come out now and try to dry off.'

Jeph tossed his apple core over the hedge, where it was set upon by a couple of young pigs, and pushed himself away from the tree. 'Right you are,' he said. 'I'll leave you two lovebirds to it.'

'We're not lovebirds,' said Sebastian to Jeph's retreating back, and turned to Emma for support.

'Oh, and keep an eye out for Old Geronimo,' Jeph called over his shoulder as he headed up the hill into the village.

'Why does everyone keep calling us lovebirds?' said Sebastian. 'It's so embarrassing.'

'Embarrassed of me, are you?'

'I didn't mean…' he began, but her lopsided smile stopped him. She was teasing him again. 'Shut your face,' he said, and waded back to the shore, his jeans heavy with water.

As they sat by the willow tree, drying slowly in the warm sunshine, Sebastian was struck by how wet Emma's clothes and hair were. After all, he'd only embraced her for a few seconds. He was also surprised at how see-through her dress had become; he'd heard that such things happened when women's clothes got wet, and DeVere had told him about a college party he went to where the girls had lined up to have buckets of water poured over them, but he'd never witnessed it himself. Until now.

'Do you want to hear my plan,' said Emma, 'or are you going to spend the whole afternoon staring at my breasts?'

Sebastian's eye snapped, with a little regret, to her face, where he was met with a *meaningful* look, eyebrows raised, lips in a slight pout. 'Sorry,' he said. 'I was just thinking about something…'

'About Mac and my mother?'

'Good grief, no!' he said, and couldn't help his eyes dropping again for the briefest of moments. Part of him wished her dress would hurry up and dry so it didn't present quite so much of a distraction. 'Let's hear it then, this plan of yours.'

'It's actually quite simple,' said Emma, in the business-like tone she had used on the brewing evening. 'I've booked them a table at the Green Man tomorrow night and have arranged with Donald to get some proper food in for them, instead of his usual rubbish.' Sebastian nodded, remembering the somewhat disheartening menu. And the tagine. 'I thought he'd be a bit put out by the suggestion, but it seems *someone's* got him thinking seriously about improving the place at last.' Emma nudged him with an elbow and Sebastian tried not look at her dress. 'He's been proper busy and even mentioned hiring a part-time chef.'

'Good for him!' said Sebastian. 'But how exactly is this going to work with your mum and Mac? It's all very well booking them a table, but there's no chance of Mac actually asking your mum to dinner. And you said your mum's too old-fashioned to do the asking.'

'That's easy,' said Emma. '*We* do the asking for them.'

'We? Us? You mean, *we* ask them out on a date?' Sebastian pushed his mostly dry, but still floppy fringe out of his face so she could see his confused look. 'How exactly do imagine that's going to work?'

'Beautifully! I'll tell my mum that I saw Mac and he invited her to the Green Man tomorrow night, and you can do the same for Mac. Tell him she gave you the message when you came to see me at the shop or something.'

Sebastian lay back on the grass, staring at the cloudless sky and the willow branches as he considered Emma's proposal. He sensed her copying him, stretching out beside him in the sun, her shoulder brushing against his. 'You really think they'll buy it?' he said at last, after a long pause. 'You think they'll believe that they just suddenly decided to ask each other out?'

'Doesn't matter if they believe it. It just needs to be enough to get them there. They can sort out the rest themselves.'

There was another pause, as he stared upwards, listening to the familiar birdsong, the river as it murmured across the rocks and the gentle sound of Emma's breathing. After the sliver of sleep the previous night, the warm, still air began to lull him into a stupor. The sound of what he assumed was Old Geronimo bellowing from the other side of the field roused him for a moment.

'Worth a shot,' he said, half-turning his head to look at Emma. 'When should we deliver our messages? Now?'

She turned to shake her head at him, and Sebastian noticed the sunlight accentuated her freckles. On the narrow strip of grass between them, she hooked her little finger around his. 'There's no rush, is there?' she said.

Sebastian was almost dry as he pushed open the door of the butcher's and joined the queue of elderly ladies, all of whom took forever ordering tiny quantities of far more products than seemed necessary. He caught Mac's eye, but didn't say anything; he wanted to wait until they were alone.

'And the same to you, Miss Standfield,' said Mac, as the last of the customers headed to the door, her purchases tucked into a basket.

This threw Sebastian for a moment. 'Miss *Standfield?*' he said. 'Any relation to...?' He nodded in the general direction the Village Shop.

'Cousin or something, I believe,' said Mac and started sharpening one of his lethal-looking, long knives. 'And what can I do for you, boy? Come to help with some more butchering?'

'Hardly. Not that I was much of a "help" the other day. Funnily enough, I'm here on behalf of *Mrs* Standfield.' Again, he nodded towards the shop. 'I've got a message for you.'

The knife didn't even pause as it swept across the steel. 'Oh yeah?'

Sebastian cleared his throat, wishing he'd spent more of the last hour working out what to say and less time daydreaming, holding Emma's hand. Now that he was actually here, alone in the shop with this huge man and his knives, it suddenly seemed like a really rubbish plan indeed! 'Yeah,' he said, trying to sound nonchalant and failing miserably. He cleared his throat again, making a sound not entirely dissimilar to that of the knife sharpening. Surely the wretched blade should be done by now. 'So, yeah. Um... I just happened to, you know, pop into the shop just now-'

'Buy anything nice?' asked Mac, laying down the knife before taking up another to sharpen.

'Oh, nothing special. Just browsing.' Breezy, that was the effect Sebastian was going for. Breezy. But he wasn't sure it was working. 'Anyway... er, while I was in there-'

'-browsing-'

'That's right, browsing. While I was in there *browsing*, Mrs Standfield asked if I'd pop in here on my way, you know, back to the farmhouse,' he nodded again, this time in the other direction, 'and ask you, Mac, if you'd... go to the Green Man with her tomorrow night.' This last phrase was blurted out as though it was formed of a single, eleven-syllable word. It was followed by a silence, broken only by the rhythmic scrape of the knife as it slid across the steel.

'What time?' said Mac at last, fixing Sebastian with a narrow-eyed stare.

'Sorry?'

'What time did she ask to meet me at the Green Man?'

'Seven-thirty?' said Sebastian, wishing it didn't sound so much like a question.

'Right.' Again the silence and the swishing knife, though it was a different knife this time, a short one with a wickedly thin blade.

Sebastian cleared his throat again. 'Well?'

Mac laid down the knife and the steel, and started untying his apron. 'Guess I'd better go and deliver my answer.'

'You can't!' said Sebastian, panicking. 'I mean, you don't need to. You've got your shop to look after, customers to serve.' He gestured to the empty shop, knocking one of the dangling birds with the back of his hand. 'I've got to nip back to the shop, anyway. I forgot... to get more gloves. I'll pass on any message to Mrs Standfield.'

'Alright,' said Mac, tying up his apron again. 'But it'll need to be more like eight, as I've got to supervise the hog roast at tomorrow's fayre and I'll need time to get ready.'

'Sure!' Sebastian turned to leave.

'One other thing…'

Sebastian stopped, his hand on the door handle. 'Yes?'

This time it was Mac's turn to clear his throat and Sebastian turned to see him looking sheepish again, as he had when trying to explain why he was skulking in the dark on Monday night. 'Well, you're clearly a man who knows how to present himself for this sort of thing, you know, what to wear and that.' He flapped a hand to indicate Sebastian's clothes, despite the fact neither they nor he were looking that presentable at the moment. 'So, er, I was just wondering if you'd be free maybe to give me a hand getting ready… if it's not too much trouble, of course?'

'Mac,' said Sebastian, smiling with relief, 'I'd be honoured.'

He almost skipped up the road the Village Store, though he held himself back for the sake of his "real man" image. Catching sight of him through the window, Emma hurried out to meet him, shutting the door and the sound of the bell behind her.

'Well?' she asked, and Sebastian was mildly disappointed to see her dress was completely dry. Unlike his underwear.

'He bought it!' he said. 'But he can't make it until eight o'clock, because he's doing the hog roast at the fayre.'

Emma frowned. 'What do you mean "until" eight o'clock? That's the time we agreed on them meeting anyway.'

Sebastian, who had clearly drifted off when that was being explained, shrugged. 'Exactly,' he said. 'So that's all sorted. And your mum's on board?'

'She'll be there.'

'Good.' He flicked his fringe out of his face and smiled at her. She was looking slightly cross again and he decided he quite liked her that way. 'I feel good about this. I guess it wasn't such a bad plan after all. And now, I need to get changed into some dry clothes before Neil drags me off to feed the animals, or whatever delights he's got in store this evening.'

'You mean you don't know?' asked Emma, smiling in a way that caused Sebastian's mood to deflate somewhat.

'Of course I don't know. No one tells me anything. Care to enlighten me?'

The smile grew larger. 'Not afraid of needles are you?'

'There's no way I'm doing that!' said Sebastian, shaking his head at the syringe in Neil's hand. 'No flipping way.' He was hanging onto the side of a livestock trailer, which was almost filled with the vast bulk of Major Tom. It had taken them roughly twenty minutes - an amount of time Sebastian didn't want to think of in association with this particular pig - to coax him into the trailer, and now that they had him all boxed up, Neil had produced a hypodermic and a bottle of worming medication from his pocket and presented them to Sebastian.

'What's up, lad?' asked Neil, turning the syringe point upwards and flicking it in much the way they do on television. He pushed gently on the plunger and a brief jet of liquid spurted out of the end. 'Anyone'd think I was asking you to inject yourself. This is for the Major's benefit. You wouldn't want all those nasty tapeworms eating him up from the inside now, would you?'

'Well, no…' said Sebastian, unable to tear his eyes away from the syringe. 'I'm just not great with needles, that's all.'

'Ah, there's nothing to it. You just grip it in your fist and punch it down into the Major's backside. Once it's in, just push down the plunger and pull it out. Job done.'

Sebastian frowned at Neil, unsurprised to see him grinning from behind his moustache. 'If it's so simple, why don't you do it yourself?'

'You didn't come all this way just to watch me do everything, did you?'

'I wouldn't have come all this way at all if I knew I'd have to inject a huge pig in the arse! That said, most of the stuff I've done this week has been pretty grim - killing chickens, butchering pigs, putting elastic bands round lambs' testicles. I've done quite well, really, wouldn't you say?'

Neil reached across the trailer and patted Sebastian on the shoulder with his non-syringe-holding hand. 'I think you've done amazing, lad,' he said. 'I barely recognises you as the primped up dandy I collected from the station last week.'

Sebastian allowed himself a smile. 'More rugged, would you say? More manly?'

'More bloody messy,' said Neil. 'But I reckon you've proved yourself, right enough.'

'So there's no need for me to do this injecting thing, is there?'

In response, Neil held out the needle. 'Nice try,' he said as the pleased expression slipped from Sebastian's face. 'Won't take half a mo. And then you can add it to your impressive list of accomplishments.'

Sebastian sighed, knowing he wasn't going to get away without doing it. 'Alright!' he said and snatched the syringe out of Neil's hand, being careful not to jab himself.

'That's it, lad. Grip it in your fist and ram it into him. Got to do it hard and fast, mind, otherwise…' He stopped, looking down at Major Tom's backside. 'Otherwise *that'll* happen.'

Sebastian, who had screwed his eyes shut as he attempted to perform the injection, looked down to see the needle bending outwards, its point stuck on the pig's thick, hairy skin. He withdrew it enough to allow the needle to straighten and tried a second time. Again, the metal bowed as the point failed to pierce the skin. 'This is ridiculous,' he said, pulling back his hand. 'It's like trying to thread cotton through a brick. I can't do it.' He held out the syringe to Neil, but he pushed his hand away.

'Try like I said. Grip it.' He balled up one massive fist. 'Ram it into him.' He brought his fist down hard on the side of the trailer. 'And push down the plunger with your thumb.' He mimed the action, then opened his hand to Sebastian. 'Your go.'

Taking a deep breath and trying not to imagine the needle snapping off in Major Tom's rump, Sebastian gripped the syringe as tight as he could in his not-quite-so-massive fist and slammed it down onto the pig. There was a muffled squeal as the creature registered the blow, but it made no attempt to pull away.

'Plunger!' said Neil, miming again, and Sebastian forced his thumb down.

'It's not moving,' he said. 'It's stuck or something.'

'No, no. That's perfectly normal. Takes a fair bit of pressure to force the medicine into the muscle. It'll go. Just keep pushing.'

Slowly, so slowly that it defied observation, the plunger sank into the body of the syringe until, just as Sebastian felt as though his thumb was going to give up, it touched the bottom. He yanked out the needle and staggered away from the trailer, his knees shaking from the effort of the procedure. By the fence behind him was a large log, slowly being consumed by brambles, and he sat on it, wiping the thin sheen of sweat from his forehead.

'See?' said Neil, thumping him on the shoulder. 'Nothing to it, lad. You'll soon get into your stride.'

Sebastian smiled weakly up at him, then frowned. '"Get into my stride"?' he said. 'What's that supposed to mean?'

Neil gestured towards the other enclosures. 'It means there's all the girls to do yet.'

PREPARATIONS

The farmhouse was deserted by the time Sebastian surfaced on Friday morning, though he found another scribbled note on the kitchen table, informing him his hosts were "pimping for the fags", which he eventually worked out actually said "preparing for the fayre", and asking him to join Neil at ten-thirty for what probably said "pig feeding". He turned to look at the living room clock. It was almost ten already.

After an uneventful visit to the chicken run, he wandered up to the Village Store to deliver the eggs.

'Good morning, Mrs Standfield,' he said as he nudged the door closed behind him, slightly disappointed to find her there instead of Emma.

Mrs Standfield glanced up from the stack of paper bags she was arranging on the counter. 'So you're always telling me,' she said. 'Though there's precious little of it left now.'

'Only twelve eggs today,' he said, as he placed the boxes on the counter. He glanced over her shoulder to peer into the corridor of the house beyond, but couldn't make out anything moving.

Mrs Standfield caught his eye. 'Emma's out. Helping get things ready over on the green.'

'Really?' said Sebastian, going for nonchalant and breezy again.

'I'm not in the habit of lying, young man!'

'Sorry,' said Sebastian, then noticed she was smiling. He shook his head. 'So *that's* where Emma gets it from.'

Over the road, the village green was alive with activity, not quite on the scale of Covent Garden or Hyde Park, but it was still an impressive change from previous days that week. As he crossed the road, he was met by Donald wandering over from the pub. Sebastian was not entirely surprised to see him still wearing his slippers.

'Ah!' said Donald, catching sight of him. 'And how are we today, young Sebastian? Looking forward to the village fayre? It's pretty much the only thing what drags people out of their homes around here. Some from as far away as Chittlehamholt and Bratton Fleming. Couple of years back there was a whole family came all the way from Withypool. Ever been to Withypool?' Sebastian opened his mouth, not to answer, since it had to be a rhetorical question, but to ask if Donald was just making these places up. The landlord, however, barely paused for breath. 'Funny place, Withypool. A little mess of buildings clustered together out in the middle of nowhere. Not my sort of thing at all.' Sebastian, who thought the description could well have applied to Steepleford, just nodded. 'But I guess people have got to live somewhere, and I take my hat off to them for coming all the way here for our little fayre, since most of the people here,' he frowned back at the village green, 'can't even be bothered to drag themselves as far as the village pub, what's right on their doorsteps, the lazy bast-'

'So how're things going at the Green Man?' Sebastian broke in, mindful of the time. 'I hear you're making a few changes.'

'You bet I am,' said Donald, his frown dissolving as he puffed out his chest. 'Trying out a new chef this evening, following your excellent suggestion. Got a table booked for an *anonymous* couple,' he tapped his nose in a way Sebastian couldn't quite interpret, 'so I'm going to test his cooking on them. Not only that, my lad, but I went to the decorating shop up Barnstaple yesterday morning and spent the rest of the day sprucing the place up, with a little help from the vicar. Sid's grandson does something to do with computers in Exeter and is going to help sort out a...' he looked down at the ground, clearly trying to remember something, 'a worldwide webpage, er... site. And the pair of them, Sid *and* Harry, have been advising me on what real ales I should get in.'

Sebastian smiled at the thought of Sid and Harry offering a rambling stream of confusing and no doubt conflicting advice to Donald. He almost felt sorry for him. 'Sounds like they're being helpful!' he said.

Donald rolled his eyes. 'To be honest with you, they're being a bit *too* helpful. They keep following me around offering their suggestions and arguing with each other about what I should be doing. But I'd rather have them that way than whining away all the time about how the Green Man ain't what it used to be when my father ran it. Anyways, don't mean to keep you. I'm sure you've got better things to do that stand around listening to my ramblings and I'd better get back and change into my shoes before someone accuses me of being a crazy, what with wandering around the streets in my slippers.' And with that he turned on his slippered heel and stalked back towards the pub, leaving Sebastian in the middle of the road, watching the villagers busy with their preparations on the green.

Around the edges of the field, wooden trestle tables were being loaded up with cakes, books, bottles and other items, and in between these stood various activities, most of which Sebastian didn't recognise, though he could make out the clear shapes of coconuts perched on metal poles. There was no obvious sign of Emma, but Virginia was there, stacking jars of preserves and chatting with a number of ladies he thought he recalled peering out beneath the driers in the Head Mistress. Mac was there too, standing next to a smouldering fire over which a pig was turning slowly on a spit. The vicar was tapping at a microphone on a half-erected stage, and Mrs Farley was running around with a clipboard and a worried expression on her face. In the middle of the green there was a roped off area around which people were positioning bales of straw and a small man was leaning against a Punch and Judy tent, smoking on a pipe. In the morning sunlight the scene looked to Sebastian like something out of a period drama or one of those murder mysteries shows that are set in idyllic villages full of psychotic killers and interwoven grudges.

He glanced at his watch and sighed. He was going to be late.

'You're late,' said Neil as Sebastian hurried along the path towards the pig runs. 'Think you're ready to face these little lovelies again?'

Sebastian eyed the seething mass of piglets with suspicion. He hadn't entered this enclosure since his first morning in Steepleford, and he remembered only too clearly the desperate scrambling through their toilet area and the shock of that electric wire. 'Possibly,' he said, touching his cheek at the memory.

'Good. Here's the food.' Neil tossed a sack to him, but Sebastian fumbled the catch, spilling a few pig nuts into his boots. He carefully tipped them out before venturing into the enclosure, just in case. 'Remember,' said Neil as he marched up through the trees to fill the water trough, 'chuck a handful of food to keep them occupied, then dump the rest and back away.'

Sebastian, who didn't really need the reminder, scooped up some of the pig nuts in his hand and tossed it into the far corner of the run. Immediately the piglets scurried over to the food so he seized the opportunity and upended the sack. The food had barely struck the muddy ground, before the sea of piglets swarmed over, leaving two of the more stubborn ones behind. By this time, Sebastian had retreated uphill, leaning against the large pig house as he watched the piglets jostling and squealing in their frenzied search for food.

'Probably not the best place to stand,' called Neil, and something about the tone of his voice made the little hairs bristle on the back of Sebastian's neck.

'What is it?' he asked, glancing round. 'And where's Lucy?' Even as he spoke the words, he knew what the answer was. And a nudge in the back of his thigh confirmed it. Lucy, the monster mother of these sixteen piglets, was in the house. And she wanted to get out.

Sebastian, who had been admirably cool up to this point, launched himself from the pig house, where Lucy's enormous, wrinkled face was pushing its way out, and scurried down the hill in a curious series of hops, slides and twists, like a drawn-out collapse, though somehow he managed to stay on his feet this time.

'Back in their toilet area, then?' said Neil, picking his way down the muddy slope. 'It's like a magnet to you, ain't it? Here you go,' he added, handing Sebastian his empty bucket. 'You can do the water from now on. You never know, you might survive the week yet.'

Together they fed and watered the remaining pigs, before turning their attention to the poultry, the goats, the horses and, after scrambling up a steep, half-hidden path, the sheep, all without incident, except for Amy the goat having a nibble on the back of Sebastian's jacket. And the horses terrifying him in the usual way.

It was just after midday when they entered the farmhouse to get lunch. It was strange to find the kitchen lacking Virginia's presence, but she had left two sandwiches for them in the fridge, together with a plate of ham, a few small tomatoes, half an apple pie, and a bottle of beer each.

'She's a good lass, my Virg,' said Neil, settling himself down at the table and gripping his sandwich in one, massive hand. He snatched up a tomato with the other, which he held out to Sebastian. 'See this little beauty? Surprising to see one so ripe this early in the season, eh?' Sebastian, who had assumed you could get any vegetable at any time of the year, opted for a quick raising of his eyebrows. 'We grow them in the greenhouse, out behind the chickens. Amazing what a bit of glass can do. Even on a winter's day it's warm in there if the sun's out; you can pick these straight from the source. The *tomato* source!' He nudged Sebastian, causing him to drop the small, red fruit he'd just plucked from the bowl.

Ignoring the attempt at humour, Sebastian picked it up again. 'So you grew these here?'

'Yes indeed. Nothing like picking something you've grown and eating it while it's fresh - from ground to gob.'

'Once, when I was a kid,' said Sebastian, smiling at the memory, 'my mum took me to a farm shop, somewhere near Croydon, and we did that with strawberries. Pick your own, they called it.'

Neil frowned. '"Pick your own"? Sounds more like "pick someone else's" to me.' He popped the tomato in his mouth, sighing with pleasure. 'Beautiful! Once we've finished this, I'm going to head over to the village green and give Virg a hand. Want to join me?'

'Sure,' said Sebastian. 'Though I need to get some packing done before the fayre. Might not be much time later.'

Neil nodded, chewing his mouthful. 'No worries,' he said. 'Doesn't kick off til two, anyways.'

When two o'clock arrived, however, Sebastian's case was far from packed. He was caught in a dilemma between wanting to get it all done, yet also needing to leave out anything he might need tonight or tomorrow morning. Also, he couldn't find a bag to put in his dirty laundry so as to keep it separate from the few clean clothes that remained.

In truth, though, he had failed to get packed because he didn't really want to do it, as if the act of preparing to leave somehow hastened his departure, and he wanted to delay it as long as possible. He didn't want to leave this new world he had found, this *old* world, where the days seemed to move more slowly, where life was, if not more relaxed, at least more experienced. Here there was time - time to stop, time to think, time to learn, time to listen, time to look and not feel rushed at every moment, shifting from one inconsequential activity to the next without real thought, without real purpose and ultimately without real meaning. *That* was the difference. Here life really mattered; the things people did and said, even thought, were of worth. Back in London there was the semblance of life in that it was always busy, always moving, always active, but in truth it was not life, not *real* life. It was more about using up life, about forcing yourself from day to day, month to month, year to year until, at last, that meaningless, empty existence would come to an end and you could simply vanish and be forgotten, your life used up and discarded like a spent match that never really strikes. In London there was no time to stand and stare, because the system wouldn't let you, not in the city that never slept and was never still.

'I don't want to go back,' he muttered, folding a shirt that he had already folded three times in the last hour. 'Not yet.'

A tap at his door made him look up and he was surprised to hear Emma's voice from the landing. 'You decent?'

'Depends what you mean exactly,' he said, jumping to his feet as the door swung open, revealing Emma wearing her usual shapeless shop dress.

'I meant, are you naked, of course, but I can see you're not. That window needs fixing, by the way.' Sebastian turned to look at the still-broken pane, but didn't have a chance to comment. 'So, are you coming to the fayre or what? It's started already.' She peered round him at the half-packed case lying open on the bed. 'Oh,' she said, and a cloud passed briefly across her face. 'Getting ready to leave?'

Sebastian nodded and edged back to the bed. 'Afraid so,' he said, snatching up the clothes that lay in various stages of folded-ness on the sheets, and chucking them into the case. 'My train leaves at ten tomorrow morning, so I thought I'd get packed. Won't take me a second.'

'Is this all yours?' asked Emma, picking up one of the containers from the shelf above the sink. 'What's body butter, exactly?'

'It's for super-moisturising your body,' said Sebastian, hurrying over to prise it from her grip and toss it into the case. She gave him an uncomprehending look. 'It doesn't matter. It's just some boring product. I hardly use any of these things,' he added as he swept the other jars and bottles in with the rest of his luggage.

'Why do you have them then?'

'Well...' he began. 'I... What about you? There must be things you have that you rarely use. What about... what about a pizza slicer? Do you have one of those?'

'Of course.'

'And I bet you almost never use it, do you? Even when you have to slice an actual pizza, I bet you forget about it and use a knife. And yet you keep that pizza slicer, just in case.'

Emma pulled a face. 'I guess so, but I don't take it away with me when I go on holiday!'

'Funny,' said Sebastian, pausing in his case stuffing as he sought to change the subject, 'I can't really imagine you on holiday.' This was in fact completely untrue, and he had to quickly continue with his packing in an effort to distract himself from the mental image of Emma stretched out on a tropical beach, the sun drawing out her freckles, the warm sea air caressing her smooth... He cleared his throat. 'What sort of places do you go?' he asked, his voice a croak.

'Can't really remember the last time I went on holiday.'

'Why's that? Too drunk?'

'Haven't had the chance to go away,' she said, ignoring him, 'what with helping mum look after the shop. I'd love to, though, and I keep meaning to, but it never quite seems to happen.' She bent down and picked up a pair of boxer short that had been half-hidden under the bed. 'These yours?'

'No,' said Sebastian, but they both knew he was lying, so he snatched them and shoved them deep into the contents of his case. 'Right. I reckon I'm about done with this. Shall we go?'

She nodded and he followed her downstairs to the backdoor and began pulling on his shoes.

'Silly me!' said Emma. 'I've left my purse upstairs. Won't be a minute.' And she headed back into the house, returning a short while later waving a small, red purse at him. 'Found it. Let's go and have some fun, shall we?'

And together they set out for the village green and the Standfield fayre.

21
LOVE GAMES

Neil gripped the hammer in one hand, testing the balance, his eyes fixed on Sebastian.

'Right, lad,' he said, as the head dropped into his palm once, twice. 'This is it!' He raised the weapon above his shoulder, pausing for a moment, then brought it crashing down. The chime of the bell rang out above the sounds of the fayre and there was an appreciative applause from those looking on. 'Come on, then. Give it a shot,' said Neil, holding out the long shaft of the hammer to Sebastian.

'No, no,' he said, holding up his hands as if to fend it off. 'It's not my sort of thing.'

'Not your sort of thing?' Neil gave him a look that suggested this was a ridiculous statement. 'Don't be ridiculous. Just give it a good whack. I'm sure you can ring that bell, no problem.'

'Yes, go on,' said Emma, who was nibbling a cloud of candyfloss in a curiously alluring way. 'You don't have to do it one-handed like Mr Show-off here.'

'I thank you,' said Neil, with a slight bow, still holding out the hammer.

Sebastian hesitated, battling with himself between not wanting to look like a coward for refusing and not wanting to look like an idiot for being rubbish at it. 'Alright,' he said at last and took the proffered the handle. Neil released his grip and the weight of the hammer's wooden head caught him by surprise. It dropped to the floor, just missing Neil's foot, and caused Sebastian to stumble forwards.

'Not a *great* start,' said Emma.

'Just messing,' he lied, and hefted up the hammer, shifting round to face his target, a small wooden cylinder that protruded from the base of what looked like a large thermometer, topped off with a bell. At various intervals up the thermometer's length there were words to describe those who managed to get the red puck up to the corresponding height, from 'Useless' at the bottom all the way up to 'Hercules', which was written on the bell itself. Sebastian hoped he could at least get past 'Weakling'.

'Right,' he said, gearing himself up as he raised the wooden head ready to strike. He paused for a moment, narrowed his eyes as he focussed on his target, then brought the hammer down as hard as he could.

The bell did not ring. The red marker did not move. There was no applause.

'Call it a practice swing,' said Neil, helping Sebastian yank the hammer's head out of the grass where it had half-buried itself. Sebastian's eyes flicked across to Emma, who was watching him over the top of her candyfloss. She winked in a way that he didn't find especially helpful. Distracting, yes, but not helpful.

He raised the hammer again, repositioning himself to make sure of his target this time, then slammed it down. The red puck leapt from its home at the bottom of the thermometer, shuttling up to just past the halfway mark.

'Not bad!' said Neil, joining in the smattering of applause, and read the corresponding label. '"Could Do Better". Guess it could be right... Want to give it another shot?'

Sebastian leant the hammer against the thermometer. 'Absolutely not!'

He and Emma headed off around the stalls and activities. Next there was a circle of trestle tables covered with what looked like piles of charity shop rejects, from tasselled lampshades and porcelain dogs to biscuit jars and an ancient VHS recorder, complete with its book-size remote control. Sebastian even spotted a pink My Little Pony comb and was half-tempted to buy it, as he hadn't seen the remains of his since the shooting session. But only half-tempted. Nearby, children were gathered around a lucky dip where, for only fifty pence, they were guaranteed of winning a prize worth at least five, and beyond them an old man with a disturbingly red nose and eyes veiled beneath bushy brows peered between a mountain of greenery and tried to sell Sebastian a tray of runner bean plants for his non-existent garden.

One of the strangest attractions was a fenced enclosure in one corner of the green, in which gridlines had been painted across the grass. In the middle of this the largest and most ferocious-looking monster he had seen all week - even more intimidating than the horses - stood immobile, idly chewing on something unseen; probably a passing dog, Sebastian thought, or a stray child. A sign on one of the fence panels declared, "Guess The Mess! Where Will The Cowpat Fall?" A young lad Sebastian hadn't seen before had his work cut out taking people's bets, and around the enclosure, a number of middle-aged men were trying to coax the bull towards them, no doubt in an attempt to move his back end over their chosen square.

'Is that Jeph's bull? Geronimo?' asked Sebastian,

watching as the creature continued to chew contentedly, completely unfazed by all the attention.

Emma nodded. 'That's right. Last minute substitute for the pony ride.'

They continued their round of the green, with Sebastian trying to avoid taking part in anything he might look stupid at, which as far as he was concerned meant everything, and with Emma trying to talk him into having a go. He almost tried his hand at the coconut shy, but when he saw a girl of about six knock one off with her first throw, he changed his mind. The wellie throwing was definitely out as burly farmer-looking types queued up to flick them far into the distance with barely any discernible effort. The crockery smashing was another throwing game that required aiming skills which Sebastian was fairly sure he didn't have, and though he was tempted by the skittles, there was quite a crowd gathered around, who seemed to be taking it far more seriously than was necessary.

'What's this thing?' he asked, pointing to where an elderly lady was clutching a bundle of what looked like lengths of firewood. As he watched, she drew out one of the sticks and tossed it at a wooden doll that was perched, a short distance away, on top of a long pole.

Emma, who was busy opening her tombola tickets, glanced across. 'That's Aunt Sally.'

'I meant, what game is she playing,' said Sebastian. 'Oh, you've won something,' he added, pointing at the ticket she had just opened, number 245.

'Thank goodness you're here,' she said, her words laced with sarcasm, and handed the ticket to the woman behind the stall. 'And the *game* is Aunt Sally. You should definitely have a go. It's very traditional.'

When she had finished with the tickets and received her prizes, a bottle of red wine and, to her amused delight, a tub of body butter, they wandered across to the Aunt Sally as the old lady, who probably wasn't called Sally, took her last couple of throws, missing the target altogether with the first, but managing to knock the whole structure down with the second.

'Oh, well done,' said Sebastian, nodding his encouragement.

'You're not supposed to knock it *all* down,' whispered Emma, disconcertingly close to his ear.

He stopped nodding and whispered back, 'How was I supposed to know? Unlucky,' he said out loud, but the lady just ignored him and shuffled off towards the tea tent, no doubt to drown her misery in caffeine. 'So what are the rules, then?'

'Glad you asked,' said Jeph, emerging from the wings to gather up the sticks. 'All you has to do is knock off the Aunt Sally, *without* toppling her pole as well.' He ambled up to Sebastian and dumped the five sticks into his arms. Sebastian wasn't ready, however, and a couple of them dropped to the floor. 'Should I count them as throws?' asked Jeph.

'What?' said Sebastian, bending to pick them up. 'I didn't mean I wanted a go, I was just asking-'

'All you've got to do is knock her off three times,' Jeff interrupted, ignoring him and pointing to the Aunt Sally, 'and you'll get double your money back.'

'But I haven't even given you any money.'

Jeff smiled. 'Quite right. That'll be one pound, please.' Sebastian, who wasn't entirely sure how he'd ended up in this situation, scrabbled in his pocket for some change, eventually fishing out a bundle of coins from which Jeff pecked out three twenties, a couple of tens and some fives, tutting his disapproval as he did so.

Sebastian shrugged. 'Sorry about all the small change.'

'This should be interesting,' said a voice behind them, and Sebastian turned to see Sid and Harry approaching, each gripping a pint of what looked like real ale.

'You ever played before?' asked Harry. Sebastian gave him what he hoped was a withering look. 'Something wrong with your eyes, boy?'

'Shh,' said Sebastian, 'I need to concentrate.' He lined himself up in front of the Aunt Sally. Teasing one of the sticks out from under his arm, he hefted it in his hand, trying to work out if he should throw it horizontally as if rolling it through the air, or vertically like a knife. He opted for the latter, chucking the stick in a high arc, sending it spinning towards the target.

'Wow!' said Emma, as the stick caught the doll in the head, knocking her cleanly from her perch. 'That was amazing! Do it again.'

Sebastian took out the next stick and threw it in much the same way, and again Aunt Sally toppled, leaving the pole still standing. Emma tried to join in the applause from the small crowd that was watching, but it was hard while clutching her tombola winnings. Sebastian, surprised that neither Sid nor Harry had made a comment about 'beginner's luck', turned to see them staring at him, mouths open.

'Beginner's luck!' said Jeph, wandering over to place the doll back on her pole.

'It's got to be,' Harry agreed, shaking his head. 'Takes years to master the Aunt Sally, don't it, Sid?

Years.'

'Course it does, Harry. Remember old Nobby Clarke, what lived behind the forge? He had is own Aunt Sally and everything, all set up in the backyard and there was barely an evening except you'd find him _'

'I'm sure it's a fascinating story,' Sebastian interrupted, 'but could it wait til I've taken my shot?' The old men fell into a sullen silence and he turned back to the game, drawing out another stick. He took aim and threw, hitting the doll, but catching the pole at the same time.

'Unlucky,' said Jeff, grinning from the wings. 'Only two more left.'

Sebastian took the fourth stick, deciding to have a go at throwing it underarm instead. It didn't work, the stick sailed past, missing its target by several inches.

'Guess you was right,' said Sid. 'Beginner's luck was all.' He lapsed back into silence at a look from Emma.

'Come on,' she said, giving Sebastian another of those unhelpful winks. 'You can do it.'

Sebastian took the last stick in his right hand, deciding to revert to the overarm, knife throw, though it suddenly seemed like an impossible task - the doll was so far away and so easily missed and the pole so easily caught. As Harry had said, it must take years to master. 'Here goes,' he said, and tossed the stick. Everyone held their breath as it turned over and over in the air, whirling towards both Aunt Sally and her pole. Sebastian was certain it was going to knock them both down, but somehow the spin caught the doll at just the right moment, sending her tumbling to the floor once more. The edge of the stick, however, brushed against the pole and it teetered on its plinth. 'Nooooo…' said Sebastian, the word coming out like a long groan through gritted teeth, but just as it seemed about to topple, the pole began to right itself again, eventually coming to rest still standing upright.

'Well done!' said Emma, as the crowd of onlookers burst into applause. 'You did it!'

Sebastian turned to Sid and Harry, unable to suppress a grin of satisfaction. They were both wearing their stunned expressions again.

'That,' said Harry, 'was bloody amazing.' And took a swig of his beer.

'Amazing,' echoed Sid. 'Are you sure you've never done this before, boy?'

'Never. I'm as surprised as you are. I've never won anything before in my whole life!'

'Must be your lucky day,' said Jeff, looking slightly put out. 'Here's your winnings.' Sebastian held out a hand and Jeff dropped a pile of silver coins into it. 'Two pounds. Sorry about all the small change.'

A short while later, Sebastian and Emma emerged from the tea tent, each carrying a steaming mug of tea and a plate of scones lavished in jam and clotted cream, and headed to the straw bales that ringed the central area of the green. The Punch and Judy show was drawing to a close, with the eponymous baddie getting his comeuppance for assaulting not only the devil, a clown and a crocodile, all of which surely deserved it, but also his wife, a policeman and his own infant son.

'Should all these children really be watching this?' asked Sebastian, as Punch took a bow and flounced off with his string of "saus-um-ages". 'It doesn't seem entirely appropriate.'

'Oh, the kids love it,' said Emma, nudging him towards a free bale.

Sebastian sat down, frowning. 'I'm not sure that's a relevant answer.'

Emma smiled. 'You think *that's* odd? Just you wait for the Morris dancers.' A scream of feedback rippled across the green, killing conversations and drawing all eyes, including theirs, to roped-off area, where Vic was fiddling with the microphone. He tapped at it before announcing, to the accompaniment of further feedback, that the dancers in question would be performing in a matter of minutes, so would people please gather around the central arena.

'Arena?' said Sebastian, nodding at the roped-off area, his hands filled with the various components of his cream tea. 'Bit of a grand title, isn't it?'

Emma shushed him. 'Here they come.' She pointed with her scone in the direction of the church. Sure enough, a troupe of thirteen men and women were heading across the grass, three bearing instruments, the rest kitted out with an assortment of tassels, bells, handkerchiefs and sticks. They all wore knee-length socks and their faces had been painted to match their green and red patchwork attire. Some of them had hats.

'Look at these jokers!' Sebastian grinned at her. 'They actually do look like jokers - from some creepy deck of cards.' Emma's mouth was full, so she nudged him in the ribs, which he interpreted as another request for him to shut up.

And even though the Morris dancing was weird, and the combined noise of the accordion and fiddle sounded to Sebastian more like a session at the dentist than a song, he couldn't think of anywhere else he would rather be. He was sitting on a village green next to a girl whose company, and pretty much everything else, he adored, bathed in warm sunlight beneath a bright, blue sky, assailed by the mingled smells of grass, candyfloss and roasting pig, and surrounded by the gentle movement and conversation of people enjoying the fayre. And as he leaned gently against Emma, he would have happily sat there, watching the dancers skipping around smacking their sticks together in vague time with the musicians, forever.

'Have you fainted?' said Emma, nudging at him with her shoulder. Sebastian, who was quite comfortable and was not about to be pushed away so easily, mumbled for her to be quiet and carried on watching the display.

'How're you two lovebirds enjoying the Morris dancing, then?'

'We're not lovebirds!' said Sebastian, jerking upright and turning his scathing look towards Neil, who grinned back at him.

'Something wrong with your eyes, lad?'

'No. And yes, I am enjoying the Morris dancing. Well,' he glanced back at the group whose hopping, skipping and tapping was at last coming to a somewhat jumbled close, '*kind of* enjoying. It is a bit odd though.'

'Odd's right,' said Neil. 'Bunch of weirdoes the lot of them, if you ask me. Wouldn't catch me prancing about like that! Anyways, can't hang around chatting all afternoon. I've got to help out setting up for tonight.' And with that he stomped off across the green towards the stage.

'Did he seem a little anti-Morris dancing to you?' said Sebastian, leaning towards, but not quite against, Emma.

She leaned forwards also, in a conspiratorial

fashion. 'Maybe they turned him down; refused to let him join in, or something. By the way, when you insist we're not "lovebirds", could you try not to sound *quite* so outraged? It is a bit hurtful.'

'It wasn't anything against you!' he said, pulling away in alarm. 'I didn't mean, you know... I'm sure you'd be a wonderful lover, er, lovebird. It's just... I didn't want to assume, I mean, I didn't want *Neil* to assume...' He petered out and resorted to coughing to hide his embarrassment.

Emma smiled, laying a hand on his. 'I know,' she said. 'Just teasing. Anyway, it's getting on for five o'clock and I also have to get ready for this evening. And help my mother get ready to.' She raised her eyebrows suggestively. 'Big night tonight!'

'That reminds me,' said Sebastian, jumping to his feet, the awkwardness vanishing as he stood on tiptoes to peer over at the hog roast. 'I'm supposed to be helping Mac get ready later, too.'

22

MIRROR, MIRROR

Sebastian paused, his fingers on the handle of the butcher's shop door, and peered at his reflected face looking back at him. The bruises were still showing from the late night tent-wrestling, his shooting accident and his drunken head-butting, and they were joined by the beginning of dark rings beneath his eyes. Worse than this his hair looked more like a scruffy dog than the usual not-a-hair-out-of-place artwork. Instinctively, his hand went to his pocket, but it came back combless - maybe he should have bought the pink one, after all, though he wasn't sure it would have made much difference. It simply took too long to sculpt his hair, and since it would no doubt be destroyed mere minutes later just by *being* in Steepleford, it wasn't worth the effort. The scruffy dog look would just have to do.

Letting his fingers slip from the handle, Sebastian side-stepped to look at the whole of himself in the window he had spattered with egg only a few days, and a whole lifetime, ago. The view of his face had given him an idea of what to expect, but he was still surprised by the sight of his clothes and the worn-out shape of his body. He was slouching. Slouching! He pushed back his shoulders in an effort to regain his usual, Alexander-technique-straight frame, and winced at an ache beneath his right shoulder blade.

'What's that all about?' he muttered, reaching

across with his left arm to massage the area in question. He frowned at the sight of his shirt sleeve which, evidently in some unconscious moment of madness, he had rolled up to the elbow. He couldn't even remember doing it. The dirty streaks across his cargo trousers, however, he *could* remember doing, especially the patch of purple spray that had stained them, probably irrevocably, on the night of the lambing.

Slouching shoulders, rolled up sleeves and grubby trousers. What had these people done to him? Even his birthday boots had lost their new-wellie shine and still bore the marks of where the piglets had tried to eat their way through to his flesh. Worse than that, he wasn't especially bothered by how countrified his appearance had become. At least he wasn't until he realised he was starting to look like Neil. At this rate he'd be growing himself a moustache!

He ran his fingers across his stubbled chin. In the butcher's shop window, his reflection shook its head at him.

'You need a mirror,' it said.

In the echoing entrance hall of the vicarage, Neil nodded approvingly at the heads of bison and gazelle, eyeing him glassily from their wooden mounts - relics of past parish incumbents with a good eye, a steady rifle hand and a typically Victorian attitude towards big game conservation. He had been out shooting with the current vicar several times during his three years overseeing the parish and he'd never known him to miss even the most zigzagging of rabbits or twitchy of deer. Neil couldn't work out when Vic practised, but he supposed the man couldn't spend the whole time praying!

He smiled at his recollections and how fortunate Steepleford was to have a man like Vic in the God-seat, even if his preaching did lean more towards the "It's great to be nice to each other" than the usual "Thou shalt not enjoy thyself!" stuff. For some reason Neil felt more comfortable with the fire and brimstone sermons. Still, Vic was one of the good guys, and he certainly tried to practice what he preached, without being too holier-than-thou and making everyone feel bad about themselves. Not like that Mrs Farley, always racing about the place, fussing around at everyone like a Jack Russell trying to herd sheep. He smiled again, imagining Mrs Farley scurrying around his top field on all fours.

Neil was distracted as he caught sight of himself in the vast and garishly ornate mirror that hung next to a list of the previous occupants of the vicarage. He rarely bothered to check how he looked; after all, why should it matter to him? It wasn't him that had to put up with looking at his face. For a moment, he considered himself, quite content with the image that met his gaze.

'Not too ugly today, old boy,' he told himself. 'A bit greyer than I recall.' He ran a hand through his hair, smoothing it back into the style that had graced his head since he was a teenager, then paused, narrowing his eyes as he leaned towards his reflection. He leaned in closer, a frown creasing his forehead. There, nestling just off-centre in his otherwise black moustache, was a single white hair. It had definitely not been there the last time he'd seen his moustache, whenever *that* was. Clearly a long time ago, if the length of the offending hair was anything to go by. 'Let's have you!' said Neil, raising a hand to tear it out. And then stopped, blinking at himself as though waking from a trance. 'It's that lad,' he muttered, 'with his insidious London ways. Start going down that route and you'll end up like some primping pansy.' He peered in again at the stray white hair. Maybe it would be best just to get rid of the wretched thing. His hand still hovered in front of his face, and with a shake of his head he shoved it into his pocket. 'Good God!' he said.

'Did you say something?' asked Vic, appearing from a doorway at the back of the entrance hall. Neil jerked away from the mirror, embarrassed.

'Nothing, Vic,'

'Right. Well, if you come on through, we'll take the beer out through the back way. Quickest route to the green. No, don't worry about the boots,' he added, as Neil bent to heave them off. 'A bit of dirt won't matter. And it'll give me something to do in the morning. Can't spend the whole time praying!'

Upstairs in the Village Store, five middle-aged women fussed around the seated figure of Virginia. Margaret, Verity, Patricia, Beatrix and Constance had been swift to vacate their usual perches beneath the domed dryers at the hair dresser's as soon as they heard about Virginia's desire to surprise her husband with a *new look* at the fayre. Word had arrived through the usual Steepleford channels, an overheard conversation here, some whispered gossip there, though it was not difficult to trace it back to its source, since it was young Emma who had suggested the ladies gathered here and Sebastian's name never seemed far from her lips.

'We should really be doing this in the Head Mistress,' said Verity as she worked away on the back of Virginia's hair. 'It's got all the facilities we could need.'

Virginia raised a hand, causing Beatrix to pause in whatever she was doing with her nails - probably something to do with cuticles or canticles. 'With everyone peering in at me through that huge window? No, thank you.' She lowered her hand. 'This'll do just fine.'

'It's so exciting,' said Margaret, who had spent the previous evening altering a summer dress for Virginia and was even now putting on the finishing touches and checking over the seams. 'I've been dying to do this for years.'

'We *all* have,' added Constance, perching on a stool to Virginia's left, an open magazine on the dresser and an array of eye-liner shades open on her knees. 'Ever since you married your dashing, young beau.' Virginia's eyes widened. She hadn't thought of Neil as either dashing or young for a long time, and probably *never* as a "beau", yet Constance's words reminded her that he still was all those things to her. As they fussed and cooed over her, their excitement at giving her a make-over (as she was trying *not* to think of it) was infectious, and Virginia felt a thrill as she imagined Neil's reaction when he saw her. Oh, he'd attempt to hide it, try to cover his surprise with some off-hand remark, but he could never hide that look in his eye, that little glint that would betray his delight. Even if everyone else fell for his pretence, *she'd* still know.

'I suppose we've got that lodger of yours to thank, have we?' said Patricia, the oldest and most demure of the five. 'The boy from London?'

Virginia considered this, tilting her head slightly, which elicited a tutting from Verity. A week ago, the thought of getting dressed up couldn't have been further from her mind. She'd given up on being a princess years ago, but after seeing all Sebastian's hair, skin and who-knew-what products all lined up in the guest room, it had stirred something in her, awakened a long-forgotten dream.

'I guess so,' she said at last and around her the ladies nodded away to each other as though they'd had bets on this being the case. 'And why not?' she thought, frowning at her reflection as though it was about to challenge her. 'If a man can take such pride in his appearance, why shouldn't I?'

There was the sound of a zip being drawn, and her eyes slid to Margaret's reflection as, behind her, she opened a large carpet bag and began rummaging through its contents.

'I believe you're a size seven,' said Margaret. 'I have some lovely shoes in here that belonged to my Gillian. Much more ladylike than those dirty great boots you go stomping around in.'

In the Green Man, Donald paused, glass halfway to the optic, and caught sight of himself in the large mirror behind the bar, installed two days earlier to add, as Sid and Harry had put it, 'a bit of depth to the ancient dump, and to give customers something to look at other than Donald's ugly mug.' He had to admit the old boys had a point, the mirror really did make the place look bigger. And today, it needed to be. He could hardly believe how many people had not only bought drinks in the pub but also *stayed* inside to drink them. Usually, at the village fayre, everyone headed to the beer tent instead, and even those who made the mistake of heading into the Green Man tended to hurry outside the moment they'd bought their drinks. And didn't come back.

Donald pushed up the glass, producing a brief golden jet of whiskey, and turned to look around his domain. It was only his first day of business after the refurbishments he'd made so far and already he counted twenty-three people in the bar, some sitting at tables and chatting loudly as they sipped at their drinks, others leaning against the bar or peering out of the window at the comings and goings on the green. There was even one couple perusing the menu, giving off definite about-to-order-something vibes. At this rate, he might even be able to cover the cost of the new chef, which admittedly wasn't that much, since he'd found himself a young lad, straight out of college, whose wages were half-covered by Donald letting him live in one of the Green Man's bedrooms; bedrooms which he hoped would soon be the brief homes of guests - real, genuine, paying visitors to Steepleford.

Pulling open a drawer, Donald scrabbled around for a *Reserved* sign and, having dusted it off on a bar towel, hurried over to the table he had mentally set aside for Mac and Mrs Standfield's dinner, and set it down. He made sure it was straight, smiling at the novelty of the thing, before heading back behind the bar.

'Cheers,' he said, snatching up the whiskey and toasting his reflection in the mirror. He knocked it back with a well-practiced flick of his wrist, savouring the burn in the back of his throat.

'Going to stand around serving yourself drinks all evening,' said Harry from the other side of the bar, 'or is there any chance of me and Sid here getting something to sup before we die of thirst.'

'I don't know, Harry,' said Sid, shaking his head in mock-sadness. 'Guess you can't change everything with a bit of paint and a new menu!'

In her bedroom over the shop, Emma stepped out of her unflattering dress and folded it neatly onto her bed. The floorboards creaked in the room next door as her mother got ready for her date with Mac, while the voices of the women fussing away over Virginia drifted from upstairs. She smiled at the unfamiliar sensation of her house being filled with women making themselves beautiful for their men. And she was no exception.

Unhooking the dress that hung on the back of her door, she held it up against her body, smoothing it out as she considered the pattern of small red flowers against the white background. It was short, but not too short - after all, evening's could get quite cold even in May, and she was planning on staying out late tonight.

Her breath caught at the thought and she felt a tingle of excitement mixed with sadness at the idea that it was Sebastian's last night in Steepleford. Tomorrow, the train would sweep him away back to the city, leaving her behind, stuck in this village where nothing ever happened.

She unzipped the dress, tossing the hanger onto her bed, and slipped it on. As she tugged awkwardly at the zip, she shifted across to her dresser, tilting the mirror up to catch as much of her in the reflection as possible. It really was a nice dress, and it fit her well, even if it did show off just a little too much of her spindly arms than she would have liked. And then there were her freckles.

'Stupid brown spots!' she muttered. She'd always hated the way the sun brought out her freckles as though they were dirty, little flowers blossoming across her face. Hopefully Sebastian didn't hate them as much as she did!

She smiled then, as she thought of the letter she'd slipped into his suitcase, of his face when he found it. But that would be tomorrow, and tomorrow was a lifetime away. Tonight was what mattered.

At a sudden thought, she tugged open the top drawer of the dresser and rummaged through various small items of clothing. At the back of the drawer, half-hidden inside a sock, was a long, green ribbon. Her dad had bought it for her many years ago, a gift from a visit to the city when she was seven. 'To go with your beautiful eyes,' he'd told her, as he tied it in her hair before lifting her up onto his shoulders. She smiled at the memory, one of the few clear ones she still had of her dad.

With quick, well-practiced fingers, she gathered up her long, red hair behind her and tied it up with the ribbon, the long, green strands hanging almost to her waist. She stepped back and turned her head slightly in the mirror.

'That should do it,' she told her reflection. 'That and a quiet spot to watch the fireworks.'

In the room above the butcher's shop, Mac pulled open

the door of his wardrobe and, ignoring the butchering attire, drew out the only dress shirt from the rack. He fumbled with it, struggling to drag it onto his arms, and pushed out the wardrobe door with his foot so he could see what he was doing in the full length mirror that hung inside. The buttons slipped from his sweaty fingers and he growled, partly in despair at himself, partly in an attempt to stop his mind going to places he didn't want it to go, to times that he did not wish to remember.

'It's just a damn meal!' he told himself. 'You ain't a teenager no more.' But he hadn't been a teenager back *then* either. He'd been a young man with good prospects, with a future. He'd risen up from the black hole of the Locksley Estate to become a butcher's apprentice. He'd got himself his own place after his father had lost his job on the docks, and was in the process of getting everything ready to ask her, to ask his *Sally*...

Mac felt the sweat prickle on his palms at the thought. Only that week, he had been going to pop the question. He'd been meaning to for ages, but he hadn't been ready. Not quite. And then the opportunity was gone, just like that. No warning. No signs that he'd noticed. Nothing. And then she was with Steve, the guy who'd been his mate since forever, and his world fell apart...

'Shut up!' Mac bent back to the task of worrying at the shirt buttons, breathing hard. It had been months, maybe years, since he'd allowed himself to think about his life in London and those old wounds that still yawned open deep inside him, buried under years of suppression and denial. But he'd been battling with it every day since Virginia had told him she was expecting a visitor from London. He'd been furious at first, resenting the intrusion of the city into his quiet corner of England, and he hadn't even tried to disguise his animosity when Sebastian had arrived. But he had to admit, he couldn't help liking the boy, even if he *was* something of a dandy.

At last, he got the shirt buttoned up, straining against his vast chest, and considered the spectacle looking back at him from the mirror. He shook his head again and this time it was *only* in despair as he took in the bald head, red with worry and glistening with sweat, and the tangled mess of his beard. What could Julia possibly see in him, the lumbering butcher, already the wrong side of fifty? And what were the chances that, after his years of cowardice, she would suddenly ask him to dinner the very week London elbowed its way back into his life?

The sound of the shop door opening roused Mac from his reverie and, taking a deep breath to calm his nerves and kicking the wardrobe closed, he stepped out onto the landing.

'Hello?' said a voice from below and Sebastian appeared at the foot of the stairs, peering up at him in the half-light.

Mac folded his arms and tried to look stern, though he felt he probably just came across as a bit childish. 'I ain't going,' he said. 'I look ridiculous!'

Sebastian opened his mouth to argue, but closed it again, when he couldn't think of anything to say that wasn't an agreement. Mac *did* look ridiculous. But there was nothing they could do about that now, not unless there was a decent tailor nearby.

'There aren't any tailors around here, are there?' he asked. Mac glared at him. 'Well, what's the problem? What do you think looks so ridiculous?'

In response, Mac raised his arms, flapping the cuffs of his shirt, which clearly dated from an era when men in lace was all the rage. The Victorian era, perhaps. Or maybe the Civil War.

'Where's your wardrobe?' asked Sebastian and Mac led him upstairs to a small bedroom above the shop. It was surprisingly neat and clean, but also on the spartan side, the only furniture being a single bed, a bedside table and the wardrobe. Sebastian heaved the doors open to find the hangers almost entirely occupied by white trousers, white shirts and white jackets, Mac's butchering attire. On the left, however, huddled together for company, was a handful of normal clothes. Normal-*ish*, anyway. 'You don't go out much, do you?' said Sebastian as he leafed through them, like the pages of the most unfashionable magazine in the world, before pulling out a shirt and holding it up as distasteful exhibit A. It was brown. Or mostly brown, anyway. 'Paisley? I didn't even know they still *made* paisley shirts.'

Mac shrugged. 'Wouldn't know. I bought that in seventy-nine.'

'I see,' said Sebastian, hanging the shirt back up and considering the rest of the wardrobe's contents. 'And did you happen to buy anything else in the decades since?'

'A few aprons, I guess. And my butchering whites. Got six sets of them in all.' He puffed out his chest with pride and Sebastian was sure he heard the sound of tearing fabric.

'You aren't thinking of wearing them on your date, though, are you?' Sebastian gave him a "don't even answer that" look and, with a sigh of resignation, lifted out a brown suit that looked like it was about as new as the paisley shirt. 'Does this still fit you?'

Five minutes later, after a fair bit of effort but a surprising lack of ripping, Mac had it on. He had refused to let Sebastian snip any of the lace off the dress shirt, so he was now wearing one of the normal, plain white shirts. The one with the fewest blood stains.

Mac looked at himself in the wardrobe mirror. 'Needs a tie, wouldn't you say?' he asked.

'That depends if you're thinking of wearing one of *these* ties.' Sebastian gestured to the cluster hanging on the inside of the wardrobe door. They were decorated with identical blue and gold diagonal stripes, which reminded Sebastian of his old school tie. 'They're not your old school ties, are they?'

Mac snatched one off the rack and began threading it round his broad neck. 'Don't be ridiculous,' he said. 'I get them direct from the butchery supply place. What about my hat?'

'Your butcher's hat?'

Mac nodded. 'Course.'

'The straw boater?'

Mac nodded again.

Sebastian tried not to smirk. 'Depends if you're thinking of taking Mrs Standfield for a punt on the river.'

'Stop smirking!' said Mac, glaring at him as he slipped the knot up his tie and tucked it into his jacket. 'What about the beard? Should I do something with it?'

Sebastian took a step back to consider the huge mass of hair that clung to the butcher's chin as though he'd been shot in the face with a black sheep. He ran a hand across his own chin and wondered what it would be like to have such a magnificent growth himself. Unfortunately, the sparse tufts of stubble that he had produced in the last couple of days were unlikely to become anything more than a collection of straggly wisps, and showed few signs of improving the further he got from puberty.

'It looks fine,' he said. 'Your eyebrows, however, could do with a little threading.'

'Threading?' Mac frowned at him. 'Onto a needle? What are you trying to say about my eyebrows?'

Sebastian leant forwards to present his own, immaculate eyebrows for Mac's inspection. 'Threading will help to tidy up the stray hairs and add a clear edge. You know, to give definition.'

Mac bunched his bushy, undefined eyebrows into a frown. 'I reckon I'll pass. Anything else? Sensible things, I mean.'

Sebastian turned back to the wardrobe, but there was little there to give him inspiration. 'Dunno,' he said, backing it up with a shrug. 'Like what?'

Mac rolled his eyes and headed through the door and back down to the shop. 'How would I know? I haven't been on a date in years. Decades, even.' He paused on the staircase. 'What sort of things do you young lot wear when you go on a date?'

'No idea. I've not been on a date *ever*!'

The pause on the staircase continued and Sebastian was slightly gratified by the look of genuine surprise on Mac's face. Then the butcher turned and continued downstairs. As Sebastian followed him into the shop, a splash of red from a cluster of flowers caught his eye and, though he didn't know anything about flowers and certainly couldn't identify the make and model, he sneaked over and pulled one of the heads free.

'Here you go,' he said, and deftly slipped it into the button hole of Mac's suit as he turned. 'This might draw attention away from your tie.' He patted the jacket front and stepped back to consider the whole picture and saw a huge man stuffed into a small suit, like a side of ham crammed into a fingerless glove. Mac's bald head was glistening with sweat and the flower was only slightly redder than the portions of his face that were visible peering out from the beard. 'Talking about the tie,' said Sebastian, stepping forwards and reaching for it, 'it might be an idea to loosen it, just a little? And you might want to undo that top button.'

Mac slapped his hands away. 'It's fine,' he growled, though the growl may have been more the product of his restricted windpipe than any actual crossness.

'You ready?' asked Sebastian, checking his watch. 'You don't want to keep the lady waiting.'

Mac ran a finger around his tight collar, looking suddenly nervous. 'I ain't sure this is such a good idea,' he said. 'What if I muck it all up, or she decides she don't like me? What if-'

'What if it all goes fine?' Sebastian interrupted. 'Which it will. What's not to like?' He stepped back again to gesture to Mac with both hands, presenting him to himself, and tried not to think about that image of the gloved ham. A bead of sweat trickled down Mac's face. 'Let's get you out in the fresh air,' said Sebastian, 'before you catch fire.'

They parted at the crossroads, and Sebastian watched as Mac walked with a stiff gait, that was probably a combination of tight trousers and panic, towards the Green Man.

'How the hell did you get him into that suit?' said Emma, slipping out of the shadows by the village shop.

Sebastian gave her a cocky smile. 'It's amazing what you can do with butchery supplies,' he said, which earned him a look. He ignored it, watching Mac hovering outside the pub, clearly having some final second thoughts. 'I can't help but feel a bit sorry for him. Is your mum already in there?'

'She sure is. Dressed up in all her finery.'

'Like a Victorian duchess, no doubt!' He chuckled, only slightly concerned at how similar it sounded to Neil's. He slipped a hand behind Emma's head and flicked the strip of green material that hung from her ponytail. 'And yet you manage to look amazing wearing only a ribbon!'

'*Only* a ribbon?' She arched her eyebrows in mock offence, before giving him a brief once over. 'It's a pity not *everyone* made an effort.'

'What do you mean?' He glanced down at himself. His clothes weren't quite up to his usual standard, but they weren't *that* scruffy.

Emma shook her head and set out towards the village green. 'You need a mirror!' she said.

CRYSTAL BALLS

Sebastian snatched up Emma's hand and led her across the road to the village green, which had changed somewhat since he'd left it only a couple of hours before. While the various stalls were still lined up around the edge of the green, they were no longer home to the tombola, second-hand book sales and the like, but had been replaced by sellers of hot drinks, henna body artists and what looked like an elderly fortune teller.

'It's Madame Petrovia,' said Emma, sounding as excited as a young girl spotting a pony. 'Let's go and have our fortune's told.' She dragged on Sebastian's hand, pulling him into the path of a broad, surly-looking man in a dirty wax jacket.

'Sorry,' said Sebastian, almost tripping over his own feet. The man drawled out a few surly-sounding words, but his West Country accent was so thick that Sebastian couldn't make any of them out. 'What did he say?' he asked Emma.

'He *sort of* told you to watch where you were going.'

'Sort of?'

She shrugged. 'Sort of. Would you like to know *exactly* what he said?'

'Yes, please.'

'Give me two pounds.'

'Two pounds?' he said, sounding slightly indignant. 'I don't want to know *that* badly.'

Emma stopped and held out her hand, palm upwards. 'Two pounds so Madame Petrovia can tell our fortune.'

'Madame Pet-' Sebastian stopped as he caught sight of at the fortune teller, seated across the trestle table from where they now stood. It wasn't the vast quantity of jewellery, fingers filled with rings, chest adorned with coils of necklaces, or the faux-gypsy clothing, swirly patterned dress, twinkly shawl and turban-like hat, that had stunned him. It wasn't even the curls of red hair the spilled from beneath the headwear and across her shoulders. It was the fact that she was very much a *he*. And had a big, bushy beard to prove it. Sebastian opened his mouth to point this out, but closed it again as he noticed Madame Petrovia's arms. Not only were they covered in thick, black hair much like the bristles on Major Tom's back, but they were also massive, with forearms like planks of oak and biceps that wouldn't have looked out of place on Geronimo. He shifted his gaze to Madame Petrovia's face to find eyes narrowed back at him, as though daring Sebastian to say something he'd regret. 'Hello,' said Sebastian, his voice reduced to a mere squeak of its usual self.

'Going to stand there staring,' said Madame Petrovia, in a voice that couldn't have been further from a squeak, and held out a huge, leathery hand, 'or are you going to cross my palm with silver?'

Sebastian frowned, thrown by this request. 'Silver?'

'Well, a bit of copper, zinc and nickel, then? It's two quid for a reading.' At a nudge from Emma, Sebastian fumbled in his pocket and managed to produce two pound coins, which he dropped into the slab-like palm. The coins vanished somewhere about the fortune teller's person and he gestured to the seats across the table. 'Sit down, then,' said the gravely voice, 'and give us your mitts. You first, young lady.'

With a sideways grin at Sebastian, Emma held out her hand, which, once cupped in Madame Petrovia's palm, looked even more slender and dainty than ever. To Sebastian's secret delight, they were also slightly freckled. The fortune teller ran a finger, that wouldn't have looked out of place inside a bun with a coating of fried onions, across the lines of Emma's hand, then grunted. 'And yours, hunky boy.' Sebastian held out his hand without comment, though he noticed Emma's grin widening.

Madame Petrovia's finger caressed the lines of Sebastian's hands, which did not look quite as soft and clean as usual, and there was the start of a callus where his third finger met his palm, no doubt caused by shovelling straw and dung around. He looked up at another grunt from the fortune teller and his hand was returned to him, callus and all.

'Well?' said Emma, as Madame Petrovia sat back and stroked away at her beard. 'Let's hear it then.'

'Both your lifelines is good and strong,' said the fortune teller, 'so nothing much to worry about there. But it looks like there are long journeys ahead for you.'

'Long journeys?' said Sebastian, finding himself drawn in despite the fact he thought it was all nonsense. 'Where to?'

Madam Petrovia slipped a purple silk covering from what was obviously supposed to be a crystal ball. The effect was slightly spoiled by the fact the ball was balanced on an old coffee mug with the faded words

"World's Okayest Dad" printed on it. She ran her hairy hands around it and affected a mystical air. 'The destination is of little importance. It is how the journey shapes you.'

'Uh huh?' Sebastian rolled his eyes at what he considered to be airy-fairy-ness. 'So are we talking about car or train journeys? Or maybe an ocean voyage? Or a rocket to the moon?'

The fortune teller peered at him over the crystal ball. 'Some journeys takes us no further than our own homes, and yet all the same, we may leave ourselves far behind.'

'You mean, like the journey of life?' said Emma, who was gazing wide-eyed at the crystal ball, like a child seeing a television for the first time.

'Brilliant,' said Sebastian, his tone ironic. 'Well worth two pounds.'

'Do not be too hasty to dismiss what I've told you,' said Madam Petrovia, still wafting hands over the crystal ball. 'As the first of your journeys draws to an end, young Sebastian, the foundations are already laid for the next.'

'I've not-' He stopped and gazed at the fortune teller. 'How do you know my name? Is that some sort of psychic trick or something?'

'Neil told me,' said the fortune teller, with a wave, which clipped the crystal ball, knocking it off its coffee mug plinth. 'Damn it!' he said, ducking down as the ball rolled off the end of the trestle table.

At that moment the vicar's feedback-laced voice echoed across the green, announcing the start of the evening's entertainment, and Sebastian took the opportunity to grab Emma's hand and leave while the fortune teller was distracted.

'What's the matter?' asked Emma, struggling to keep up as Sebastian hurried towards the stage at the rear of the green, where the action was focused. 'Didn't you think what she said was interesting?'

'*She*? You know that was a man, right? Madame *Petrovia*?'

Emma laughed. 'Course I do! His real name is Peter Babbage. He lives somewhere near Barnstaple. But that doesn't mean she, or he, can't read fortunes.'

Sebastian turned to see if she was joking, and almost tripped over his own feet. 'Actually, I think that's *exactly* what it means. Did you see that mug?'

'Maybe he's better as a mum?' They pulled up on the outskirts of the crowd, which had gathered in front of the stage to see the first act of the evening, a troop of singing pupils from one of the nearby secondary schools. There were around thirty children in all, singing a medley of show tunes from musicals Sebastian had seen, but was struggling to recognise. On the grass directly in front of the stage stood a short, bald man conducting their performance with far more enthusiasm than was really necessary.

'He's going to have his eye out, if he carries on like that,' said Sebastian.

Emma sniggered, but managed to cover it up as a cough. 'That's my old music teacher, Mr Paul. He accompanied us on a school outing to Glastonbury once and broke his arm falling down a hole. He ended up having to conduct the school orchestra with his arm in a cast and I swear he kept punching himself in the face with it.'

They listened for a while, catching snatches of what Sebastian identified as "Memory", "Supertrooper", and something which sounded suspiciously like "The Time Warp". He leant towards Emma, speaking quietly.

'What other spectacles have they got lined up for tonight?'

She shrugged, brushing a distracting shoulder up his arm. 'Not sure,' she said, 'but I have no doubt the Steepleford Band will be playing their usual mess of folksongs.'

'I'm imagining accordions, fiddles and maybe a big box as a drum?'

'Throw in a guitar and that's pretty much it. I suspect we'll have a school band first, though.'

Sebastian nodded slowly, processing this information. 'Want to go and grab something to eat?'

'Yes, please.'

'And how're you two lovebirds doing?'

Sebastian twisted round to find Neil's moustache smiling down at them. And winking.

'We're not...' he began, then caught Emma looking at him, her eyebrows arched in a meaningful way. He cleared his throat. 'We're not too bad, thanks. Are you enjoying yourself?'

Neil raised a hand, filled with a large roll stuffed so full with chunks of pork that the apple sauce was spilling out of the edges and dripping from his fingers, and took a massive bite, chewing on it slowly as he considered the question. This took so long that the expectant look on Sebastian's face drained away, replaced by one that was sighing in every way except actually breathing out loudly.

At last Neil swallowed. 'Yep!' he said, licking apple sauce from his fingers.

Sebastian sighed.

'Aren't you supposed to be supervising the fireworks?' asked Emma.

Neil flapped his hand dismissively, and Sebastian felt flecks of the sauce hit his cheek. 'All under control,' he said. 'It's going to be spectacular. But the band have a couple more numbers to get through. It's not nine-thirty yet.'

Sebastian looked at his watch. 'How do you even know that?' he asked. 'You don't have a watch or a phone or anything. Do you tell the time by some... country... folklore thing?'

'See them stars?' said Neil, gesturing to the sky with his roll. Sebastian looked up and, between a few wisps of cloud drifting overhead, he made out the faint glittering of stars. He nodded. 'Well, you see that bright one just above the church tower there?' Sebastian shifted his gaze and could indeed make out a star hanging directly above the building in question. He nodded again. Neil shifted round to point over Sebastian's shoulder, dropping a blob of sauce onto his knee in the process. 'Follow the line down with your eyes.'

Sebastian did so, wiping at his knee. 'Onto the tower itself?' he asked.

'That's right,' said Neil. 'And as you do, you'll notice there's a bloody, great clock on it.' He chuckled, clearly pleased with himself, then straightened up and bit off another huge chunk of the pork roll. 'Saints alive!' he said, through the mouthful. 'What in the..?'

Sebastian looked up to see him staring off to the left and turned to look himself.

'Wow!' said Emma, leaning back to look past him. 'Is that Virginia?' It was, and even Sebastian, who had at least been prepared for something of the sort, was amazed by the transformation. Gone was the unmanageable frizz that kept falling across her eyes, replaced by hair that cascaded in clearly defined waves, framing a face that was, for the first time since Sebastian had met her, and maybe for the first time in years, accentuated with lipstick, mascara and other delicate shades of makeup, all applied with what looked like a well-practiced hand. Virginia's hair sat comfortably across her shoulder, from which hung, not her usual dungarees over one of, what Sebastian suspected were, Neil's old shirts, but a dress. An actual dress. And while it was not in the most fashionably up-to-date design, it suited her well and showed off a figure that Sebastian hadn't even considered might be hidden beneath. But then, she was at least fifteen years older than him, so he tried not to think about them now either.

'This is your doing!' said Neil, jabbing a finger at Sebastian. 'You've been putting all this… pretty-fying into her head.'

'I don't think I can really take responsibility-' Sebastian began, but Neil cut him off.

'Look what you've done!' Neil gestured towards Virginia, who had spotted them and was heading their way. 'You've turned my wife into… into a woman!'

'Well, I'm definitely not responsible for that!' said Sebastian, confused by Neil's apparently disapproving reaction.

A moustache-stretching grin spread across Neil's face. 'Well, I won't bother thanking you, then, lad,' he said and, laughing like an excited child, he hurried away to sweep Virginia off her feet. Sebastian was pleased to note the feet in question were wearing shoes, rather than wellies.

'You're going to miss him, aren't you?' said Emma, turning to smile at him.

'Unfortunately,' he said, 'you're probably right. Where on earth did Virginia get all those nice clothes?'

Emma tapped the side of her nose. 'Word gets around,' she said. 'A few of the ladies in the village helped her out. They've been itching to spruce her up for years.'

'Spruce her up?' Sebastian chuckled. 'Well, it looks like she "spruces up" pretty well. I feel just a little bit proud, actually.'

'Along similar lines,' said Emma, dropping an excited, and somewhat exciting, hand onto his knees, 'you up for spying on Mac and my mum?'

Sebastian nodded. 'I thought you'd never ask.'

ELEVATION AND ELATION

Hand-in-hand, they sidled across to the Green Man, creeping up to the window that faced the fayre. Emma was about to peep through when Sebastian caught her shoulder, holding her back.

'Your face is going to be all lit up if you're that close,' he said, demonstrating by reaching out a hand towards the window until it was bathed in the light from inside the pub. 'The secret is to stand back a bit, so you keep in the shadows.'

'Oh, really?' said Emma, in a voice that was only slightly accusing. 'Do a lot of peering in through people's windows, do you?'

Sebastian was glad of the shadows, as he felt his face flush at the memory of his night time peep at Emma. He cleared his throat. 'Do you not?'

She thumped him on the arm, before circling around to look in through the window from the shadow of a holly bush. 'They're still in there,' she said and pulled him over by his sleeve. He peered into the room beyond and the first thing he noticed was how clean it looked. Instead of the gloomy forty-watt glow of earlier in the week, the light was crisp and bright, drawing his eyes to what appeared to be freshly painted walls. They had been done in light, neutral colours which emphasised the dark wood of the panelled bar, now thankfully free of the garish lager posters. Even the threadbare carpet had been whisked away to reveal the ancient-looking stone-flagonned floor.

The second thing that caught his attention was the clientele. The few times Sebastian had been in the pub, he could have counted up the number of customers on one hand, with fingers left over. Now, however, he was hard pushed to count them at all. At least thirty, he reckoned, mostly hanging around the bar, including Sid and Harry, and others sitting at tables. The furniture hadn't been updated yet, which would be quite an expensive venture, but now that there were people gathered around them, even the odd assortment of chairs and tables didn't look that bad. And there, nestling in the back corner at a table for two, complete with a candle in a wine bottle and a posy in a half-pint glass, were Mrs Standfield and Mac.

'Are they..?' Sebastian began. 'Are they holding hands?'

'Yes,' said Emma, in such a quiet tone that he turned to look at her. Her eyes were sparkling in the light reflected from the pub.

He gave her a surprised look. 'Are you crying?'

She glared back. 'I am female, you know!'

Sebastian, who was all too well aware of this thanks to being pressed up against her in the dark, cleared his throat. 'So, if they've liked each other for ages-'

'Which they obviously have!' added Emma.

'-then why have they never done anything about it before?'

'You mean apart from Mac being a coward and my mum being old-fashioned?'

Sebastian turned back to the window, where the

couple were still holding hands in a way that looked neither cowardly nor old-fashioned. 'Yeah, apart from that. Surely they were *aware* they liked each other?'

In the shadows, he felt rather than saw Emma shrug. 'I reckon there's hundreds, even thousands, of people around the world who like each other, but take years to realise it.' She was silent for a while, watching Mac and her mum chat across the table, gazing at each other, their desserts evidently forgotten. 'Must be fun finding out though!' she said at last, and slipped a hand into Sebastian's. 'Let's leave them to it. I fancy going for a stroll.'

'I thought it was you two peering in through the window!' Sebastian and Emma span round with the speed, and facial expressions, of the guilty, to see Donald emerging from the side door of the pub.

'We weren't *peering*,' said Emma, trying her best to sound indignant. 'We were...'

'Peeping?' suggested Sebastian, realising too late that this was not an improvement. He hurried on. 'I mean, we were just admiring your new décor. I have to admit I'm amazed at how much you've achieved in only a couple of days. It looks great. Very apropos.'

Donald nodded at him for a bit, then replaced it with a frown. 'No idea what you mean, but the general consensus seems to be favourable. Not that that rowdy rabble in there know anything about style, but they do know what they like, I'll give them that, and it turns out they quite like the new menu and the real ale and even the *décor*, as you call it, so I can't be going too far wrong, I reckon. But I thought as how you might have been looking in on Mac and your mum,' he nodded to Emma, 'to see how their date was getting on, and between you and me and the doorpost,' he kicked out at the pub door and Sebastian was surprised to see the landlord's feet were no longer slippered, but instead sported what looked like a pair of black and red bowling shoes, 'I'd say it was going pretty well. Not only that, but Mac's offered to meet up with my new chef and talk through the menu with him, so good news all round, eh? Worth a celebratory drink.' Donald fixed Sebastian with an expectant, slightly pleading look. 'How about a pint on the house?'

'I...' Sebastian began, then turned to Emma. A drink in the pub was certainly tempting. But even more tempting was the thought of some time with Emma. *Alone* time. 'Could we maybe take you up on that a little later, Donald?'

It was as if someone had flicked a switch on in the Landlord's face. He went from a disappointed frown to a look of *Eureka!* enlightenment. 'Ah!' he said, grinning from Sebastian to Emma and back again. 'Yes, of course. It's your last night here, ain't it!' He stepped backwards towards the door and Sebastian could feel the embarrassment spreading across his cheeks. 'Well, yes. Run along them. Don't let me keep you. And I might see you later for a couple of beers.' And with that, he pushed the door open and slipped inside.

Emma turned to Sebastian. 'At least *that* wasn't awkward,' she said, and squeezed his hand. 'Come on!'

The sound of the evening's entertainment was muffled as they headed along School Road, towards the western edge of the village. Away from the lights of the pub and the green, the world had grown dark, the last of the evening sunlight painting a fiery glow across the rooftops nearby and the fields and trees in the countryside beyond.

'So?' said Emma, shifting to tuck her elbow behind his without letting go of his hand. 'What's it like in the big city, then?'

Sebastian, distracted by the soft female-ness that now brushed against this arm, cleared his throat. He didn't really want to think about the home that would so soon be tearing him away from here, drawing him back across the miles to swallow him again. 'There's not much to tell, really. It's kind of the opposite of here.' He paused to gesture towards the buildings around them, the quaint stone cottages, the former school and post office. 'Look at it! So calm and peaceful.' The door of the Old Forge chose that moment to burst open, and three children spilled out, laughing and shouting at each other as they scampered across the road, passing the couple as they raced each other towards the green.

'You were saying?' asked Emma, as their voices and running footsteps echoed away.

Sebastian took her hand again and they continued their walk towards the edge of Steepleford. 'It *is* calm and peaceful, though,' he said. 'The whole way of life here is slower and more... I don't know, gentle, I guess.'

'Gentle? London is the opposite of "gentle"?'

'Exactly! The city's a brutal, aggressive place that wants to swallow you, all of you, body and soul. It chews you up and spits you out, and every day it's a fight for survival.'

Emma steered him to the right towards a narrow opening in the hedge and the strip of woodland beyond. 'You make that sound like a *bad* thing! Shouldn't life be about survival? Isn't it that struggle that grows and shapes us?'

'But what good is that if the struggle destroys you in the end? Or destroys your soul.' He sighed. 'Imagine what it's like to walk along streets where the buildings tower above you like cliffs, where the crowds pack the streets so that every moment you are forced to touch and brush up against other people. The background drone of traffic is endless, as the cars, buses, taxis, lorries and any other vehicle you can mention-'

'Boats?' suggested Emma, but Sebastian ignored her.

'-push between the hoards of pedestrians like a slow-flowing river of metal and exhaust fumes. Below London, there are tunnels filled with people rushing this way and that, cramming themselves into squat trains as they head off to feed the city's insatiable appetite for human flesh. No one dares to look at or speaks to anyone else - it's heads down, keep on moving. And dropped into this vast machine, an insignificant speck in the whirring, shoving, violent, filthy works, is me. Or you. That's what London's like. The streets are never still, the noise never fades, the lights never dim and the city never sleeps.'

'While Steepleford never really wakes up!' said Emma. 'It's over this stile here.' In the twilight, Sebastian could just make out a break in the trees ahead that opened out onto a hedge. Instead of a gate, however, there was what looked like a short bench stuck sideways through a gap in the hedge with a wooden plank above it, bridging the gap. Emma went ahead of him, using the bench to step up and over the plank and into the field beyond. The action caused her skirt to tighten across the back of her legs and, even in the half-light, Sebastian couldn't help noticing.

'Not staring at my backside are you?' said Emma,

not even looking round at him.

Sebastian swallowed. 'Just get a move on!' he said, glad the darkness was there to cover his embarrassment. 'Where are we going anyway?'

She dropped into the field and turned to face him. 'Embercombe Hill,' she said, pointing. Sebastian stepped onto the stile and peered up ahead. The field they were entering swept steeply uphill, north of the village, and though the woodland they had come through ceased, the top of the hill was fringed with trees.

He looked back at her. 'Why?'

'Why not?' she asked, and started walking up the hill. 'Just fancied a walk is all.'

Sebastian clambered over and hurried after her. The field was even steeper than he had realised and, here and there, he could just make out the shadowy figures of cows, which probably explained why there were dark, suspiciously soft patches on the ground.

'I have to say, you're not really selling the city very well,' said Emma as he drew alongside her. 'Earlier this week it was all, "country people are medieval weirdoes" and "London's so full of life and wonderfulness".'

'I don't sound like that!' said Sebastian, indignant at the whiny, high pitch voice she put on.

'Of course you do! And now, here you are, going on like you hate the city.'

'It's not that,' he said. 'It's just… I don't know, I guess I quite like it here in the country.'

Emma let out a strange, almost fierce, laugh and picked up the pace. 'Well, I don't!'

Sebastian stopped and stared after her, stunned by this sudden revelation. 'You what?' he said, and jogged after her. 'What do you mean?'

'I mean, I don't like it here. Living in this village - it's so… dull!'

Sebastian pulled an incredulous face, but it was lost in the gathering dark. 'I thought you loved it here, working in the shop and brewing beer and all that stuff.'

'It's like you said. Steepleford is just a sleepy little backwater, stuck out in the middle of nowhere.'

'I'm pretty sure I never said that! *Sleepy*, yes, but not the rest of it. Any chance we can slow down a bit?' He added, struggling to speak and breathe, while hammering up the hill at this pace.

'Sure,' said Emma, stopping suddenly and turning to face him. 'We're here. Have a seat.' A few paces ahead, obscured slightly by some scrub, was the trunk of a fallen tree, and once they were perched on it, side by side, it provided them with a perfect view of the village spread out below them. The lights and activity on the green were clearly visible, the crowd gathered in front of the stage while others milled about, visiting the stalls or the pub. Sebastian leant forwards slightly to see if he could recognise any of them, and thought he could just make out Virginia, in her new dress, heading towards the stage with Neil. He must have been staring for a while as, when she spoke, Emma's voice almost made him jump.

'It's not that I hate it here,' she said, resting her hands behind her and leaning back. 'It's just that I've been waiting to leave for so long. I'd planned to leave at eighteen, but things didn't work out.'

Sebastian recalled her mentioning before. 'Because your mum was ill?'

She nodded. 'And now I'm twenty-four! Six years

of working in the shop, of waiting for an opportunity to get out, but it never comes.'

'But where do you want to go?' he asked. 'Not the city?'

'Why not? Why shouldn't I go to the city? You think I'm too... medieval? Too provincial to survive?' Emma sounded cross and, when Sebastian looked at her, he could see she was frowning.

He held up his hands as if trying to stop a runaway conversation. 'Not at all,' he said. 'I just can't imagine why you would *want* to go.'

'I have been to a city, you know,' she said, only slightly mollified. 'Not London, of course. Exeter. But it's a big city all the same, especially when you've spent all your life in Steepleford, with occasional outings to Barnstaple or South Molton.'

'I don't know where that is,' said Sebastian.

'It doesn't matter. I was talking about Exeter. I presume you know where *that* is?' When he didn't respond, she continued, 'It was back when my dad was alive. He took me and mum to the city one afternoon, to watch the carnival. I was only seven, but I remember it as clearly as yesterday. Bright lights and beautiful people.' She gazed into the distance, as though she could see it all again. 'The press of the crowd, the laughter and excitement. It was all so... so alive. Like you said, it's the opposite of here.'

Sebastian tried his incredulous face again, hoping it would have more impact now that he was out of the shadows below. 'But it's alive *here*!' he said, and pointed to the village green. 'Look down there and tell me there isn't laughter and excitement and all those other things. If anything it's *more* alive here than in the city. Here, the grass is growing beneath your feet, there's life all around, both wild and,' he glanced at a small cluster of cows a short distance away, 'every so slightly less wild. There are birds and trees and cows and pigs and goats and… hedges and… everything else that I can't think of immediately, everywhere you look. This…' He held up his hands to present Emma with the panorama before them. 'This is alive! The city is nothing more than a concrete coffin, a prison of bricks and mortar and machines that's designed to keep *real* life out. And if I had the choice, I wouldn't go back.' He paused, noticing Emma staring at him strangely. 'Not yet anyway. I don't want to leave tomorrow.'

She slid a hand onto his knee. 'Why ever not?'

He shrugged. 'Coz I'll miss it,' he said. 'I'll miss collecting the eggs and bringing them to the shop. I'll miss hanging out at the Green Man with crazy Donald and his slippers. I'll miss Mac being all huge and intimidating, while at the same time actually being a soft git. I'll miss Virginia's amazing cooking, and Neil's constant chuckling every time I end up falling over in the pigsties or getting goat's milk squirted in my eye. I'll even miss all those damn, crazy animals that love nothing more than trying to peck me, crush me, kick me or eat me.' He turned to Emma and, though she was already so close that her shoulder was pressed up against his, she craned her neck towards him, and he was amazed at how large her eyes appeared to be.

'What about *me?*' she asked, and her breath brushing his cheek caused an involuntary shiver down his spine.

He cleared his throat, not trusting himself to speak without croaking. 'You?' he said at last, moving closer and trying to ignore the piston-pumping quiver in his chest. 'I'm going to miss *you* the most.'

The last few millimetres between them disappeared as Emma leaned in and kissed him.

Sometime later the fireworks began.

25

HOME AGAIN, HOME AGAIN

One thing Sebastian wouldn't miss about life in Steepleford was the early morning sunlight cutting between the curtains to spear him awake through his eyelids. He couldn't even recall which direction his window faced back in London, and it didn't really matter considering the short gap between it and the wall opposite - the sun *never* found its way in. But, as he tugged the curtains open and looked out across the road and hedgerow to the fields and river beyond, he knew this view was one thing he *was* going to miss.

He paused for a while, leaning with his hands on the windowsill and his forehead against the non-broken glass, drinking in the blue of the sky and the various greens below, the scattered poultry and other animals nosing at the ground in search of something good to eat that might have cropped up during the night. Through the tree cover to the right he could just make out the occasional shapes of pigs up to much the same.

With a yawn so big that it made his jaw click, Sebastian turned away to find something to wear. He eyed the suitcase against the dresser, which contained the only clean clothes he had with him, then shifted his gaze to the jumbled mound of yesterday's clothes that had half-tumbled off the chair. The need to solve two bodily demands made up his mind - the crumpled jeans and t-shirt would have to do.

Having visited the bathroom to deal with the first demand, he headed downstairs to sort out the other with a glass of water. Memories of the night before bubbled up in his mind: fireworks that would have rivalled the New Year celebrations in most capital cities, pints with Donald at the Green Man, the horseshoe throwing match against the neighbouring villages of Filleigh and West Buckland, dancing - *barn* dancing! - and some local brandy drink made out of apples. His head ached at the memory, though the overriding memory of Embercombe Hill did much to raise his slightly hung over spirits.

'Morning,' said Virginia, bustling in through the backdoor and kicking off her wellies. Sebastian placed his glass in the sink and turned to look at her, pleased to see that, though she was back in her usual dungarees and checked shirt, her hair looked almost as good as it had last night. 'You're just in time. Neil will be up once he's finished sorting out the pigs, and I'll get the breakfast on. A nice big fry up for your last morning.'

Sebastian's stomach grumbled with a mix of hunger and slight nausea at the thought of a fry up, and he had to stifle a belch. He needed some fresh air. 'I'll go and collect the eggs,' he said.

It was as uneventful an affair as usual since the poor Psycho Hen had been dispatched, and the cluster of hens barely glanced at him while he loaded the twelve eggs into boxes. As he pulled the door of the run closed behind him, he noticed two figures making their way up the road towards the village. It was Mac and Mrs Standfield, though why they would be walking in this direction so early in the morning, he couldn't work out.

'Good morning,' he called, waving foolishly at them as they neared the farmhouse driveway.

Mac grinned at him through his beard. 'Alright, boy. Ready for the off?'

Sebastian managed a half-hearted shrug. 'Guess so,' he said.

'Those are for me, are they?' asked Mrs Standfield, nodding towards the eggs boxes. 'Might as well take them as I'm heading up to open the shop.' Sebastian, who was hoping to take them up himself and deliver them personally into Emma's waiting arms, hesitated, his mouth open, but no words coming to fill it. 'If you were hoping to see Emma,' she continued, causing a slight blush to colour his cheeks, 'I'm afraid you're out of luck. She's in town this morning on a grocery run. I was going to do it, but she told me she didn't want to come and say goodbye. Said you'd know why.'

'Oh.' Sebastian, who had no idea why Emma didn't want to say goodbye to him, felt an almost overwhelming stab of grief at the thought of not seeing her again. He must have looked as wretched as he felt, because Mac stepped forward and placed a huge hand, gently, on his shoulder.

'Don't fret, boy,' he said. 'I'm sure you'll see her again soon enough.'

Sebastian, who felt that even "immediately" would be nowhere near soon enough for him, shrugged again, then, remembering he was still clutching the egg boxes, he handed them over to Mrs Standfield.

'Well,' she said, once she was all loaded up. 'I can't stand around chatting all day. Some of us have a business to run.'

Mac beamed at her. 'May I walk you to your door, Julia dear?'

'I would expect nothing less, Victor,' she said, but with that same mischievous look Sebastian had noticed her wearing before. It reminded him of Emma.

As she started off up the hill, Mac leaned in to whisper to Sebastian. 'Thanks for last night, by the way,' he said, nudging him with his elbow and possibly bruising a rib or two. 'I owe you, lad.' Sebastian opened his mouth to protest his innocence and claim he had no idea what Mac was talking about, but the butcher was already hurrying away after Mrs Standfield.

'Sure you've got everything?' asked Neil as Sebastian heaved his suitcase into the rear of the Landrover. 'I ain't going to find a pair of your old pants under my bed, am I?'

Sebastian shook his head. 'Only if you put them there.'

'I wouldn't put it past him!' said Virginia as she emerged from the back door, wiping her hands on her apron. She stopped a few paces in front of Sebastian and gave him a wistful look. 'I'm really going to miss having you around,' she said. 'You've been such a wonderful guest, and a willing and very capable pupil. Not only that, but you've been an inspiration to me with your knowledge of hair products and the like.' She patted her hair, which she'd tied back in a ponytail while washing up.

'If you call smelling like a tart's handbag and shedding forty quid for a manicure an *inspiration*!' said Neil, climbing into the driver's seat.

'Shut up, you,' said Virginia, and stepped forward to give Sebastian a hug.

'Thank you,' he said, hugging her back. 'For

everything. You've both been so kind.'

Neil chuckled through the open car window. 'Come on then, you big pansy. Before you get me all choked up.'

'Wait!' Virginia broke away from Sebastian and hurried back into the farmhouse, reappearing a moment later with a brown paper bag swinging from her hand. 'Almost forgot. I made you up some sandwiches and a few other bits for your journey home.'

Sebastian, who was stuffed from breakfast, took the bag, thanked her and walked round the Landrover to join Neil.

As they reversed out of the drive onto Holders Hill, Sebastian took one last look around, at the familiar hedgerow and the overhanging trees, at the vegetable garden, a thick patchwork of green with flashes of reds and whites, at the chickens pecking the dusty ground in the run beyond, and at the farmhouse, with Virginia still standing in front, her apron rippling in the morning breeze, one hand shielding the sun from her eyes, the other waving as the Landrover headed down the hill and away from Steepleford.

'So how's it been for you, then, lad?' asked Neil, pulling the vehicle onto the main road. 'Quite an adventure, I'd reckon.'

'I guess you could call it that, yes. Certainly more of an adventure than the chore I had expected. To be honest, this time last week, I was dreading it.'

'Really?' said Neil with a smirk in his voice. 'I'd never have guessed! But you seemed so suited to the country way of life.' He laughed and flicked Sebastian's thigh with the back of his hand. 'Say, lad, do you remember scrabbling around in that pigsty, crawling on your elbows in all that sh-'

'It's not something I'm ever *likely* to forget, is it?' Sebastian interrupted.

'Not if I get to remind you now and again!'

'Those first days were pretty bad. I'd have given almost anything to get out of here and get back to the city.'

'So what changed your mind?' Again he flicked at Sebastian's leg. 'Anything to do with young Miss Standfield, perchance?'

Sebastian flicked Neil back with a slow, deliberate action. 'Maybe,' he said. 'In part, at least. But it wasn't *just* Emma.' He looked out of the window for a moment, considering the source of his change of heart as he watched the hedgerows zipping past. It hurt his eyes to look at it, so he shifted his gaze to a distant patch of trees. 'I think it had to do with being part of something... something real.'

'Real? What do you mean, *real*? Ain't life in the city real?'

'Look at it like this,' said Sebastian, turning to look at Neil. 'My days are spent sitting in an office where I try to devise ways to make companies hire us to write software - computer programmes - for them. They don't really want or need it, but I have to work out ways to convince them that they do. Mostly it's nothing more than rather unsubtle manipulation, like suggesting it'll make their business more efficient or better than their competitors, but actually we're just after their money. *That* is not real. Nothing I do in the city is real. I live in a concrete box, I have a view through my bedroom window of a brick wall, I walk through streets where nothing grows and hang out with people that I will never *really* know. In fact, apart from my family and a couple of my old school friends I see about once a year, I know you, Virginia, Emma - even Mac and Donald - better than I know anyone else. And I only just met you last week!' Neil opened his mouth as if to comment, but instead he smoothed his moustache and said nothing. 'The things I've been involved with this week,' Sebastian continued, 'felt a hundred times more real than anything I've done in the city. With the exception of milking the goats, of course.'

'That's only because you wasted so much milk!' said Neil, tutting at him. 'I don't know what you were thinking, squirting it all over the place. Disgraceful.'

Sebastian grinned. 'I apologise. Anyway, in answer to your original question, my week here has been an unforgettable experience. I wish I could do it all over again.'

'I'm glad to hear it,' said Neil, glancing at him. 'And between you and me, it's been a delight having you with us for the week - though if you tell anyone I said that, I'll deny it and then set fire to you. You've made quite an impact on our sleepy little village, you know, what with giving Donald the good kick in the arse he needed, turning my Virg into a woman... and a little bird told me you had a hand in a certain dinner date, last night.'

'I don't know what-' Sebastian began, but Neil cut off the denial.

'You should've seen Mac grinning away this morning,' he said. 'He looked like a dog what'd got all the sausages.'

Sebastian laughed at the image, remembering how sprightly Mac had appeared. 'Yeah,' he said. 'I saw him. That's exactly how he looked.'

'And when all's said and done, I have to admit,

I've enjoyed your company and it's been a pleasure to see the change in you as the week's gone on. I'm proud of you, lad.' Sebastian turned to look out of the window again, to hide the embarrassed, choked up look he was sure was visible on his face. 'You're welcome here anytime,' Neil continued. 'On one condition, though.'

Sebastian frowned. 'What's that?'

'I want a shooting rematch,' said Neil, 'after your outrageous cheating!'

Twenty minutes later, the train lurched away from the station and Sebastian, who was still trying to stuff his suitcase into the overhead luggage rack, nearly lost his footing.

'Sorry,' he said, letting go of the sleeping man's shoulder he'd used grabbed hold of. The man peered at him through one, tired-looking eye then lapsed back into his doze without a word. Sebastian sat down in the opposite seat, gazing out of the window as the fields slid into view.

In his pocket his phone had clearly found a signal at last and started buzzing away as the texts, emails and voice messages of the last week queued up for his attention. There was an urgency to its vibration that made him, almost involuntarily, drag it out of his pocket, but he couldn't be bothered to go through the stack of messages. Instead he held down the power button until the screen went blank and, for good measure, he stood up, unzipped his suitcase and shoved the phone inside.

As he did so, he noticed a piece of paper sticking out from between the legs of a pair of trousers. Frowning at the presence of something he was sure he hadn't packed, he tried to tease it out by a corner and, when it proved to be caught on something, he tugged at it. It came free, ripping open as it did so, revealing itself to be an envelope. Inside was a letter.

He sat back down in his seat and unfolded the sheet of paper, his eyes sliding down to the signature. It was from Emma.

'*Dearest Sebastian,*' it began. '*I'm sorry I won't be around to see you off, but the thought of saying goodbye makes me sad. I know you have to go, I've known it since I first saw you, but I've been trying to pretend it won't happen. Anyway, I know this isn't really goodbye. Who knows, if things work out with mum and Mac, I might be able to escape this place! For now, I want to thank you for a great week, and for bringing much needed and welcome excitement into this girl's boring country life. I'll miss you. Love, Emma. PS, I might try and steal a kiss at the fayre tonight, but I guess you know that already.*'

Sebastian read the letter through a few more times, a smile easing its way onto his lips as he did so. Then, as though handling some ancient, fragile document, he folded it and slipped it into his pocket, before leaning back into his seat and, with the smile still locked in place, closed his eyes and dreamed of wonderful things.

Sometime after four o'clock, he was jolted awake as the train announced its arrival at Clapham Junction. Around him, passengers bustled around getting themselves and their bags to the doors in time for them to open, evidently desperate not to waste a second of onward journey time. Moving like a sleepwalker trapped in a dream of mundane reality, he unfolded from his seat and reached up for his suitcase, hardly registering the weight as it dropped into his arms, and shuffled along the aisle behind the other passengers, staring at the floor. He registered brief surprise to find the carriage was carpeted instead of coated in lino like the Underground trains, but the thought slipped away like a bright fish darting into the depths of the ocean. Mostly he thought of nothing.

'Would you look at the state of *that!*' shouted a voice, and a flicker of recognition caused Sebastian to look up. There, lined up against the black railings that surrounded the platform's stairs, stood the very people who had sent him on his week away in the country, his so-called friends.

Brillig stepped forwards and clasped Sebastian by the shoulders, keeping him at arm's length for inspection. 'You scruffy git!' she said. 'It's good to have you back.'

'Yeah,' said Little Pete, sidling up and thumping him on the arm. 'When we didn't hear nothing, we was worried them country types had done away with you. Sacrificed you to the spirit of the forest or something.'

DeVere popped out from behind him, a slightly worrying grin on his face. 'Pity,' he said. 'I had twenty quid riding on you getting eaten. Looks like they did a job on you, all the same. Did they steal all your fancy clothes and your perfume? You smell like a pig's arse.'

'You look like one, too,' added Little Pete. 'Your hair's all over the place, your clothes look like you borrowed them off of a scarecrow, and you've got the remains of a black eye. You almost make *me* look smart.'

Brillig jabbed him with her elbow. 'Shut it,' she said. 'Let the guy talk.' And turning to Sebastian, she also peered at his bruised face. 'So, how was it then? Was it as life-changingly awful as you thought it was going to be?'

Sebastian sighed as he thought about his stay in Steepleford, about the tent wrestling and bread baking, about milking goats and birthing lambs, about the Psycho Hen and its harrowing demise, and about the other animals and experiences on the smallholding. He thought about the brewing session at the vicarage. He thought about the day of butchering pigs and lambs, and struggling with the sausage machine. He thought about music and fireworks and dancing. About Neil, Virginia, Mac and Donald. About Emma.

He blinked and looked at the expectant faces of his friends. 'Life changing?' he said, at last. 'You could say that.'

When it seemed evident there was no further information forthcoming, Little Pete stepped forward and slapped him on the arm. 'That it then?' he asked. 'Did nothing of any actual interest happen?'

'Yeah,' said Diesel from the back of the group. 'I want to hear about, you know, all those animals you had to work with.'

'Did you get to kill anything?' asked DeVere. 'Like with an axe or a shotgun? What about sticking your hand inside a cow? They love all that stuff out in the country.'

'Meet any nice girls?' asked Little Pete, which seemed to amuse the others and earned him a thump on the arm from DeVere.

'Don't be stupid,' he said. 'They don't have *girls* out in the country. It's all like hags and witches and stuff.'

Little Pete gave him a withering look and pushed him by the shoulder. 'Like *you'd* know anything about the countryside, DeVere. Closest you've ever been is the fruit and veg aisle at Sainsbury's.'

DeVere shoved him back, straight into the path of someone hurrying across the platform. 'Watch where you're going, Peter!' he said loudly.

'Pack it in, you two,' said Brillig and turned back to Sebastian. 'We're all going down the pub this evening, about eight-thirty, if you want to join us. You can come and regale us with tales of your adventures.'

'How Sebastian Became A Real Man!' said Diesel, with a grand sweep of her hands as if presenting the words on an imaginary banner.

Sebastian felt like a balloon that had lost half its puff, and the last thing he felt like doing was going to the pub and talking about his week on the smallholding, but he nodded anyway. 'I'll see,' he said. 'If I've not passed out, I'll meet you there.' The first flecks of rain had started to fall so he excused himself and, without a backward glance, dragged his suitcase away towards the stairs.

He fumbled the key into his apartment's front door, almost toppling inside as it swung open. Kicking it closed behind him, he shrugged his shoulder bag off onto the kitchen sideboard and dragged his suitcase into the bedroom. When he got there, however, his noble idea of unpacking his clothes and putting them away nice and neatly evaporated. Instead he dumped it on his bed and perched next to it, staring blankly at the wall.

A sudden brightness caught his eye and he turned to peer out of the window, surprised to see the light on the wall opposite had switched on. No doubt the black clouds he had seen gathering from the train window had arrived, casting their shadow across the city and adding to the gloom that hung over him.

He sighed and walked across to the window, leaning on the sill and stared, unseeing, at the brick wall opposite that had, only a week ago, brought such comfort and security to him. Now it felt less like protection than a prison, hemming him in, trapping him in this brick and mortar and concrete tomb. There were no animals grazing in the distance, no trees swaying in the sunlight, no sunlight even, nor any life whatsoever. Just the bare, harsh wall gazing back at him, unseeing, uncaring, unblinking.

Another sigh cast a haze of condensation across the window for a moment, and Sebastian's eyes focussed not on the wall, but on his own reflection. He was struck by how different he looked, with his hair sticking out in all directions, his chin unshaven, his t-shirt skewed to one side and the faded bruises of the week still evident on his cheeks and eye. No wonder his friends were taken aback. He looked like he'd slept for days in his clothes, like some kind of apprentice tramp.

Outside the window, the rain fell harder, gathering to form a network of large drops that ran, one-by-one, down the glass. As he watched them, it looked so like his reflected face was crying that he raised a hand to his cheek, and as the rain and the glassy tears continued to fall, Sebastian stood and stared, and dreamed of life in the country.

EPILOGUE

The afternoon sun glinted off Mac's head as he carried the enormous suitcase, as though it was nothing heavier than the morning paper, from the car. Behind him, Mrs Standfield fussed over her daughter.

'Are you sure you have everything you need? Your luggage seems far too small for a whole week. Have you packed enough underwear?'

Emma sighed. 'Will you stop worrying, mum? I'll be fine.'

'But what if you've forgotten-'

'The girl's going to the city, Julia,' interrupted Mac. 'I'm sure they have everything there she could possibly need. She ain't being sent out into the wilderness.'

Emma picked up her tickets from the station house and followed the other two onto the platform, where the train was already standing, its doors open. Mac stepped inside and slipped the suitcase into a rack.

'Right,' said Emma, turning to her mother. 'I'd better get going.'

Mrs Standfield, dispensing with her usual formality, wrapped her arms around her daughter and hugged her. 'Please be careful,' she said, her voice creaking with emotion. 'I worry about you.'

Unseen in the embrace, Emma rolled her eyes. 'For goodness' sake, mum, I'll be fine. One week from now, I'll be right back here, on this very platform.' She broke away and gestured through the train to the other side of the tracks. 'Or over there, I'm not sure. Either way, I'll see you then, so stop worrying!'

Mac, stepping back off the train, bent to kiss Emma on the cheek. 'Don't worry,' he whispered. 'I'll keep her occupied.'

'Thanks,' said Emma, turning to board the train.

Along the platform, the guard blew on his whistle, and another signalled its response from further away. Doors slammed and a few people started waving at the train windows.

Mrs Standfield pulled a tissue from her sleeve and used it to blow her nose in as genteel a fashion as she could manage, and from her finger there was the briefest flash of diamond. Mac put a comforting arm around her shoulders, while he too began waving at the train as it pulled away.

From inside, Emma waved to them both until the train turned south and the platform was cut from view, then she let out a long breath and sagged back into her seat. She smiled for what felt like the first time that day, and felt a quiver of excitement mixed with a sense of unreality at the thought that she was, at last, escaping, if only for a week.

The old lady in the seat opposite had pulled some unfinished knitting from her bag and set at it with a rhythmic ticking of the needles that Emma found strangely hypnotic.

She looked up, noticing Emma watching. 'Going far, dear?' she asked.

'Yes,' she said. 'London.'

The lady gave her a half-toothed smile. 'Very nice,' she said, then turned her attention back to her work as Emma gazed of the window.

They were picking up speed now, the trees and the fields and the life she knew slipping into the distance, as the train carried her on and away towards the far off sprawl of the city and something new.

ACKNOWLEDGEMENTS

There is so much more to writing a novel than just shovelling a load of words onto a page, so many stages between the first draft and the finished work. One of the key roles in this process is that of the beta readers and I would like to thank mine, Karen and Lorraine, who provided vital and insightful feedback.

I would also like to thank my proofreader, who also happens to be my mother (blame her for any grammar and spelling errors), Alyshells for drawing the chapter headings, and Jon, who drew the cover image and the map of Steepleford. Lovely work!

This seed of this story was sown one rainy weekend in 2008, when I visited Hidden Valley Pigs in Devon for their first smallholding course. I recommend such an adventure for anyone, whether you want to prove you're a real man or not.

And yes, I did have to kill a chicken!

If you have enjoyed this book, please consider reviewing it on Amazon or Goodreads (or both) Your review makes all the difference for independent authors like me.

And feel free visit my website for other titles, free audiobooks and stories:

www.phinhall.net

12913540R00180

Printed in Great Britain
by Amazon.co.uk, Ltd.,
Marston Gate.